The author, Tarn Maley, is a recently retired police officer who lives in East Sussex, England. During the COVID pandemic lockdown, he has gained some international notoriety from dressing up daily and posting a variety of costumes to the Australian Bin Outing site. This has provided entertainment and distraction to lift the spirits of people suffering most in very difficult times.

A Giant Tale is the author's first published works, with a view to continuing the story in further publications in the future.

Tarn Maley

A Giant Tale

AUSTIN MACAULEY PUBLISHERS™

LONDON * CAMBRIDGE * NEW YORK * SHARJAH

A CIP catalogue record for this title is available from the British Library.

ISBN 9781398421684 (Paperback)
ISBN 9781398421691 (ePub e-book)

www.austinmacauley.com

First Published (2021)
Austin Macauley Publishers Ltd
25 Canada Square
Canary Wharf
London
E14 5LQ

1. The Golden Army

Eitak La Doog lived in the small fishing village of Monrith, one of the southern most points of the northern continent of Glomorosa on the planet Kennet. As he stood on the sand looking out to sea on what was a beautiful, calm and clear night, his mind drifted. Today had been his 20th birthday and just as he was about to remember the events of this special day, he caught a glimpse of something on the horizon. At first, he couldn't quite make it out, a dark shadow which seemed to glimmer now and then like the light of a fire and as his eyes became accustomed to the darkness, he noticed another shadow and then another and another. He began to count them and before long he had reached 20. Eitak strained his eyes and squinted to see if he could make out what these shapes were and as they came closer, he could see that they were in fact several sailing boats which were heading towards the shore with their sails full and billowing as if being blown by a great storm. *Strange,* Eitak thought aloud; there was no wind on shore at all. He was stood on the beach in a short-sleeved tunic and could not even feel a breeze, yet here were these boats under full sail. Eitak stood for a while looking at the boats and wondered who was sailing them and why were they heading towards the little fishing village of Monrith.

Just as he considered going to get someone else to take a look with him, he saw a bolt of light rise into the sky from the leading boat. It looked just like a firework, except that it wasn't going straight up but was heading towards the shore. The light from its tail lit up the sky so that Eitak could now see the boats clearly. They were small war galleons, battleships of sail and they were, in fact, travelling at some speed towards the beach. As Eitak's eyes gazed from the top of the masts to the level of the sea, he gasped in astonishment. For there, wading across the sea up to their shoulders in water were several giants. Eitak had never seen a giant before; yet, here they were wading across the sea, blowing the sails of the ships and helping them across the water. The giants were huge and dwarfed the ships which looked tiny by comparison. Eitak's attention now came back to the firework heading straight towards him. The flare of light was travelling at great speed, its burning tail filling the sky in front of him. Eitak instinctively dropped to the ground, just as the bolt of flame whistled over his head and landed firmly in the thatched roof of the single storied 'House of the Midday Moon' which immediately burst into flames.

Eitak, shocked, looked back out to sea towards the ships which were now a lot closer and looked a lot larger than they had when he had first caught a sight of them. He could now see several new bolts of light rising from the bow of each vessel. Eitak in a semi state of panic, rose to his feet and shouted at the top of his voice, "Help, Help, we are under attack!" And he ran towards the houses to the right of the pub repeating his words over and over again.

The window of one of the cottages opened and an angry voice shouted down to him, "Why don't you just shut up and go home? Can't you see that we trying to sleep here?" Eitak, sweating from a mixture of fear and excitement, looked up and saw 'Thaddeus, the butcher', looking back at him. Just as he was about to tell Thaddeus what was going on, another bolt of fire landed, this one smashing right through the roof of Thaddeus' tool shed.

"What in Kennet's name is going on..." Thaddeus said angrily.

"We are under attack!" shouted Eitak. "Run for your life!"

Thaddeus looked out from his upstairs window and could see the ships coming ashore. The sky was now filled with bolts of fire which rained down all over the small fishing village.

Eitak could hear the screams of people as they became aware of what was happening. He saw men, women and children running in all directions away from the fires which now raged over most of Monrith. Eitak now shaking turned back to the water's edge just as the first of the boats landed. From each craft jumped a group of golden metal soldiers. At first, they appeared to look like men but to Eitak's disbelief, he could see that they were, in fact, made entirely of metal and armour plate. Each of the soldiers emitted a whirring and clunking sound as if a large clockwork mechanism was at work inside. The automatons held in their hands a variety of weapons, from axes and swords to pikes and crossbows and received orders from sinister looking figures dressed in black robes that stood at the bow of each ship giving directions.

By now, the giants had waded out of the sea and were stood on the shore looking down at the metal army at their feet. They were not actively involved in the invasion and just seemed to be taking it all in. One of the robed figures turned and looked in Eitak's direction. Eitak could see that beneath the robes was a golden facemask, smooth and featureless apart from two slits for eyes. The robed creature shouted to one of the giants and pointed at the now burning 'House of the Midday Moon'. The giant shook his head and took no notice of the creature. However, the creature shouted something further and with some reluctance, the giant headed towards the pub.

Just then someone ran past Eitak; it was Thaddeus, the butcher, dressed in his nightgown, large boots and nightcap. "Run, you fool, run," he shouted as he disappeared down a path which led towards the main road, leading out of town and to the hills beyond, the bobble of his nightcap bouncing as he went. Eitak was still running on pure adrenaline and he ran in the opposite direction to Thaddeus, towards several small fishing boats which had been dragged up onto the beach. As he ran, he saw the giant raise one foot which he then brought down on the roof of the burning pub. The building collapsed, the roof caved in and burning eaves and rafters crashed through each floor to the ground. The walls gave way and crumbled under the enormous weight of the huge foot which stamped on the building and smashed it to the earth. The metal army ran amok, chasing, grabbing and capturing people, indiscriminately men women and children, all suffered the same fate; those who were not able to run were caught and shackled by the clockwork machines. These people now fleeing for their lives; they were Eitak's friends and neighbours.

Eitak approached the first fishing boat that he came to and hid underneath, tucking his body tightly against the rudder of what actually appeared to be one of the larger vessels. He had a safe but restricted view through the gap between the rudder and hull and from here, he was able to get a good look at the mechanical army swarming past him on the other side of the boat. Each clockwork soldier wore varying degrees of golden armour ranging from welded chain mail to heavy, full metal plate. Many wore helmets of differing shapes and descriptions; some full faced, some open, some with horns while others had elaborated plumes. He noticed that beneath their helmets, the soldiers did not have proper faces. Their heads were a lattice work of welded metal with a cage protecting the internal workings of their mechanisms. For eyes, each solder had two short glass telescopes which glowed blue in the dark and behind these eyes, Eitak could see a mysterious blue glow. All the soldiers differed in size just like a conventional army but the one thing they all shared in common was that they were all made of glistening gold. Eitak could see that each was extremely intricate and beautifully crafted and had obviously been made with great care and attention to detail.

Eitak's heart began to slow down from the racing pace which had been set by the circumstances. He realised that he had just spent the last few minutes on pure adrenaline and had not really had time to take it all in. Instinct had taken over and his fight or fright mechanisms had worked perfectly. Now he felt himself sweating and he began to shake, fear was setting in. How had such a wonderful day turned to this?

Eitak shook his head, trying to refocus from the horrors in front of him. The giants still stood on the beach head, were huge oversized men who towered over the galleons. Dressed in furs, which dripped water like huge waterfalls onto the sand, they huddled in a group talking amongst themselves, only one of these massive creatures was engaged in the destruction of Monrith and even he did not seem to be doing so with any great enthusiasm.

Eitak's mind began to fill with questions, who were this army? Where had they come from? What did they want with Monrith? Or for that matter…were they even from this world? Eitak considered this for a moment and then decided that as he lived on Kennet and because he had heard of giants before, then these machines must have come from there.

Kennet was a beautiful planet which was host to a variety of life forms and creatures of all shapes and sizes, not all of which were pleasant. Amongst the races, there were the humans of whom Eitak was one. Now 20, he considered himself to be at the peak of his physical fitness, he was also the talk of the town. Quite handsome and also very eligible, he stood six feet tall and was fairly athletic. He had short dark brown hair but most unusually, he had one brown and one blue eye and this caught the attention of both the available and sometimes, problematically, the unavailable women of Monrith. Next there were the Wirral, a human race comprising only of females. The women of the Wirral were the huntresses of Kennet and lived for the most part in the vast forests and woodlands. No one had ever seen a male Wirral which led to speculation and myth as to how their species perpetuated. Then there were the Nagraal, the people whose spirit inhabited the bodies of the recently departed, their own bodies having died years ago but their souls refusing to move on. The Nagraal feared the day of their judgement, most felt that they had failed in this life and were desperate to make amends for their past deeds and wanted to do something to change their ultimate fate but for now, they lived a cursed life and as each of their bodies began to decay, so they were forced to take a fresh one from those who had recently died. For some, this soul hitchhiking had been carried out many times over and therefore, the Nagraal were some of the oldest and wisest of the life forms on Kennet.

Next, there were the Dust Dwellers, the peoples of the great sandstorm of Kennet. They followed the great hurricane as it made its way across the equator of the planet, hiding in the dust and preying on those foolish enough to pass by or be caught up in the great storm. They had small eyes with extra eyelids and nostrils with small flaps of skin across each one to protect them from the clouds of dust and assist them in filtering out the choking sand.

Then there were the giants of Kidder Doon. They were a race of enormous human like creatures, who were flesh and bone during the day but according to legend, turned to stone with the full moon. They lived in the lands to the east of Kennet and only merchants dared to venture there. Most of the giants were craftsmen, blacksmiths, goldsmiths, silversmiths and skilled metallurgists. They were a shy and peaceful race and kept themselves to themselves, only making their way from the hills in order to peddle their crafts with the few travelling merchants, brave enough to make the journey. Other than the merchants, no one had seen a giant for centuries and due to their size and scarcity, myth and legend surrounded them. What people didn't know, they made up, but what everyone did agree upon was that not seeing a giant suited them just fine.

There were also the Magistan, eccentric and gifted with great insight and the ability to read the stars; they were renowned for their inventiveness and were the scientists and magicians of the world.

The other creatures of Kennet varied enormously, amongst them were the Terror Soar's, a large flying reptile from the foothills of Kidder Doon. The Wisp Warblers, creatures of vapour and mist from the marshlands who could invade the minds of men and turn them mad. The Widget Hunters of the desert floor, a small carnivorous mouse with razor like teeth, designed for stripping the flesh of carcasses and then there were the Hasty Hagraals. The Hasty Hagraal was a cross between a dog and a bear, renowned for their awesome speed across land; when they moved, it seemed as if they just left one place and then materialised in another with nothing having happened in between. The Hasty Hagraal had the reputation of being the most feared of all lifeforms on Kennet.

Eitak had enjoyed his birthday and in particular, the evening of festivities at the 'House of the Midday Moon', he patted his belly as he remembered the great feast of fine foods and wines. Eitak had no family, his parents having passed away several years ago but his friends had made him proud this day and now he could walk the lands of Kennet as an adult. His mind wandered, he had especially enjoyed the lighting of the huge bonfire on the beach in front of the pub and had stood on the shoreline watching the sky darken, the only light filling the sky being that of the raging bonfire. The fire was a massive beacon which would have been visible for miles around. This, Eitak decided must have drawn the army to Monrith and as a result, he began to feel that he may, inadvertently, have been the cause of the current predicament.

Eitak was just wondering where the army had come from, when he became aware of a presence behind him. He hadn't noticed anyone creeping up and he reeled around quickly and there crouching behind him was a middle-aged man. Eitak jumped, startled by this sudden intrusion. As his pulse began to slow, he studied the character before him. He was a tall rotund gentleman and Eitak estimated him to be around 50 years old. He had a fine crop of hair which was turning white and he wore the clothes of a merchant. About his shoulders sat a rich crimson coloured cape, fastened at the neck by a golden brooch and beneath this was an equally lavish waistcoat of many colours and a flamboyant shirt with full and flowing sleeves. The merchant wore green velvet trousers and long black socks and, on his feet, he wore a pair of expensive looking patent leather shoes. Before Eitak could say anything, the man spoke in a very calm manner, "I am Sirod Spa."

"Eitak, Eitak La Doog," Eitak replied.

There was no time for proper introductions as one of the metal soldiers that had been left behind to guard the ships, began to take an interest in the beach and the fishing vessels which had been dragged up onto it. Sirod looked along the shoreline to the west of the invading fleet and caught sight of a small fishing boat bobbing up and down in the shallow waters close to the shore. He turned to Eitak, who was now watching some of the metal army as they returned with captured villagers and loaded them into large cages on one of their ships.

"The way I see it is like this. We have one chance to get out of this as free men and that is aboard that boat," Sirod said and he pointed to the small fishing boat. "There is an offshore breeze blowing and if we can set the sail, we should be able to make it." Eitak considered Sirod for a moment, thinking that he could not believe this man was acting so calmly in a situation like this.

Sirod waited for the enemy to disappear out of sight behind another vessel and then he whispered to Eitak, "Run. Follow me." They both ran as fast and quietly as they could towards the shoreline. They waded out to the boat and began to climb in. They had no sooner clambered aboard when they saw a pair of hands appear from the opposite side of the boat; these were followed by the hair covered face of a very weathered looking fisherman. On seeing the two castaways, he appeared annoyed and said in a loud voice, "What are you doing in my boat?"

"Ssshh!" Eitak waved his hand in a downwards motion, desperately trying to keep the fisherman quiet so as not to attract the attention of the scout on the beach. Now speaking in a quieter voice but still rather angry, the fisherman said, "This is my boat, what are you doing in it?"

"The same as you, I should imagine," Sirod said sarcastically. "Look, we're all in the same boat here. Can't we just get going and argue about this later?"

Eitak managed to get to the solitary rope at the back of the vessel which was tethering it to the beach and unhitched it from its cleat. Just as the fisherman was about to make a further protest, a flare whistled overhead and plopped into the sea beside him, hissing as it hit the water. The three occupants of the boat looked towards the beach and could see that the soldiers were setting fire to all the fishing fleet, presumably to flush out any villagers hiding amongst them.

"Look, if we don't get out of here now, we are all going to die. Now, shall we forget our differences and get going?" Sirod suggested.

The fisherman quickly pulled on a rope and a sail popped up from the deck of the small boat. He reached down and grabbed two oars and threw one at Sirod, the other at Eitak. "Right," he said. "Seeing as you are here, you'd better get rowing."

Eitak and Sirod rowed for their lives, another flare whistled overhead that had been fired from one of the enemy ships further along the coast. The fisherman raised another sail and before long, despite its small size the fishing boat managed quite a turn of speed and soon the act of rowing became pointless.

Eitak looked towards the shore, none of the enemy boats were following, and Eitak presumed that it was because they had insufficient crew to set sail with their army laying waste to the village.

With the danger over, both Eitak and Sirod withdrew their oars and they turned to look at the fisherman. Eitak spoke first, "Look, I'm sorry about that back there but we had no other choice."

The fisherman viewed the two stowaways looked them up and down and then as the scowl on his face softened, he laughed out loud. "Ha, look we are all in the same boat here…Ha, now that's funny." He looked straight at Sirod who didn't have a clue what he was talking about, then all of a sudden, he realised that the fisherman was repeating what he had said when they first met and he too joined in the merriment. Before long, all three were laughing loudly on the deck of the fishing boat as the shoreline became a distant memory.

Sirod introduced himself first, "I am Sirod Spa and this is my friend, Eitak La Doog…" He offered his hand and continued, "…Pleased to meet you."

The fisherman accepted the gesture and shook with a firm grip. "Bones is the name, pleased to meet you too."

Although weathered from years of battling with the sun and sea, Bones was around 30 years old, was quite short and tubby and had a thick head of unkempt brown curly hair which continued on down his cheeks and below his nose to form a thick beard and moustache.

Eitak shook hands with Bones and asked, "So, now, what do we do?"

Sirod answered, "I suggest that we go to Illya and seek an audience with Malarog the Magistan, he will know what to do. I've heard rumours about this Golden Army but I'd never seen it for myself until this evening…"

"Yes, we must go to Illya…and attend the Grand Observatory."

Bones was busy with the sails, making sure that everything was running to its optimum efficiency whilst keeping half an ear on what Sirod was saying. "So, do I take it that I set course for Illya then?" he said and with that he went to the bow of the boat and stood looking up at the sails. As he brought his gaze back again, he caught the sight of a small speck of light on the horizon. Quick as a flash he ran to the door leading to a small hold beneath the boat.

As he opened the door, Eitak received a terrible waft of something rotting below deck. "What in Kennet's name is that?" he asked.

Within a few seconds, Bones re-appeared with a small brass telescope. "It's an instrument for looking at things in the distance," he said.

"No, not that, I meant…"

Eitak was stopped, mid-sentence by Sirod who had seen the telescope and putting two and two together interrupted with: "What have you seen?"

Bones pointed to the speck on the horizon which was now growing a little brighter and larger. All three stood at the back of the boat looking out to sea.

Bones put the telescope to his eye and within a few seconds shouted in panic, "Get the oars, quick, they're coming."

Sirod took the telescope from Bones and looked for himself. He slowly lowered the instrument from his eye and said calmly to Eitak, "He's right, we must prepare." He turned to Bones and asked, "What weapons do you have below deck?"

Bones shrugged his shoulders, shook his head and outstretched his hands palms up. Eitak ran to the door and clambered down into the hold, the smell of rot was overwhelming. He looked around in the cramped conditions, desperate to find anything which remotely looked like a weapon but all he managed to find was a pile of decaying fish piled up on one corner. After several minutes he could stand the smell no more and he went back onto the deck for fresh air. "Nothing..." he announced. "There is nothing down there apart from rotting fish."

Sirod looked back towards the boat which was now gaining on them. "Think..." he said to himself. "Think..." And then it dawned on him. "Quick, get the fish."

Eitak looked bemused at the apparent futility of their situation. "What are we going to stink them into submission?" he asked.

Eitak and Bones went below deck and began filling a large metal bucket with rotting fish. The smell was terrible, so bad that Eitak gagged several times. He turned to Bones and said, "I don't know how you can live like this." Bones just ignored him and carried on filling the bucket. Once back from the hold, Eitak handed the bucket and its contents to Sirod, who poured them straight over the side of the boat.

"What are you doing?" Eitak couldn't believe that Sirod had just emptied the bucket which potentially contained the only weapon they had over the side of the boat.

"All will become clear in the fullness of time," Sirod answered.

The small fishing boat continued on, away from the rotting fish which had by now fanned out to cover a substantial area of the sea behind them. Eitak stared in disbelief but then all of a sudden, the sea began to broil and come alive. As he watched, he saw the huge black shiny bodies of several large sea creatures as they thrashed around feasting on the disgusting cast offs that he been thrown to them. These monsters were at least twice the size of Bones' boat and had large mouths filled with rows of razor-sharp teeth, each the size of a small hunting knife.

Eitak was now worried more than anything and he looked over the side of their boat to see if there were any more of these creatures. As he did so he saw the shadow of another monster just below them, heading towards the feast. This one was the largest yet at well over four times the size of their fishing boat.

By now the wind had increased and Eitak felt happy that they were a safe distance from this new peril that Sirod had conjured up.

"Just what do you call them?" he enquired.

"They are Death Eels," said Bones.

Just then Eitak remembered the metal army pursuing them and looked towards the enemy vessel which was now gaining fast. He was just about to say, 'We will never outrun them'. When the small warship reached the area of water, where the Death Eels were just finishing off the last scraps, the monsters turned their attention to this new delicacy which had presented itself before them and they began to bite large chunks out of the wooden boat. At the bow of the stricken craft was the shadowy figure Eitak had seen back on the shores of Monrith, Eitak saw the glint of its golden mask as it thrust a large sword towards the Eels. All of a sudden, one of the largest eels propelled itself high out of the water and tore the figure from its vantage point and holding it in its jaws; it plunged back into the dark waters and was gone. The monsters quickly ripped a gaping void in the side of the enemy vessel which promptly sank beneath the waves, taking the metal soldiers with it.

Eitak, Sirod and Bones sat back onto the small benches of their fishing boat and sighed with relief that Sirod's plan had worked. Eitak was just about to ask Sirod where he had come from, when he noticed that Sirod's face looked somewhat distorted and that he suddenly looked a lot older than he had previously. "What's happened to your face!" he exclaimed.

Sirod looked down at his reflection in one of the small puddles of water on the deck of the boat. He put his hand to his now wrinkled face and said, "I'm afraid that this is the price to pay for using someone else's body." Eitak looked at Bones in puzzlement and then turned to Sirod.

"What do you mean? Someone else's body?" said Eitak.

Sirod took in a deep breath and then said, "I am one of the Nagraal and I can't leave this world until I have made amends for something I once did. My own body decayed two centuries ago and now I must use the bodies of those who have recently departed but each time I take a body, I am limited by how long it stays fresh."

"That's gross," said Eitak. "So how long does a body last then?"

"It depends on how hot it is. In the winter I can get about a month out of a really fresh one. But in the summer, a lot less."

Eitak continued, "So how much longer will this one last then?"

Sirod took another look at himself in the puddle. "About two more days by the look of it."

"And then what?" Eitak asked.

"Then we will have to see," replied Sirod.

2. The Market

The next morning Bones sighted the port of Illya and the small fishing boat settled down against one of the moorings alongside the main jetty leading to the market square.

Eitak walked ahead of Sirod, who was now being helped along by Bones. Illya was unusual in that, it was not only a port but was also one of the capital cities of Cylesia. There were only three land masses on Kennet, the inhabitable ones being Glomorosa to the north and Cylesia to the south, then there were the icy wastelands of Sivestol at the extreme South Pole but no one ever went there. Glomorosa and Cylesia were separated by the narrow sea which the three travellers had just crossed. Each of the main land mass was not divided into countries but rather had various walled cities and citadels throughout, Illya being one.

Illya was a thriving city of trade and commerce and was renowned for its market places where pedlars and merchants met to sell their various wares.

As Eitak approached the market square, his senses were immediately confronted by the brilliant colours of fine silk and cloth from a nearby draper's stall, he could smell the rich aromas of the various spice merchants and hear the sounds of pigs, sheep and goats being traded. Everywhere he looked, people rushed around, chattering and bartering and it took him a moment to take it all in.

After he became acclimatised to his surroundings, his attention was caught by a commotion coming from one corner of the square. He managed to push his way through the congregation of onlookers until he saw several large wagons with cages on top and in the cages were a variety of creatures from all over Kennet.

In the first cage he saw a creature which he had only ever heard of but had never actually seen. It had the size and coat of a brown bear, apart from its head which was emblazoned with a very distinctive flash of white fur. The creature's overall appearance was that of a large and savage dog with very powerful hindquarters and around its neck, it wore a thick leather collar studded with glowing red crystal gems. Eitak immediately recognised the animal as being a Hasty Hagraal. The Hagraal was pacing up and down, its eyes fixed on one person and that was the man stood facing the crowd, apparently, selling the animals in the cages. He was a short, slightly built man with thin features and a small mouth. In his hand, he held a wooden staff with a crystal at one end which glowed with a bright blue light. From time to time and for no apparent reason he would poke the crystal into the flank of the Hagraal which at first would cause the crystal to dim slightly, but then it would suddenly burst into a brilliant blue spark. The Hagraal snarled and salivated at the sudden pain inflicted upon it. Eitak walked over to the cages until he came to a smaller one with a creature huddled in one corner. He strained his eyes to look at the figure, cowering in the shadows which slowly lifted its head to face him. Eitak couldn't believe his eyes and was shocked to see that it was a pretty young girl. He looked around to make sure that no one else was looking and then he brought his head up slowly so that it was now level with the girl in the cage but as he did so, she cowered further into the shadows and away from him.

Eitak spoke, "Who are you?" The girl slowly turned her head to face him and realising that he had no stick and was not going to hurt her; she moved towards him out of the shadows. Now that he could see her face properly, Eitak thought that she was very pretty, a little grubby maybe but still very pretty. She had golden blonde hair and blue eyes and appeared to be around his age. "Who are you? And why are you here?" he repeated.

"I am Arwie, Arwie Willowbreeze," she said, "and I'm here to be sold as a slave."

"A slave!" Eitak shouted in disbelief. "I thought the slave trade was abolished long ago."

"Not here," Arwie replied.

"Well, I'm Eitak. Wait here and I'll be back." Eitak realised as soon as he had said this, how stupid he must have sounded; after all where else was she going to go.

Sirod and Bones had now made their way to the market square, Sirod still leaning heavily on Bones as his condition worsened. Eitak suddenly burst out of the crowd and ran up to them in an animated state. He could hardly get his words out fast enough as he told them about the slave girl he had found across the square.

Bones looked at Eitak and said, "I'm sorry to hear about the girl, but we really must do something for Sirod…and now."

Eitak looked at Sirod and could see that he needed another host and soon. Looking around he read the names of the various establishments forming the perimeter of the market square. In the opposite corner from the slave trader, he read the word "Undertaker."

"Follow me," he said and helped Bones lead Sirod to the other side of the marketplace.

As soon as they reached the undertakers, Eitak suddenly had an idea. He told Sirod to act dead and he went into the building. Once inside, he went up to the reception desk and said, "I have been sent over here by the slave trader over there. One of his slaves has died and he needs somewhere to put him until later. He will settle up any bill when the market closes." The undertaker looked sceptical but seeing an opportunity to make some money for not much work, he beckoned for Bones to bring in the 'corpse'.

Glancing at Sirod, the undertaker said, "A bit well dressed for a slave, isn't he?"

Thinking on his feet, Eitak replied, "The slave trader likes to make his slaves look their best for the auction."

The undertaker nodded in approval and said, "Just put him out the back and close up behind you, I'm off to lunch." and with that he left.

Behind a curtain in the back of the undertakers, there were several slabs of marble and on some of these were blankets covering the bodies of those recently departed from the city of Illya. Bones placed Sirod on one of the empty slabs and both he and Eitak then left and waited outside where they stood watch.

After several minutes the front door opened and a Sea-maiden dragged herself out onto the wooden decking at the front of the establishment dressed in nothing but a pink furry bikini top. Eitak and Bones both looked at the Sea-maiden's fish-like tail and when they realised it was Sirod, they shook their heads.

"No way. How do you think you are going to get about like that?" they protested in unison.

Sirod, held his body up from the decking and said, "Well, when I pulled the blanket back, I could only see the top half." and with that he dragged himself back into the undertakers. A few minutes later, a very handsome young man opened the door and stood before the two companions who were eagerly waiting outside. He was slim, tall and aged in his early 20s with a fine head of black hair which was slicked back in a ponytail. He was wearing knee length black leather boots, which had baggy folded cuffs and shiny silver buckles which sat on top of straps across each foot. He also wore lose fitting black trousers and a collarless, flowing white shirt with billowing sleeves which had flamboyant cuffs. On top he wore a black leather waistcoat.

"Excellent," said Eitak.

"Aye, it'll do." Bones agreed.

With that, Sirod jumped down from the decking and the three of them headed back into the market.

"The best thing," said Sirod, "is that this one has recently been embalmed and should, therefore, last me quite a while."

Eitak told his friends again about the slave girl he had seen and they agreed to see what they could do to help.

They made their way towards Arwie, just in time to see the slave trader poking her with his blue crystal staff as he walked past her cage. As soon as he had walked off again, Eitak inspected the lock securing the door. They all agreed that the only way to get into the cage was with the keys which the slave trader had tethered to his waist. "We will have to distract him." Eitak decided and with that Bones began looking around, trying to think up a plan.

Sirod spoke calmly, "I can help with this, now listen carefully and trust me. When the trader stops talking, take the keys from his belt as quick as you can because we won't have long."

Sirod then went to a small table upon which sat several glass jars. Each of the jars contained a mysterious swirling mist. Sirod picked up a jar and went over to stand by the slave trader. As the slaver looked at Sirod, Sirod opened the glass jar allowing the mists to escape and swirl around the trader's head and within a few moments, the vapours disappeared up the man's nostrils as he breathed in. The slave master just stood there totally motionless as if he was in a trance. Eitak and Bones, who had been watching with great interest, went over and carefully Bones removed the keys from the man's belt whilst Eitak grabbed his staff.

Bones now held the keys and together with Eitak he made his way over to Arwie's cage. By now, the last of the mists had swirled from the slave trader's nose but he still stood where he was unable to move. Saliva began to dribble from the corners of his mouth and then he began to mumble nonsensically. Eitak's hand shook nervously as he turned the key in the lock that fastened Arwie's cage and with that the door flung open and Arwie jumped out.

Eitak couldn't help but wonder at her beauty. She was tall and slim and wore a pair of tan coloured, hand crafted leather trousers and a slightly tattered white shirt. Her long blonde hair now cascaded down her back and glistened in the sunshine but across her face, Eitak noticed she wore a long scar. Eitak hadn't noticed this at first but the scar ran from just below her left eye to the left corner of her mouth.

Sirod had now come over and joined the group. "Wisp Warblers," he said. "I saw them sitting on the table as we came over and I knew that they would keep the slave trader occupied."

Arwie gingerly took Eitak's hand and looked into his eyes and said, "You must give me the keys." Eitak handed the small bunch of rusted keys over and watched as Arwie ran behind one of the cages close to where the slave trader stood. She fiddled with the lock and then ran back to her new friends who were still stood by her old cage. "Quick," she said in a desperate fashion. "Jump in the cage." Her three saviours looked at each other and were about to protest when she pleaded, "Please, trust me." Strangely, they realised that they did trust her and they all climbed in. Once inside, Arwie pulled the door closed and only just in time as the other door, the one to the cage she had just unlocked, opened.

All Eitak saw was that the slave trader was stood motionless, muttering to himself one moment and that the Hasty Hagraal had pinned him down to the ground the next. He hadn't even seen the Hagraal move from its cage. The crowds in the market square began screaming and ran in all directions away from the Hagraal, which was now tucking into its market trader meal. Within a few minutes, the market place was completely empty. The Hagraal looked up. Its eyes fixed upon Eitak, it bowed its head and then disappeared, a cloud of dust being the only 'tell-tale' sign of the direction in which it had run.

Once the coast was clear, Eitak, Sirod, Bones and Arwie climbed down from the cage and stood in the now totally deserted market place. "Right..." announced Sirod. "Shall we go?" Eitak, his heart pounding once more, picked up the market trader's staff and the group headed off out of the market place and through the city. As they left, Arwie approached a stall selling furs and winter clothing.

"I have always wanted a fur jacket," she said and proceeded to try a silver jacket on with a matching hat, she then spun around in front of Eitak.

"You look even more beautiful than ever." He gasped at her in wonderment and Arwie blushed and lifted her shoulder to cover the scar on her face. Bones had managed to find a bright yellow fisherman's coat which he tried on.

"We are trying…to be inconspicuous," Sirod announced, looking at Bones. Bones muttered something under his breath, about not seeing what was wrong with the yellow coat and then rummaged around in another pile of clothing. He found a dull black leather jacket with a fur collar and a black woollen hat. "Much better." Sirod nodded approvingly. Eitak chose a fur jacket with a hood which complimented Arwie's new attire nicely. "I'm quite happy with my cape," announced Sirod and they all set off. They had only gone a few paces when Eitak turned back to the stall and dipped his fingers into a small leather pouch he had hidden in his shirt. He pulled out a gold coin which he then left on the counter and then followed the others out of the market place.

Not surprisingly, the streets were now deserted. Just the odd face appeared now and then from behind the curtains of a closed door here and there but Sirod expected this, especially with the Hagraal on the loose and the four friends walked to the far side of the city, where they followed the dusty road towards the large observatory building, which was built at the top of a very steep hill.

3. The Grand Observatory of Illya

On the way, Arwie walked side by side with Eitak. "So, tell me how you ended up in the marketplace?" he asked her.

"I am of the Wirral," she announced. Eitak had heard of the Wirral and tales of their hunting prowess. He had also heard stories that they killed their men after mating. Unconsciously, Eitak found himself stepping sideways and away from Arwie.

Yet still curious, he said, "Are the stories true?"

"That we kill our men?" she asked, confirming that was what he had meant and then she laughed. "Ha-ha, is that what you believe, Eitak?"

"Well, I don't…" Eitak didn't want to offend his new friend and was careful in choosing his next words. "What I meant was… Do you have a man in your life?"

Arwie blushed again and hid her scar with her shoulder. "No, I have not chosen yet, there is plenty of time for that sort of thing later on; for now, I have too much to do and too many things to see. I lived with my kind in the huge forests of Rampor, at the foot of the Thunder Mountains. We comprise only of females between 20 and 30 years of age. Rampor is our hunting ground but the forest there is the most dangerous place on all of Kennet and is filled with creatures that you could only imagine in your worst nightmares. I am 21 and had only just begun my time in Rampor when one day while I was out hunting, I heard a strange whirring noise, as I got closer, I was ambushed and captured by golden metal soldiers, I tried to escape but it was no use and I was taken to a wagon where several creatures wearing robes and golden masks forced me into a cage. After that I was taken to the slave master of Bagdoon who held me in the city dungeons until market day when I was sold to the slave trader…the one you found me with but while I was a prisoner, I learnt of the Golden Army and heard rumours of how it came to be…" As she finished her sentence, she turned and looked at Sirod.

Eitak was mesmerised and as he looked at Arwie, he couldn't help but think that she was beautiful, sure she had a scar but that didn't matter and it did nothing to put him off, in fact, if anything, it just made him curious as to how she came by it. Eitak thought about that and decided that it would be best not to ask at this early stage and thought that he should get to know her a little better first. "Carry on." Arwie caught him staring at her and again hid her scar but then she realised that he was more gazing than staring and she smiled.

"One day I overheard the slave trader talking, he said that one of the giants of Kidder Doon had been captured and that he had been forced into making an army for 'The Master'. I later found out that the giant was taken into the hurricane's eye and that he is being held there against his will."

Eitak's mind swirled with all of the things that Arwie had told him. He knew of the giants but like everyone else he had never actually seen one…That was, of course, until last night. He also knew of the great hurricane which permanently swept across the equator of Kennet. Vast and with tremendous power, it tracked the desert plains as it made its way around the planet. The only beings able to survive that hostile environment were the Sand Dwellers, who lived in the great sand storm where they preyed upon anyone crazy enough to venture into its path.

Eitak suddenly thought of Monrith and his friends, he had been so preoccupied that he hadn't even considered their fate until now…and sadly he wondered if he might ever see them again. Arwie could see that Eitak was upset and she held out her hand towards his and they gently touched. Eitak desperately wanted to hold Arwie's hand and although he had held the hand of many women in his past, he got a strange feeling when he touched Arwie; a feeling of awkwardness and he slowly withdrew his hand. Arwie felt this too and she touched her face wondering if her scar had made Eitak uncomfortable and then in silence they walked together as they climbed the hill towards the Grand Observatory of Illya.

The huge bulk of the observatory building grew larger with each step and once at the top of the hill, the travellers could see the Thunder Mountains to the east and the snow-capped mountains of light to the west. Eitak looked up at the observatory and could see that the huge doors at the top of the white dome were open and the end of a massive telescope was protruding out into the bright sunshine, which he thought looked like a strange creature emerging from its shell.

"Well, it looks like someone's in," Eitak said. By now the others had now caught up and they all stood at the two large oak doors at the entrance. The doors were very elaborate and had beautiful carvings of planets and stars on each one and some sort of inscription in a strange language he could not read.

"Heaven's Gate," Sirod said as he read the words out loud.

"How can you read that?" asked Bones.

"It is written in the ancient language of the Magistan," he answered. "There are many things I can do which might surprise you."

Eitak dropped the metal ring which surrounded a black planet making up the large door knocker in the centre of the right door. He waited for a while and was just about to knock again when the door slowly opened.

A very short and stout man stood in the doorway, sucking on a lollipop. Eitak thought he looked to be in his 60s and that he couldn't possibly be a Magistan. They were much taller or so he had heard. This man was mainly bald apart from two tufts of fluffy white hair on each side of his head. To his right eye, he wore a monocle which fell and was caught by a chain around his neck as he viewed the four-people stood on his doorstep.

"What do you want? Can't you see I'm busy?" he said rather curtly.

"That's a charming way to greet an old friend," Sirod announced. "It's me, Sirod, you, old fool."

The old man's eyes narrowed as he squinted to get a better look, he replaced the monocle to his right eye, removed the lollipop from his mouth and then said, "Sirod Spa, is that really you? I seem to remember you being somewhat older the last time I saw you but then again being a Nagraal, I suppose I should come to expect anything of you." He then hobbled from the doorstep and embraced Sirod with a hug. He then turned to the others impatiently and said, "Well, don't just stand there, come in."

The inside of the observatory was just as grand as the outside. The entrance hall was a large open space painted white, the main focal point being a large spiral staircase leading to the upper floors. This had all the known planets of Kennet's solar system, intricately carved into it and hanging from the ceiling were more celestial bodies, suspended by chains of different lengths which spun slowly around in the slight breeze created when the front door had been opened.

"Wow, this is amazing!" Arwie exclaimed.

"Now that we are inside, I had better introduce myself. I am Mallard Sly, otherwise known as Malarog, the Magistan." Looking towards Arwie he continued, "And my dear, if you think this is amazing, just wait until I show you the observatory room." Eitak, Bones and Arwie formally introduced themselves and removed their coats. Malarog led them up the spiral staircase to the first landing where two massive white doors faced them. These doors were quite plain in comparison to those at the entrance with just a single carving of Kennet on the left door and Lunari, Kennet's only moon on the right. Malarog grasped the crescent moon handles of each door and opened them together. Eitak was the first to follow Malarog into the observatory room. The first thing that struck him was the enormity of the space which now presented itself in front of him. The centre of the room was taken up by the most beautiful optical instrument he had ever seen. He just stood with his neck craned skywards in total awe of his surroundings. The huge golden telescope reaching to the heavens took his breath away; on each of the three massive tubes that made up its structure were the engravings of further celestial bodies.

Once again hanging from the ceiling were numerous planets, moons and stars similar to the ones he had seen at the entrance, except that these were attached to an intricate system of cogs and rails. This caused them to revolve slowly around in a clockwise motion above his head. Eitak instantly recognised most of these from books which he had read back in Monrith but others appeared totally unfamiliar. There was a low-pitched humming noise with the odd whirr and click coming from the mechanism, as each of the large globes made its way around the room and swinging from the planets and jumping from one to another was a small monkey. The monkey had beautiful golden coloured fur and was wearing a collar with a glowing blue crystal jewel pendant, just like the stone in Eitak's staff. The monkey stopped swinging and sat on top of one of the smaller planets in order to get a better look at the new visitors.

Arwie was also taken aback by what she found in this room and gasped.

"The Magistanian Telescope of Illya. The only one of its kind," Malarog announced proudly.

"Aye, it's a pretty thing, all right," said Bones as he poked around at several items scattered on a large table in one corner of the room. "I bet you could see Monrith from here."

"If that were only possible," Malarog answered, "but I have only ever viewed the stars with this magnificent piece of machinery. I helped to make it you know. After all, there is only so much travelling a person can do and when I decided to hang up my walking boots, I assisted in creating this magnificent work of art. I can claim credit for the configuration of the lenses which give much greater power than a normal telescope." Malarog muttered on, caught up in the moment, having finally got a captive audience to share his enthusiasm for his achievements.

Bones had lost interest, his attention distracted by what appeared to be a small metal dragonfly amongst the apparent junk scattered around the table. He picked it up and viewed it closely. Once again it was beautifully designed and must have taken its creator a long time to make. Protruding from one side was a small key. 'A musical dragonfly' Bones mused as he wound the tiny mechanism. Suddenly, the eyes of the dragonfly began to flicker with light and its four wings beat gently in his palm. "Wow, this is amazing," Bones said excitedly and he held the dragonfly aloft in his left hand and turned his head towards Sirod who was standing in the middle of the room talking to Malarog. He failed to notice that the dragonfly's eyes were now brightly pulsing with light and its wing speed had increased dramatically. There was now a loud humming noise coming from his left hand as the mechanical creature slowly rose into the air. Bones quickly turned his gaze back, just as the dragonfly broke free of his grasp and took off flying wildly around the room.

Malarog shouted, "Get down, quick." and the entire group crouched on the floor beneath the flight of the clockwork insect, which was now whizzing around the room at great speed, crashing uncontrollably into everything and anything in its path. As it passed by the planets hanging from the ceiling, the small monkey took a swipe at it with its paw but missed. As metal hit metal, sparks began flying from objects that the insect collided with.

"How many turns did you give it?" Malarog asked in a stern voice.

"I don't know. A couple I guess." Bones felt like a naughty schoolboy and began to sulk just as the dragonfly's eyes grew dim and it spiralled on a collision course towards him.

"Look out!" Eitak threw himself on top of Bones, knocking him flat on the floor, the clockwork menace narrowly missing them both as it buzzed overhead and finally hit the table where it had come from and stopped amongst the many other items lying there.

Malarog rose to his feet and looked at Bones, his left eyebrow rose slightly. "On that table are my failed and unfinished projects and I see you have found one of them."

"Perhaps, now would be a good time to talk about why we are here," Sirod said softly, trying to take the attention away from Bones.

"Oh, but I already know that," replied Malarog, "it's about Usurpus, isn't it?"

Sirod's eyes widened and he listened intently to what Malarog was about to say.

"Usurpus Sly, he now calls himself the 'The Grand Master of Cylesia.' His side of the family never were much good. The last I heard was that he had a group of followers who he calls his Magistanian army and that he had captured a giant who he keeps hostage in the great hurricane. Clearly, it is he who has forced the giant into making this Golden Army that I have heard so much about. Usurpus' side of the family always did plan to take over Kennet. The only reason that we have escaped is because he knows that I am here, plus, we are protected by the Thunder Mountains to the east and the Mountains of Light to the west. I dare say it will not be long before his metal army sets sail from Monrith and attempts to take over Illya." He then took another lollipop from his pocket and placed in in his mouth.

By now the monkey had become a little bolder and felt that the visitors must be friends. Realising that Bones clearly wanted to play, he swung from planet to planet until he reached the telescope; he then slid down the optical tube and then jumped onto the floor where he made his way across the room until he reached Bones. Underneath the table, which contained Malarog's inventions, was a small silver metal orb, lavishly decorated with various inscriptions; it had a series of lenses running through the middle like a small telescope and on the top was a single button. The orb had been knocked from the table by the metal dragonfly and the monkey picked it up and handed it to Bones. Bones inspected the item and put the glass to his eye. He realised that it was indeed a kind of small telescope and as he looked around the room, he spied Malarog through the small eyepiece. Subconsciously feeling that Malarog blamed him for the dragonfly incident and believing that he probably held a grudge, he pushed the button on the top of the orb as if pulling the trigger of an imaginary crossbow. All of a sudden, the monkey disappeared, vanished in a split second only to reappear on Malarog's shoulder. As soon as it realised where it now was, the monkey quickly reached forward and snatched the lollipop from Malarog's mouth.

"Put that down," shouted Malarog, now quite cross with Bones for meddling with his inventions.

Bones panicked and dropped the orb on the floor. It rolled along the ground and each time it rolled over, the small button on the top depressed. With each press of the button, the monkey disappeared and then re appeared wherever the glass lens pointed and wherever he materialised, he grabbed out and took whatever was within his arms reach. By the time that the orb came to a rest, the monkey, who was now clinging to one of the planets with one hand, had quite a collection of items in his other.

"Another of my failed experiments!" Malarog exclaimed.

"It looked like it worked to me," said Bones. "What does it do?"

"It's a transporter," Malarog said, "except it won't work on anything bigger than a monkey and that's why I use it on my pet monkey 'Bonsai'. I wanted to move people really but I just can't seem to make it work on a bigger scale and Bonsai is the only useful small thing worth 'transporting'. It works by looking into the orb and pointing wherever you want him to move to, then you press the button and hey presto. The power source is the Orillion crystal that he wears around his neck. I couldn't help but notice your staff Eitak, where did you get that crystal?"

"I…just picked it up in the marketplace," replied Eitak.

"There is great power in a crystal of that size, be careful with it." Malarog warned.

"So, what do we do now?" asked Eitak.

"I will consult with the Planispherium and see where the Hurricane will be three weeks from now. By then you will have thought of a way to free the giant and if grateful, he will help you to defeat Usurpus' army."

"And if not?" asked Bones.

"If not, then he will eat you," Malarog replied smirking as he moved to a lever with a long handle sticking out of the floor and pulled it towards him. The humming noise in the room gradually got louder and louder as the orbs and planets above their heads began to move faster around the room as they built up speed, Bones noticed that Bonsai was still holding onto one of the planets. The monkey's eyes widened as he struggled to hang onto all of the items of bric-a-brac that he had pilfered. Faster and faster the orbs spun. "Tomorrow, the next day, the day after…" Malarog said. Bonsai was now hanging on with all his might, the items in his arm shuddered loose and crashed to the ground with an almighty clatter. Bonsai was flung around the planet in a wide arc as the speed increased and now that he had both hands free, he actually seemed to be enjoying the experience. Eitak noticed that around the equator of the orb, representing Kennet was a groove around which spun a disc representing the great hurricane. "We're nearly there," Malarog shouted, over the din of the mechanism and then he pushed the lever forward and the orbs came to a stop. "Three weeks," he said. They looked at 'Kennet' and there was the hurricane on the equator above the Crystal Desert and directly above that was an orb that represented what would be a full moon.

"There." Malarog pointed to the hurricane symbol. "You need to be there three weeks from now. I suggest you set off in the morning."

The morning came around quicker than any of them could have imagined. Malarog had packed some food and provisions for the journey. He gave Eitak a map and a compass, he gave Sirod a bottle containing a green glowing liquid and to Arwie he handed a beautifully crafted bow and a quiver which contained golden arrows tipped with tiny fragments of the blue Orillion crystals. "The map will only show you the route ahead and not the one already travelled and the compass will show the right way to those who are good and the wrong way to those who are evil," Malarog said, "the potion I bought from a merchant just a few years ago. I understand that if drunk by a Nagraal, it compels them to stay in the body they are currently in which will fuse their soul to that body but it will then render them mortal."

"But does the body continue to rot?" Eitak asked.

"As far as I know, they can then lead a full and renewed life. But they become as mortal as you or I at the end of that life…the bow…" he continued. "…Shoots special arrows you will know when is a good time to use them but only do so at great distance." Bones looked at the others who all had presents and was just about to sulk when Malarog turned to him. "And to you, I give Bonsai and the orb. Take good care of him and bring him back to me when your adventure is at an end." With that, he handed over the magical orb, picked up Bonsai who had jumped down from the planet and gave him to Bones.

The five companions said their goodbyes and left the Grand Observatory of Illya. As they walked back down the hill, Malarog shouted, "Take care… Ursurpus is no fool… Oh and don't let him touch you, he is the only Magistan who can know all there is to know about you with just one touch."

"What now?" Bones enquired.

4. The Mountains of Light

Eitak opened the map to find a detailed chart of all of Kennet and he could clearly see the route they needed to take from Illya to the Crystal Desert. "According to the map, we need to travel to the west and take the pass through the Mountains of Light, from there we follow the Red River and then on to the slave city of Bagdoon."

Arwie drew in a quick breath of air and in a panic-stricken voice gasped, "I can't go there…I simply won't go back there."

Eitak spoke to her softly, "It'll be all right this time because we will be with you." And then he looked at the map again. "From there we must enter the wilderness, navigate the canyons and then cross the Crystal Desert until we find the hurricane."

"What shall we do 'after' dinner?" Bones enquired jokingly.

Eitak folded his map, took out his compass and looked at the dial, the arrow pointed to the west and so off they set.

Within two days they reached the foot of the Mountains of Light, around the top of which swirled a constant electric storm of swirling brilliance and colour. Bones took out his transporter orb and viewed the snowy peaks of the mountain range high above. Sirod, quite alarmed by Bones actions said, "Don't make a mistake and push the button, we don't want to freeze our golden monkey."

Bones took the orb from his eye and replied, "I don't know about Gold monkey, it looks cold enough to freeze a brass monkey to me." And as he looked at the small ball in his hand, he shivered.

The five travellers began to climb the mountain towards the path that would lead them to the other side. As they climbed higher, the weather turned colder, thick snow covered the ground and a biting wind blew around them.

After a while, Bones took the orb from his pocket again and looked around the mountain. As he scanned the snowy terrain, the eyepiece was suddenly filled by a fearsome creature. It was standing on two legs and was the size of a wagon.

The creature was covered in white fur and had a large mouth with big, sharp teeth and on its nose, it had a horn. Bones took the orb from his eye, shook it and then looked back into the snow. Somehow, he had hoped that there was something wrong with the device. Now shaking with fear, Bones accidentally pressed the button; as he did so, he saw 'Bonsai' appear on the creature's shoulder. The monster turned to look at this sudden intrusion and roared. Bonsai lifted his finger and poked it in one eye. Realising his error, Bones quickly took the orb from his eye, pointed it at the ground in front of him and pressed the button once more. Almost immediately, Bonsai re-appeared at his feet. "Thank goodness for that," he said. Bones looked back at the creature hoping that it hadn't noticed them but not only had it noticed, it was now running at full speed in their direction.

Sirod looked up and saw the creature now running forwards, its arms outstretched with large claws grabbing at the air. "A Snow Jax!" he exclaimed with panic in his voice.

The companions froze, all except Arwie, who calmly removed the bow from her shoulder, set a golden arrow into the string and let loose one of the blue crystal tipped shafts. The Snow Jax was now a lot closer.

Arwie shouted, "Follow me." And the group ran to a large boulder and hid behind it. Bones peered around the corner of the rock and saw the glowing light of the arrow whizz past the Snow Jax and head off into the thick snow above.

"You missed!" shouted Bones in horror.

A moment passed before there was a flash of blinding blue light followed by a terrific explosion which caused the ground to shake and was followed by a thunderous rumbling sound.

"Avalanche!" shouted Sirod. Bones grabbed Bonsai and huddled him inside his jacket. Eitak grabbed Arwie and Sirod covered himself in his cape. They all pushed themselves as close to the rock as they could. The torrent of snow and ice quickly caught up with the Snow Jax who was immediately engulfed in the current. Vast sheets of snow slid down the mountainside at great speed and crashed against the boulder where the companions hid. The snow disintegrated to fine dust as it collided against the hard rock and flew harmlessly overhead, whilst the main river of ice ran either side of them as it travelled down to the valley below.

When the dust settled, Bones turned to Eitak and pointing at the blue crystalline end of his staff and said, "Can I suggest that you don't drop that?"

"Nor for the same reason should you drop your monkey?" Eitak replied.

The travellers slowly stood up and looked around the boulder. The mountain path ahead of them was now completely covered in deep snow.

"Did you know that would happen?" Eitak asked Arwie. "And how did you learn to shoot a bow like that?"

"I had my suspicions…" she answered proudly. "…And I told you, I am a hunter and a good one at that."

Eitak couldn't argue the fact. Addressing the group, he then asked, "What do we do now?"

"We will have to find a way around," Sirod answered with no alternative options being available.

"But that will take us hundreds of miles out of our way," Arwie said with some desperation to her voice.

Bones had taken the orb out of his pocket again and was looking through the eyepiece, Bonsai jumped around excitedly at his feet, wondering where he might end up next. "There!" exclaimed Bones excitedly. "There's a tunnel." Sirod, Eitak and Arwie all looked where Bones was pointing and then they saw that further up the mountain was a small dark hole.

As they approached the entrance to the tunnel, it became apparent that this was not a feature of nature but had been bored by something on purpose and it seemed to disappear deep into the mountain. "It might go to the other side," Bones said excitedly.

"Then again it might not." Sirod looked into the hole and continued, "I wonder what made it?"

Bones answered, "Who cares, it's here and that's all that counts." And with that, he walked into the tunnel. Eitak and Arwie followed, Sirod shook his head and then reluctantly brought up the rear. Very soon the tunnel lost what light had been cast from the entrance and to Eitak's amazement, his staff glowed with a brilliant blue light.

"That's strange," Sirod commented. "It must release energy at night." The tunnel was perfectly round and smooth and ran deep under the mountain. After a while, the tunnel opened up to a large cavern which was lit by a strange green light. The gallery was the size of a cathedral with huge stalactites hanging from the ceiling and stalagmites of equal size rising from the floor. Feeling a little less claustrophobic, the party spread out in the cave, pleased at the extra space they now had. All around the floor were numerous crystals which glowed bright green and were clearly the source of the ambient light.

"They are just like the blue ones, only green," Bones said, stating the obvious. "I wonder if they blow up too?"

"Let's not find out," Sirod replied worried that Bones might begin throwing the crystals around as an experiment.

Seeing the shiny green stones, Bones picked up one of the larger crystals and put it in his pocket.

A short while later, the group entered another tunnel at the back of the cave which continued on further into the mountain. Eventually, the tunnel divided in two with one fork continuing straight on and the other taking a slight angle to the southwest of where they were. "Let's go this way." Suggested Bones and continued straight on.

After several minutes of walking, Arwie was the first to hear the strange sucking noise coming from the tunnel further ahead. "Can you hear that?" she asked.

"Hear what?" said Bones, more interested in walking than listening.

"That," Arwie repeated. And the whole group stopped to listen. Coming from the tunnel ahead, they could now hear a strange sucking and scraping noise which appeared to be getting closer.

"What is it?" Eitak didn't really like the claustrophobic environment of the tunnels anyway and would rather that they had found a way around the mountain as Sirod had suggested.

"If it is what I think it is, then we really need to turn around and now." Warned Sirod.

"Why? What is it?" Bones enquired.

Just as he finished his question, he turned back to look into the tunnel. Ahead and in the gloom, he saw a huge worm.

"An Ice Worm," Sirod shouted. "Run!"

Bones looked at the large, white coloured Ice worm which moved with some speed towards him. It completely filled the tunnel and was all of six feet tall. Its head comprised of four small eyes and had a large mouth with razor sharp teeth which it had opened in anticipation of a delicious feast. Bonsai who was looking out from the warmth of Bone's jacket let out a shrill scream and the four friends turned and ran back in the direction from where they had come. There was no time for Arwie to take her bow from her shoulder and let loose an arrow, the worm was gaining on them and all she could think to do was run. After a minute or two of running, they were all growing tired, Bones was gasping heavily for breath and his right leg was hurting as something was banging against his thigh. He looked down and saw that it was the pocket of his jacket which had something heavy in it. "The stone." He remembered and he reached into his pocket. He pulled the stone out and felt immediate relief from the pain. Casually, he discarded the stone over his shoulder and it landed on the icy ground behind him with a thud. "Clearly the green ones don't explode," he shouted.

"What?" replied Arwie, who was running slightly ahead of him. Unseen by Bones, the green crystal began to emit a humming noise and glowed brighter and brighter and then all of a sudden it did explode. A flash of green light filled the tunnel and green flame rushed in Bones' direction. The tunnel behind him collapsed, huge boulders of ice came crashing down and stopped the worm which had been caught up in the explosion. The green fireball gained on Bones fast, he looked over his shoulder and saw the light coming at him. Just when he thought that his life was over, he saw the fork in the tunnel. Sirod, Eitak and Arwie were first to turn right and enter the other tunnel, the one that they had seen earlier after they left the cave and as soon as they entered, they were quickly followed by Bones who rounded the corner just as the green flames rushed past him and continued ahead down the main shaft. He had only taken three steps into the tunnel when he lost his footing and fell. He now found himself sliding at great speed along the icy ground and came to realise that this tunnel was in fact a long, slippery and very steep chute. He could see the others just ahead of him, all of whom were screaming loudly. After several moments, he became accustomed to this new feeling and even started to enjoy the experience. That was until he saw the light at the end of the tunnel ahead.

5. The Red River

Sirod was the first to be shot out of the icy tube, closely followed by the others. Blinded momentarily by sunlight, he couldn't see a thing; all he was aware of was that he was falling. As his eyesight returned, he found himself in midair with a sheer ice wall behind him and a glorious view of trees and forests in front. Beneath his feet, a long way below were the crimson-coloured waters of the Red River and slightly above him he heard screams and shouts of Eitak, Arwie and Bones.

Sirod instinctively panicked and like anyone who has ever found themselves in a situation where they are falling, he began to flap his arms and kick his legs in an attempt to fly. After a few seconds and realising that he couldn't, he too began to scream. The fall was long as too was his scream which required two deep breaths to maintain and then he hit the water feet first and plunged into the icy depths of the Red River. Down and down, Sirod sank into the deep river, which although cold, was thankfully calm and slow moving. As he became buoyant and began to rise, Sirod wished that he had taken a deeper breath as he started to fight for air. He did not rise as quickly as he had hoped and clawed at the water with his hands and kicked out with his feet in a desperate attempt to reach the surface above. Just as he felt, his lungs compressing in his chest as they fought his resolve not to open his mouth, allowing them to expand, he reached the surface. He drew a breath, gasped for air and sucked in as much oxygen as he could with that first gulp of freedom. Soon he became less panicked and his breathing returned to a heavy pant. *The others* he thought and he looked from side to side across the river, looking for any signs of life. Eitak was the first to surface, followed shortly by Arwie, both of whom were also desperate for air. A few moments later, Bones threw himself from under the water and gasped his first breath. "Thank goodness," Sirod called out with great relief to his voice.

Bones suddenly panicked. Not because he found himself in the deep waters of the Red River and not because he had fallen from such a great height, nor was it for the fact that he had almost drowned. He tore at his jacket, threw his hand inside and pulled out the limp lifeless body of Bonsai.

"Bonsai!" Sirod exclaimed.

Eitak and Arwie immediately swam over to Bones. Arwie took Bonsai from him and gently began to massage his small chest with two fingers. Every so often she put her lips to Bonsai's mouth and breathed tiny breaths into his lifeless lips whilst treading water in the cold Red River. Arwie was a very good swimmer and was able to make her way to the shore on the far side whilst still trying to breathe life into Bonsai. Eitak was slightly ahead of her and using his staff, he managed to haul himself up out of the waters and onto the bank. Quickly he turned and offered his hand to Arwie but as he did so, he lost his grip of his staff which fell forward and struck Bonsai on the chest where the glowing blue crystal at the end came to a stop very close to Bonsai's collar. Eitak grabbed the staff but as he did so, he pressed a small button hidden within the handle which he had not seen before. Suddenly, a great flash of light shot out from the end of the staff and an arc of blue energy engulfed Bonsai's chest.

Bones had by now just reached the water's edge just in time to see a bolt of light enter his furry little friend. "Oh, that's just great, that is. Not only do we drown him, we try to fry him too," he said.

But then the most amazing thing happened. Bonsai dribbled water from the side of his mouth followed by several splutters and then violent coughing. He opened his eyes and saw Arwie just about to give him what he considered a kiss and instinctively slapped her across the face, he then jumped out of her arms and threw himself upon the right shoulder of Bones who was now dragging himself out up the muddy riverbank.

"Bonsai!" Bones shouted, having been so busy struggling up the steep bank that he hadn't seen his little friend come back to life. Bones and Bonsai looked at each other for a brief moment and then Bonsai threw his arms around Bones' neck and hugged him. The hug only lasted a second before Bonsai found something far more interesting and with one ear in each hand, he pulled Bones' ears out to the side and then looking at his face, gave out a shrill cry of laughter as he jumped up and down on Bones' shoulder.

"That was close," Eitak said, relieved.

"Too close," Sirod agreed.

"So, now what?" Bones asked as he wiggled a finger in his right ear having been slightly deafened by Bonsai's laugh.

Eitak took his map out of his pocket and carefully unfolded it. "I think we should wait here for a while so that I can let the map dry out and get my breath back."

Bones, Bonsai and Arwie decided to walk upstream along the riverbank to find some wood to make a fire, Whilst Eitak and Sirod stayed behind and talked.

"So, Sirod, tell me, how did you become a Nagraal?"

"That is something which pains me greatly," replied Sirod, "but it has been a long time now and I might as well share it with you. You see I am over 200 years old and I once went by the name of Seth Kai. When I was about your age, I met a girl and I fell in love, her name was Ember Firestorm; she was beautiful and had hair the colour of fire. Ember was the daughter of Oubistar, the Magistan, Malarog's great grandfather. Now Oubistar had a brother named Niastar and Niastar had a son named Kalag."

"One day Oubistar died unexpectedly and Ember went to live with her uncle, Niastar. Whilst living with him, Kalag also fell in love with Ember but Kalag was cruel and evil and in time, Ember saw this and did not share in his love. She told Kalag her feelings; however, he believed that it was his right to take her hand in marriage. Their marriage was arranged and Ember was forced to take him as her husband. Ember truly loved me and this was known to Niastar who knew of his son's cruel ways. He had grown to like Ember as a daughter and would rather that his son did not marry her to save her from a life of pain and misery. On the night before her wedding, Ember called for me to go to her. I met her in the tower of her home where she told me that she wanted to be with me and she asked me to take her with me but someone had told Kalag of my visit and he came to the tower. Kalag was furious with rage in his eyes. I stood in front of Ember to protect her as Kalag came close. Kalag drew a knife from behind his back and thrust it towards me; fearing for my own life, I moved and the knife plunged deep into Ember and her body fell to the floor. Niastar had learned of his son's intentions and burst into the room but it was all too late. He saw his son with the knife in his hand and took him away. Ember was taken too and I was told that she had died. I knew that I could have saved her, it should have been me who died that day and not her or I should have fought Kalag…even if it meant dying at his hand."

"Niastar sent Kalag away to the lands to the east of the Thunder Mountains and it was he who marched upon Bagdoon in the Kenetian wars which resulted in the building of the Great Wall. I never got over my guilt and became like a son to Niastar, the son he had always wished that Kalag could have been. In time, Niastar grew old and became ill, my grief was still great and Niastar, being one of the Magistan, gave me a potion which he told me to drink, his last words to me were that he was sure that one day, I would find peace if I searched long and hard enough. As I too grew old, I drank the potion and that is how I became one of the Nagraal."

Sirod put his hand inside his cape and pulled out the small bottle containing the glowing green liquid that Malarog had given him, he looked at it and then placed it back inside his cape.

"The one thing I didn't tell you is that Usurpus is Kalag's great, great grandson."

Eitak looked at Sirod who had tears in his eyes. "That was nearly 200 years ago Sirod and it wasn't your fault."

"Have you ever truly been in love?" Sirod asked.

Eitak immediately found himself thinking of Arwie. "No…" he replied. "…Not yet."

"Then you cannot truly know the guilt I feel and the longing I have that things could have been different."

Sirod had only just finished his sentence when Bones came running back and shouted with panic and dread in his voice, "They're coming. Run!"

Sirod sprang to his feet. "Who's coming?" he shouted.

"The Golden soldiers…" Arwie shouted. "They're on the other side of those trees." Arwie pointed to the trees where she and Bones had just come from.

"Did they see you?" Sirod asked his words tinged with a sense of panic.

"I don't think so," Arwie answered, "but they are coming this way."

Eitak picked up the map which was now a lot dryer having warmed in the heat of the sunshine. He glanced down and to his disbelief saw that the map had changed, Illya was no longer visible and the scale was slightly smaller with a little more detail of the route ahead. From what he could see, they needed to travel down river. He looked around him and could see a fallen tree on the riverbank a short distance further downstream from where they stood. "Follow me!" he shouted and the group of friends ran along the riverbank towards the log. As Eitak got to the tree, he saw that it was in fact a very large trunk which had been gnawed away from its root and had been left abandoned on the ground. The trunk had a very large hole in one side and on further inspection, Eitak discovered that the tree was hollow for most of its length and on either side of the trunk, there were two large branches culminating in some foliage at the ends.

Eitak could now hear the same whirring and clicking noise which he had first heard in Monrith. It was the Golden Army! And it was getting closer. He turned to look towards the trees where Arwie and Bones had run from and saw the first of the Golden soldiers marching towards him. "Quick!" Eitak shouted. "Help me push this log into the river." Eitak, Arwie, Sirod and Bones each grabbed a hold of one corner of the trunk and pushed with all their might whilst Bonsai sat on top of a small nodule on top of the tree. Surprisingly, being hollow, the tree was quite light and it quickly slipped into the river with ease. Once afloat, the four companions jumped into the water just as an arrow whistled through the air and embedded itself in the trunk with a heavy thud. The four travellers held their breath, swam under the log and came up on the other side. Now protected from further arrows by the wood, they allowed themselves to be carried away downstream and away from the Golden Soldiers who now stood on the riverbank throwing spears and firing arrows in their direction. The soldiers did not view the four escapees as any threat, certainly no more so than any other villager or town dweller they had already encountered and so after a short while, they diverted their attention back to their original task and that was the conquest of the Mountains of Light and the port city of Illya beyond.

Once out of arrow range, Eitak, Arwie, Sirod and Bones clambered up onto the log and sat astride it, their feet dangling in the red waters. Eitak and Arwie were tired and looked into the hole in the trunk. Inside the tree, the wood was dry, the outer shell being thick enough to stop the ingress of water. Arwie was the first and she slipped herself into the cavity and lay down inside the log. She found the soft wood inside to be surprisingly comfortable and bug free, Eitak followed and lay next to her but kept a small distance between them. As she closed her eyes, he looked at her in the dim light and found himself drawn to her in a way that he had never experienced before. Usually he was quite forward and confident but with Arwie, it was different and as much as he wanted to tell her how he felt, he just couldn't manage it. "Arwie…" he whispered.

She opened one eye as he lay close to her, "It's OK, I feel the same way too," she replied.

"Sorry?" Eitak asked, not quite expecting her response. "I was going to tell you about Sirod."

"Oh," she said, feeling embarrassed. "I'm sorry…what I meant was…just carry on."

"I was wrong about Sirod. At first I thought that he was a bit aloof, cold and unfeeling but I was so wrong…" Eitak told Arwie Sirod's story and at the end he asked, "What did you mean, you feel the same way too?"

"It doesn't matter," she replied and before long, they were both fast asleep.

Sirod and Bones sat on top of the log as it slowly travelled downstream in the direction that Eitak's map had indicated, to their left was the tall sheer rock face of the Mountains of Light and to their right was dense forests. They had been drifting for several hours when Bones noticed that the current of the waters began to increase and being a sailor, he knew what the likely cause of this increase in flow meant, however, he considered that it was not worth worrying about at this time. "So why is it called the Red River?" Bones asked.

"Because it runs rich with the blood of the many lives that have been lost to it," Sirod replied.

"Really?" he enquired. Bones was horrified as the river seemed fairly calm and not at all dangerous and he just couldn't imagine that it was capable of taking enough lives to make the water run red.

"No," Sirod answered. "It's because of the mineral deposits on the river bed, you fool."

Bones laughed more out of embarrassment at having been had over than anything else and he dipped his right hand into the water as the log continued downstream. Within a few seconds, he felt a sharp pain on his fingertip. He pulled out his hand to find a small fish with very big teeth biting down on his index finger. "Must everything around here have big teeth?" he asked shaking his hand, vigorously trying to shake off the small fish. He inspected the fish and then through the pain said, "I've not seen one of these before, what are they?"

"Biter fish…" replied Sirod. "…And wherever there's one, there are normally a lot more." And as he finished his sentence, another of the small fish appeared. This one had thrown itself out of the water and had latched onto Sirod's cape. Grabbing the fish by the sides of its mouth, he removed its teeth from his clothing and threw it back into the river. Seconds later, another fish leapt up at him, followed by another and another and another. Before long, the log and its passengers were being attacked from all directions by these tiny menaces. "Quick. Into the hollow!" Sirod shouted and with that, Bonsai and

Bones scrambled into the hole in the trunk and climbed over Eitak and Arwie who had been enjoying a pleasant nap.

Rudely awoken, Eitak asked, "What's going on?"

Sirod, who had now also entered the space in the tree replied, "Biter fish, if we stay up there, we will, very soon, be reduced to nothing." Sirod removed his cape and pushed it up plugging the hole so that the fish could not get in. The tree trunk was now very cramped with four people and one monkey squashed together. Eitak's staff again glowed bright blue as did Bonsai's collar and between the two crystals, there was plenty of light to look around. At the bottom of the trunk, Bones found a pile of nuts which he picked up and began eating.

"How can you think of food at a time like this?" Eitak asked.

"Any time's good for eating," Bones replied and then he remembered. "Now might be as good a time as any…to tell you why the river is running faster."

"And why is that?" Eitak asked.

"When a river runs fast, there is always a reason." Bones continued. "…And it's probably because of a waterfall or worse," Bones concluded.

"A waterfall…or worse!!! What could possibly be worse than that!" Eitak exclaimed.

"Well, it could be a sink hole like a waterfall but a hole in the river, where the water gets sucked in. Like a big plug hole," Bones added.

"And where does the water go?" Eitak asked.

"Down," Bones replied.

Eitak gave up. "Let's just hope that it's a waterfall then, shall we."

"Or we could abandon ship," Arwie added.

"Not with those biter fish out there, we can't," Sirod continued, "but if we plug this hole nice and tight then we could stand a chance."

As Sirod plugged the hole, Bones poked his finger at a small circular pattern he had found in the side of the log. As he pressed the circular rings, out popped a small knot giving him a view of what was going on outside.

The log was now travelling faster and faster as the river outside carried them along at great speed. The water was also becoming extremely rough as it flowed over several large rocks which stood in its way as it travelled downstream. One of the outer branches of the tree suddenly struck a large rock which caused the trunk to continue on…sideways.

Bones could now clearly see the cause of the increased current as their log cascaded towards a very large sink hole in the riverbed.

"I was right!" Bones announced delightedly. "It is a sink hole and a very large one at that."

"Oh, that's just great," replied Eitak.

Bones continued to look out through his spyhole and could see another tree just ahead of them which became trapped by the swirling waters of the maelstrom. Round and round the log circled and then suddenly it disappeared into the whirlpool.

"I think I'm going to be sick..." Arwie announced. "I never was much of a sailor."

"Hold it together if you can," Bones replied. Just then there was a large bump as their log came to a stop. Sirod took his cape away from the hole and looked out. Just ahead of him he could see the ravaging waters of the whirlpool as they made their way downwards towards the unknown. But to his amazement, he saw that the tree had become stuck between two very large rocks, the branches either side of the log were now firmly wedged and despite the rush of the current from behind, the tree could go no further.

"Quick. Let's go!" Sirod shouted and the four friends and Bonsai climbed out of the trunk and scrambled onto the rocks. Arwie was the last one out and just as she clambered onto the rock, one of the stuck branches snapped and gave way to the pressure of the river. The log immediately accelerated away at great speed, caught by the maelstrom and disappeared from view into the abyss.

The foam capped waters now smashed against the rocks trying to knock the companions from their temporary safe haven. Sirod had already picked out a route from one rock to the other which eventually led them back to the river bank. First to the bank was Sirod followed by Eitak and Arwie whilst Bones being somewhat slower, brought up the rear. Bonsai had just about had enough of water and sat on top of Bones' head. As he was about to step from the last rock, a small biter fish jumped out of the waters and headed straight for Bones, quick as a flash, Bonsai lashed out with his right hand and slapped the fish which landed, flapping on the rock, where it thrashed about until it made its way back into the river and was gone. "You're quite good at that, aren't you?" Bones said to Bonsai, who simply looked at Bones, and let out a shrill cry of laughter.

Now back on dry land, Eitak took out his map and compass. Once again the scale of the map had changed and showed slightly more detail of the way ahead and between the two items, he could see that they needed to travel through the forest which now stood in front of them to Sherpa's bridge and from there, they would take the road leading to the slave city of Bagdoon.

The night was now drawing in and Sirod was feeling the strain from the day's arduous adventure. His body was showing the first and early signs of decay, his fingertips were speckled with blue black coloured spots and his complexion had taken on a slightly yellow, jaundiced tone. Bones was tired too and to his relief, Sirod suggested that they camp down for the night in a clearing slightly southwest of the Red River. The clearing was a pleasant and welcome sanctuary from the chaos and turbulence of the water and Bones and Sirod sat down on the mossy ground whilst Eitak and Arwie went into the woods to collect firewood.

Bones lay on his back and looked up into the trees high above. In the treetops, he could see some large and succulent fruits, 'Alder apples', he said in a loud voice and jumped to his feet. He looked around him and picked up a few small stones which he threw high into the trees in a vain attempt to bring down one of the large and succulent fruits. After several minutes, Bones gave up and threw the remainder of the stones he had collected to the ground. "It's no good," he said to Sirod. "They are just too high." Bonsai had been watching the proceedings with great amusement and had even joined in throwing stones into the air. Several of the pebbles had ricocheted off the trees and had landed on Sirod who was trying to relax on the ground. Seeing Bones accept defeat, Bonsai pulled at his trousers and pointed to his collar.

"Of course!" exclaimed Bones excitedly and he pulled the orb out of his pocket and looking through the lens pointed it at the fruits high in the tree tops. He pressed the button on the top and Bonsai disappeared in a flash. Seconds later a very large and heavy Alder fruit came crashing down, narrowly avoiding Sirod's head as he still lay on the mossy ground. This was followed by another Alder fruit and another and another.

Sirod shouted, "I think we have enough, we've got enough…do you want to bring him back down here before he kills someone?" Bones pointed the orb at the ground and on pressing the button, Bonsai re appeared next to him. This led Bones to think and moments later, off he went towards the Red River with Bonsai running along behind him.

"Where are you going?" Sirod shouted quizzically.

"Fishing," replied Bones and then he was gone.

Eitak and Arwie returned with some wood and before long, a warm and welcoming campfire had been lit which crackled and popped as small flames darted into the evening sky. After several moments, Bonsai and bones returned with several fish.

"How did you manage to catch those?" enquired Eitak.

"I spied several fish through the orb and I transported Bonsai to them. Bonsai grabbed them and I transported him back, it's simple."

They all laughed and set about cooking the fish and preparing the fruit. After a satisfying meal, they all snuggled down around the camp fire and fell asleep, all that was except Arwie who looked at Eitak and when she thought that he was asleep, she moved closer and lifted her arm, she was about to put it around him when he sighed heavily, scaring her into thinking that he was still awake and she withdrew her arm, turned over and fell asleep too. Eitak wasn't asleep and had just been relaxing when he felt the warmth of Arwie's presence. He desperately wanted to feel the softness of her touch and inside himself, cursed his involuntary sigh, he then closed his eyes and before long, everyone was asleep, enjoying the warmth of the crackling fire.

With the first light, Bonsai awoke and began to make small chirping noises which awoke the rest of the group and after a breakfast comprising of more fish and Alder fruit, they set off through the forest following Eitak's map as they went. The route through the forest was a long one which took several days. They fed upon Alder fruit, nuts, various roots, leaves and fungi which they foraged and they made camp at the end of each day wherever and whenever they came upon a suitable clearing. The companions found that the climate improved as they continued south as the sun shone brighter and hotter with each passing day.

Eventually, they came to the edge of the forest and looked down upon the road to Bagdoon.

6. The Road to Bagdoon

The road to Bagdoon was nothing more than a dirt track which ran from the town of Lamorah in the north to the slave city of Bagdoon in the south. Eitak pulled out his map which now showed a detailed plan of their immediate area and he pointed to Sherpa's bridge which crossed the Red River a few hours walk to the south of their current position.

"We must cross the river there," he said. "Now that we have passed the Mountains of Light, we will have to cross the river again in order to continue to Bagdoon."

"Why can't we just go around Bagdoon?" Bones enquired.

"Because of the Great Wall," replied Sirod. "The wall was constructed after the Kenetian war against Kalag and runs from the Thunder Mountains in the east to the Lamoran Peaks in the west. It is an impenetrable barrier built to withstand any invading army and the only passage from the north to the south is through the fortified city of Bagdoon."

The road to Bagdoon was deserted, usually a busy trade route, there was now not a single person to be seen. "I wonder where everyone has gone?" Bones asked.

"I can only surmise that they have either run away and are in hiding or that they have been captured by the Golden Army," Sirod replied. "We must be careful as I'm sure that Sherpa's bridge will be guarded."

Littered along the dusty road were many abandoned wagons filled with various goods including food and wine, clothes, cooking utensils, items of ironmongery and weapons which had just been left at the side of the road, as if the owners had just vanished into thin area or had been in a great rush to leave.

At first Eitak looked through one of the wagons which contained weapons and before long, he picked up the most beautiful knife he had ever seen. It was a dagger which had a blade forged of the finest folded steel and a blue stone handle which was turned from a single piece of lapis lazuli. At the end of the handle was a beautiful pommel, made to look like a Sun Violet flower which had white gold petals and a yellow gold centre. Eitak turned the dagger in his hand; it truly was a magnificent piece of work and far too nice to just leave lying around.

Eitak went over to join Arwie, who was looking inside a wagon containing fine clothing, whilst Sirod picked through several barrels containing various fruits in varying degrees of decay. Bones on the other hand had found just what he wanted, a wagon full of rotting fish.

Inside their wagon, Eitak and Arwie found clothes of the finest silk and cloth. Eitak uncovered a collarless white shirt with flowing sleeves which he tried on unbuttoned to the chest. Over his shirt he found a black velvet jacket and finished off his outfit with a pair of fine cloth trousers and black, knee length leather boots. Arwie had managed to find a flimsy, flowing white silk blouse and a black leather waistcoat.

"Look away," she said, embarrassed, and with her back to Eitak, she took off her tattered white shirt. Eitak couldn't resist a peek and he glanced over at her. He realised that he was, in fact, totally in awe of her beauty and he watched her flowing golden hair as it cascaded down her back. She placed one arm into the sleeve of the silk blouse and tossed her head to one side causing her hair to flow over her shoulder and reveal her back. Eitak gasped in horror, across her back in several places were a series of deep welted scars. Arwie heard the intake of his breath and hurriedly brought the blouse around her shoulders and placed her exposed arm in the other sleeve. She began to fasten the buttons as Eitak stepped over to her. He gently placed his hand under the blouse and lifted it slowly to reveal her injuries. She shook her head and pulled away. "That is why I don't want to return to Bagdoon," she said and quickly tucked the shirt into her trousers.

"I'm sorry…I didn't mean to…" Eitak didn't know what else to say.

"It's all right." Arwie took the awkwardness away from the situation and continued, "They are healed now, they just make me look…ugly."

"You could never look ugly…" he said, not really knowing what to say and then he thought he might as well just come out with it: "You are gorgeous and truly the most beautiful woman I have ever seen, your wounds do nothing to take that away, we all have scars. Look." and he rolled up his sleeve to reveal a tiny burn mark on his right arm. "I got this one taking cakes out of the oven." Arwie looked down at the miniscule scar and laughed. Soon they were both laughing loudly together, Eitak reached out, put his arms around her shoulders and they embraced, he looked into her eyes and smiled and in that moment, he knew that he wanted her more than anyone else he had ever met.

"Come on," Arwie said. "You wait outside while I change properly." Eitak jumped down from the wagon, followed a short time later by Arwie who had managed to find a pair of black leather trousers and short ankle length boots to compliment her outfit.

Sirod viewed the pair as they jumped from the wagon, "Very becoming," he said and they then made their way towards Bones to show off their new outfits. They could smell the wagon Bones had gone to from several paces away. The stench of rotting fish reminded Eitak of the boat trip from Monrith. As they got closer, they saw Bones pick up a barrel of rotten fish and tip it over himself so that he was now covered from head to toe in fish slime.

"What in Kennet's name are you doing?" Eitak shouted.

"I'm covering myself in fish," Bones replied as if it was a totally normal thing to do.

Arwie looked at Eitak and turning to Bones, enquired, "Can I ask why?"

"You'll see…" Bones answered. "…And I suggest you do the same if you want my advice."

"You're all right there, I think I'll pass on that one…and you can keep away from me and my new clothes," Arwie added.

Bones brushed some of the slime from his hair and clothing and stood there baking in the heat of the sun.

"You absolutely stink," Sirod announced.

"That's the general idea…" Bones said feeling quite proud of his achievement. "…But to be honest, you don't look so good yourself." Sirod looked down at his hands; the blue-black colour had now spread from his fingertips up his palms and onto his forearms. He touched his face and could feel how thin the skin had become. He closed one eye and looked at his nose with the other and realised that his face was now quite yellow, tinged with more spots of blueblack.

"I haven't got much longer," he said quietly.

Having taken everything worthwhile, carrying from the wagons, the four travellers together with Bonsai continued along the road to Bagdoon. Bones brought up the rear, having been forced to walk a few paces behind.

Soon Sherpa's bridge loomed into view and Sirod could see that it was indeed under guard. Two Golden soldiers stood this side of the Red River; beside two human characters dressed in short chainmail vests overtop of peasant clothing. Both of the men were tall. One was skinny with a small beard on his chin, whilst the other was quite fat and had red rosy cheeks. On the other side of the bridge was a horse drawn wagon with a large, empty cage on the back.

On seeing the guards, Arwie removed the bow from her shoulder and set another of the crystal tipped arrows into the string.

"Wait," Sirod shouted alarmingly. "You might blow up the bridge…Those people are probably part of the Magistanian army. I think we should pretend to be entertainers and say that we are on our way to perform for the slave master of Bagdoon." he continued, "After all we can't pretend to be merchants…they don't seem to have fared that well from the look of those wagons back there."

On hearing the mention of the slave master, Arwie gave a shudder, however, seeing no alternative, agreed to the plan. After a moment she turned to look at Bones and then said, "What shall we tell them about him?"

"We'll just say that he's getting into character," Sirod suggested and they all walked towards Sherman's bridge.

"Good morning," Sirod announced, thinking that it would be best to get their side of the story in first and thus sewing the seed of their deception. "We are Thespians from Illya here at the request of the slave master of Bagdoon, for his general amusement and delight."

The two men stood at the bridge looked at the four companions and then turned to each other and muttered something under their breath. Sirod managed to make out the words "story" and… "one here".

"I assure you that it is the truth," Sirod added in an attempt to throw aside any doubts the men might have.

"You are them that got away up river, ain't ya?" The skinnier of the two men accused, speaking the common tongue with a deep gruff voice.

"I assure you, sir, our visit is imperative…" Sirod continued.

"Fancy words, I ate fancy words." Interrupted the skinny man. "You betta come wiv us."

"Yeah." The fat man added and the two metal soldiers suddenly sprang to life and stood across the entrance to the bridge.

Arwie turned and was just about to run when Eitak grabbed her by the arm. "Hold on…" he whispered. "…I'm sure Sirod knows what he's doing."

Sirod turned to the group. "This could be our way in to the city...if it's guarded like I think it's going to be, there may not be another opportunity to get in without serious problems."

Eitak looked into Arwie's eyes. "He's right, this could work."

"And if it doesn't?" Arwie enquired her voice trembling from adrenaline.

"Then you will be with me...and we will think of something else."

Sirod turned to the men and said, "We will come with you as your guests and would be grateful of the lift. Thank you."

"Yeah, guests. That's it, come over 'ere while I search you all," the skinny man suggested.

"Yeah," the fat man added.

Sirod approached the men and was first to be patted down.

"You don't look so good, don't think you're gonna keep," the skinny man said looking at Sirod's face.

"Stage make up," Sirod answered thinking fast.

"And what's this?" asked the man pulling out the bottle of green liquid that Malarog had given him back in Illya.

"Face paint," Sirod replied.

Arwie was next and was just about to be searched by the fatter of the two men when the skinny man threw the bottle of potion back at Sirod, pushed him to one side and announced, "I'll do this one, nice she is."

Arwie screwed up her face and held herself rigid in anticipation of being touched all over by the disgusting peasant soldier when the fatter of the two men interjected, "Nah." and pushed the skinny man who danced backwards and collided with one of the metal soldiers. The skinny man reacted by pushing his companion back and the two men began pushing and slapping each other.

Bones had by now approached the men and stood close by. After several moments of fighting, the skinny man broke away from the grasp of his compatriot and said, "What's that stench?" He turned and looked at Bones who stood there smiling. "You stink...I ain't searchin 'im, ee's yours."

The big man looked at Bones and replied, "Nah." and shoved the skinny man firmly in the chest, causing him to recoil and collide once again with the same metal soldier and once again a squabble broke out with both men pushing and shoving each other having now completely forgotten their original dispute over who was going to search Arwie.

Arwie sidled up to Eitak, who put his arm around her reassuringly. "I promise they won't touch you," he said and he opened his jacket to reveal the blue lapis stone handle of his dagger.

"Are we good to go?" Sirod enquired.

The two men stopped their fighting and released their hold of one another, the skinny man couldn't resist one final slap in the red face of his comrade who retaliated by shoving him on the shoulder as soon as his back was turned.

"Yeah, get in the cage," said the thin man as he held open the door and shoved each one of his prisoners as they climbed in. As Arwie and Eitak clambered up, he grabbed from them their bow, quiver and staff and said, "I'll take them."

"Yeah," added the fat guard.

Eventually, the wagon pulled away from the bridge, leaving behind the two metal soldiers who remained on guard.

The journey to Bagdoon was a bumpy one with each rut of the road being magnified by the suspension less wheels of the prison transport. Eitak, Arwie and Sirod, all sat up one end of the cage looking at Bones who sat with Bonsai, facing them at the back of the wagon.

"That was a smelly but good idea of yours," whispered Arwie. "How did you know it would work?"

"I didn't…" Bones replied jokingly. "…I just like the smell of fish."

As they got closer to Bagdoon, they saw more abandoned wagons at the roadside, these were being tended by numerous soldiers of the Golden Army who were picking them over, collecting anything of value that they could find, then once emptied of any valuables, they set fire to the wagons where they stood. The heat of the fires was intense as they passed by the burning hulks that were once the prized possessions of the various traders who attended the many market places within the walled city.

After having endured the most uncomfortable journey by road that anyone could remember, the four prisoners saw in the distance the imposing and impressive barrier that was the Great Wall. The wall had been built of stone and brick, stretched as far as the eye could see and was impregnable. The only crossing along its entire length was the fortified slave city of Bagdoon which now loomed in front of them, a colossal rampart with a gigantic portcullis indicating the way through the wall which led to the city beyond.

7. The Slave City of Bagdoon

Once through the city gates, their wagon continued forward along the cobbled streets lined by various houses and establishments, the doors and windows to which were boarded tightly closed. On every street corner stood a metal soldier holding a pike, its face pulsing with blue light. Eitak had never seen anything like this place and he could hardly believe his eyes. Here and there were several people from the upper echelons of society who were dressed in fine clothes, they were walking behind other less fortunate souls; some of whom wore only trousers with their bare feet treading painfully on the cobbles beneath them. Others including women wore nothing more than rags, covering their modesty but the one thing that all of these poor unfortunate souls had in common was that they were shackled with chains around their ankles and they wore leashes around their necks. The leashes were held by the wealthy who were walking behind. They held a whip and every so often they would use the whip to beat the unfortunate souls in front of them.

"Slaves," Arwie said and she lowered her head refusing to look at the spectacle any more.

Eitak considered this, he was repulsed by this sight and could not believe that anyone could be so cruel to another being. It was then that it dawned on him…whoever was responsible for the metal army was getting the soldiers to bring people here to be sold as slaves, ordinary people, people like himself and his friends and his fellow townsfolk from Monrith.

As he pondered this, the wagon moved forward through the city and it soon became apparent that there was not just one road but an entire city filled with people reduced to a life of slavery, a wretched life of servitude and torture at the hands of these others, those cruel and rich enough to afford them.

Eventually, the wagon turned a corner to reveal a huge market square. Except that this was no ordinary market, for around the perimeter were numerous horses pulling large caged wagons and inside the cages, Eitak recognised the huge muscular shapes of several Hasty Hagraals. At the far end of the square was a wooden platform with a large chalkboard standing behind it.

"That's where they sell the slaves," Arwie said pointing to the raised stage.

To one side of the market square stood a large and imposing stone built keep. As they drew alongside, their wagon jolted to a stop and the thin guard announced, "We're 'ere."

"Yeah," confirmed his fat accomplice.

Eitak, Arwie, Sirod and Bones were led from the confines of their cage towards the fortification which overlooked the market.

"What is it with these people and Hagraals?" enquired Eitak as he passed by one of the wagons. Looking in, he was certain that he recognised the same Hagraal that he had seen back in Illya, it had the same flash of white fur on its head and was wearing the same leather collar studded with the red gemstones. The Hagraal snarled and salivated as the first guard walked past but when it saw Eitak, it sniffed the air, lowered its head and made a quickened panting sound. Powerless to do anything, Eitak added, "Poor thing…it must have run south and got caught again."

Once inside, the keep was dark, lit only by burning torches which hung from holders spaced out along the walls and corridors. "This way," demanded the thin guard as he led them further into the building. They soon came to a stone spiral staircase. The area below street level smelled of damp, was dimly lit and extremely inhospitable. Looking around, the prisoners found themselves standing in a narrow corridor. Along one side ran a series of cells with thick walls and heavy metal doors. The thin guard grabbed a set of keys which were hanging on a nail opposite the cells just out of arms reach. "In there." And he pushed the four friends into a cell before locking the door behind them. "The doctor'll be here soon," he added before he hung the keys on the nail, placed the bow, quiver and staff at the foot of the stairs and left.

As he followed, the fat guard added, "Yeah."

Once alone, the new prisoners surveyed their surroundings. There was no way of escape, the walls were built of solid stone, the keys were out of reach and in any case the doors had no bars to reach through. Bonsai, who had been hiding in Bones' jacket, jumped down and began sniffing around the edge of the cell.

"What did the guard mean the doctor will come?" asked Eitak.

"I have no idea," Sirod answered, "but whoever he is, I doubt that he will be all that interested in our health and wellbeing."

"Talkative chap that big fellow," Bones said suddenly, thinking aloud. Everyone turned to face Bones and couldn't help but laugh even in a situation as dire as this.

After a while they heard a shuffling noise outside of their cell, followed by the sound of the keys being lifted and then the door opened. Two new guards stood in the doorway holding the limp and lifeless body of a young man between them who they threw into the cell and then grabbed Sirod. The companions rose to their feet, Eitak remembered the dagger in his jacket and went to grab it. "No," said Sirod as he was dragged over the young dead man's body and out of the door. The door slammed shut behind him and he was gone.

"Sirod," Arwie screamed as she tried to pull the door open. Realising it was futile she sank to the ground and sobbed.

Eitak went to her and put his arm around her shoulders. "It's OK. It'll be all right," he said in an attempt to comfort her.

"How can it possibly be all right, he's gone, they'll torture him and he'll be dead just like him." Arwie looked at the corpse lying on the floor a short distance away and as she did so, it suddenly moved. Arwie screamed, "He's alive."

Bones went straight up to the young man who was lying face down on the ground and gently pulled him onto his back. "Hello, hello, are you all right?" he asked.

The young man slowly opened his eyes and looked at Bones. "I wouldn't have been, had it not been for this poor soul," Sirod replied, now with a new host body.

"Sirod…is that really you?" Arwie shouted and then realising that Sirod had entered the dead man's body. She continued, "Thank goodness you're OK." And in her excitement, she totally forgot that one man had lost his life.

Sirod was now a tall, slim and fine-looking young man in his early 20s with blonde hair. He wore a red shirt which was torn at the back, black trousers and black leather shoes.

"Erm, won't the guards realise that your other body is dead?" Eitak asked Sirod.

"Hopefully, they will just think that I've passed out for a while, what we really need is a way out of here."

"What do you think he died of?" Eitak asked as he looked Sirod up and down. "Apart from a ripped shirt you seem to be fine."

"Some sort of fever I imagine, he felt a bit clammy when I took over but more importantly, I can't stress enough how desperately we need to get out of here and soon."

Bones had begun rummaging through his pockets looking for anything to eat. He took out the orb and placed it on the ground which caused it to roll around the room. As it rolled the button on the top depressed and Bonsai disappeared and reappeared several times around the room.

Sirod tried to keep pace with Bonsai and then the idea came to him. "Do you suppose that it would work if you looked through the keyhole?"

"Sorry?" replied Bones.

"The orb, if you look through the keyhole and then press the button, do you suppose that Bonsai would appear on the other side of the door?" asked Sirod.

"Anything's worth a try," Bones said as he jumped to his feet and rushed over to the door taking Bonsai with him. Bones pointed to the lock and pretended that he was opening the lock with an imaginary key. Bonsai looked at him and grinned knowingly and showed his full set of white teeth. Bones then put the orb to the keyhole and could see the bunch of keys hanging on the nail across the corridor. He pressed the button and bonsai disappeared from the cell. Through the eyepiece, Bones saw Bonsai materialise halfway up the wall clinging with one hand to the nail where the keys hung, he then grabbed the keys with his other hand and Bones pointed the orb back into the cell and pressed the button. A second later Bonsai reappeared with the keys.

"Fantastic!" Eitak exclaimed and excitedly he took the keys from Bonsai and unlocked the door. Once in the corridor, Arwie retrieved her bow and quiver; Eitak, his staff and they all made their way up the stairs. From the ground floor of the keep, they could hear the sounds of a woman screaming further along one of the corridors. "I'm not having that," Bones said and off he went in the direction of the cries followed closely behind by the others. They passed by several small rooms until they came to a large closed double door, behind which they could hear the tortuous screams of a woman in obvious distress.

Bones knocked on the door and quickly hid to one side whilst Eitak and Sirod hid to the other, this left Arwie stood right in front of the doorway. The door opened and there stood a very short bald man, wearing a long white coat and a pair of black leather gauntlets. On the bridge of his nose, he wore a small pair of black metal, round rimmed glasses. The man looked surprised and yet delighted to see Arwie and said, "Come in, you must be here to assist me with my experiments." Arwie could see straight over the man's head and into the room. At the back, strapped to a bench with her arms and legs outstretched was a young woman with flame red hair and beside her was a wooden trolley which contained various hammers, pliers, saws, knives and probes. The bald man stretched his hands out towards Arwie, just as the young woman at the back of the room turned her head and showed her face.

"Mia!" exclaimed Arwie. The man retracted his arms with sudden realisation that the woman in front of him was not there to assist him in any way but just before he could shout for help or do anything else, Eitak brought the handle end of his staff down hard on the back of the man's neck rendering him immediately unconscious.

Arwie rushed forward and into the room. "Mia, Mia…are you all right?" she asked as she set to work untying the heavy straps, holding the girl to the bench. The red-haired girl smiled a broad smile, happy beyond belief to see Arwie standing before her.

"I'm fine, thanks to you that is, how did you all get here? Have you escaped?"

"We are just passing through, we are on our way to the Crystal Desert and handed ourselves in to some guards at Sherpa's bridge. We managed to escape…" Arwie was then aware that her friends had entered the room after her and were now all stood looking at the pretty young girl before them. "I'm sorry." she continued. "Let me introduce you to my best friend, Mia Stormwind. She is also one of the Wirral from my home in Rampor."

"Erm…yes, hello…I'm very pleased to meet you all and er…thank you for rescuing me," Mia said in a gracious but hesitant way. She rubbed her wrists and ankles where the straps had been sat up and then swung her legs slowly over the side of the bench. Beginning at the top of her head, Sirod slowly lowered his eyes, taking in all the beauty of the most exquisite female he had ever seen. Her hair was wild and the colour of fire, deep burnt orange tied back in a big bushy pony tail. She had hazel-coloured eyes, high cheekbones and slim features. Her mouth was full with lips that were a perfect bow shape but across her face from her right eye to her nose was a deep and savage scar. Sirod took no notice of the scar passing over it as if it never existed. Mia's body was athletic, slim but with curves and she had a large bust. She wore a green silk blouse and light brown tight-fitting trousers and on her feet, she wore short brown boots with pointed toes. Sirod could not keep his eyes off her, to him she was perfect and reminded him so much of Ember.

Eitak looked at Mia and then at Arwie and he thought it was strange that both girls had a similar scar across their face although on opposite sides.

"So how did you end up here?" Arwie asked.

Thinking quickly, Mia said, "Well, Erm, when you went missing, I grabbed my bow and went looking for you. Days I searched until one day I met a travelling merchant…and…let me think now; oh, yes, that's it, he told me that he knew someone who could help. Unbeknown to me, he led me into a trap…he took me along the woodland path through the forests of Rampor until we came to a clearing; there he introduced me to his friend who turned out to be a slave trader. I was imprisoned and then brought here to Bagdoon."

"You poor thing…" Arwie said sympathetically, "but I suggest we go before someone comes."

"What shall we do with him?" Bones enquired, pointing at the unconscious bald man lying on the floor.

"I think we should put him in the dungeons," Sirod suggested.

"It would be my pleasure." Mia grabbed a hold of her tormentor by the wrist and pulled him in a rather undignified manner along the corridor and down the stairs leading to the cells below. As his head bumped down the first step, he awoke and realising what was happening began to scream. Each tread was accompanied by a satisfying thud as his head collided with stone.

"Stop," he shouted. "You don't know who I am."

"Oh, yes, I do…" replied Mia as she got to the bottom of the stairs. "You are the torturer, responsible for the suffering of thousands and now you can pay for some of their misery."

"You can't do this…I'm sick, I can't help it…I only do this work because I can't get a job anywhere else…OK, I might have grown to enjoy it a bit but I can change."

Mia dragged him into a cell and slammed the door shut. Sirod handed her the keys from the nail and she locked the door.

"Don't leave me here…I'm claustrophobic…and the floor's cold…I could die in here…no one will find me until the morning…they're all out celebrating for the Arena events tomorrow…you can't leave me here."

Eitak and Arwie decided to explore the lower level of the keep and walked all the way to the gloomy and unlit end of the corridor. Instead of a wall, the corridor terminated in a heavy wooden door. "I wonder," Eitak said thinking aloud and he removed the map from his pocket. Once again to his amazement, the map had completely changed and now showed a detailed plan of the building they were in and the immediate area around it. Beyond the door he could see a large circular shape marked 'Arena'. "Bring the keys," he called out and moments later they were joined by the rest of the group. Sirod unlocked the door and opened it cautiously as Arwie readied her bow in anticipation of what they might find on the other side.

The door slowly swung open to reveal an enormous crater. Opposite him on the far side was another keep, identical to the one he was in. Sirod left the corridor and found that he was now standing on a narrow path which ran around the craters rim. Below him were rows upon rows of seats concentrically arranged around a large circular arena far below. The arena floor was covered in sand with a high wall running all the way around the edge. Sirod assumed that this feature was designed to keep something from getting out of the sandy pit. To his left on a lower level was a boxed off area, separated from the main seating by a low wall, this separate viewing gallery contained several lavishly upholstered red fabric chairs and leading from this box was a wooden platform which jutted out, slightly overhanging the arena floor below. Opposite the platform on the other side of the arena was a set of enormous wooden doors.

Eitak locked the door to the keep behind him and then walked with Arwie and Bones around the rim to the right, whilst Sirod and Mia went to the left.

Looking over a low wall which ran around the outer edge of the crater, Eitak could see that on the other side of the wooden doors was a long ramp which had been cut out of the earth and lead from the street level down to the arena floor.

Having walked around the rim, everyone now found themselves stood in front of the keep on the opposite side from the one they had left. "Try the keys," Sirod suggested. And Eitak opened the door to an identical cell lined corridor. The cell doors were all open, all that is apart from one. Eitak looked through the keyhole, and in the darkness, he could make out the shapes of three men inside.

"Hello," Eitak whispered.

"Who's that? Who's there?" came the reply.

Eitak tried his keys in the lock; however, they did not fit. He looked at the lock and saw that it appeared newer than the others and there were also no keys hanging from a nail as had been in the other keep. "We escaped from the other keep," replied Eitak. "Who are you?"

"Thaddeus, Thaddeus the butcher from Monrith," the voice replied.

"Thaddeus…is that really you?" Eitak asked not, quite believing that he had found one of his neighbours. "The last time I saw you, you were running for the hills."

"We were captured by those metal creatures and now we've been told that we have to fight in the Arena tomorrow."

"We?" asked Eitak, wondering if any of his other friends from Monrith were inside the cell. "…Who else is in there?"

"Well, apart from me, there's Lucius, the blacksmith and Felix, the baker."

"Felix, did you say?" Eitak asked excitedly. "I love his cakes."

"I don't think you heard me right, we are supposed to fight in the Arena tomorrow and what I know about fighting is about as much as you do about baking, I should imagine," Thaddeus said with a raised voice, as he started to get a little cross that there were lots of talking and not much in the way of doing.

"Who are you supposed to be fighting anyway?" Eitak asked innocently.

Sirod tapped Eitak on the shoulder and putting his finger to his lips, shook his head.

At that moment, there came the sound of footsteps on the stairs leading down from the floor above.

"We've got to go," Sirod said urgently.

"Don't leave us." Eitak could hear the desperation in Thaddeus' voice from the other side of the door.

"We'll see what we can do." And they all quickly left the corridor and went back into the Arena, locking the door behind them.

"Who are they going to fight?" Eitak asked again.

"I assume that is why the Hagraals are here," Sirod replied.

"Oh no, no, no, we can't just leave them here, they won't stand a chance against a Hagraal," Mia pleaded desperately.

The five companions ran to the other keep and locked the door behind them.

"Help…I'm a doctor, well, sort of…" the short bald man shouted from the confines of his cell.

"Be quiet," Mia shouted, and then turning to Sirod continued, "What are we going to do. Surely, we have to do something to help them."

"Well, if the doctor over there is to be believed, then we should be quite safe here until the morning, we could sleep here tonight and think of a plan for tomorrow."

They looked between each other and nodded in agreement as Eitak opened his map.

Once they had formulated an idea and gone over it several times, the five friends settled down in one of the cells for the night and soon they all fell asleep apart from Sirod and Mia.

He sat opposite Mia and their eyes met; for the first time he found himself staring at her, his eyes penetrating into hers as if he were trying to absorb her very soul. Somehow, there was something very familiar about her, almost like they had met before; perhaps, it was because she looked so like…Ember. Their gaze held for a few moments before they both realised what they were doing. Sirod shook his head and distractingly said, "So tell me some more about you…"

Mia removed her hair from its ponytail and tossed her head to one side causing her wild fiery mane to flow down onto her shoulders, "What is to tell…I am from Rampor…and I…live there with Arwie and the other women of our kind and I, that is to say, we pride ourselves on our hunting skills and like Arwie…I am…very accomplished with a bow."

Sirod was so mesmerised by her beauty that the vagueness of her answers failed to register in his mind and her words washed right over him.

"…and are all the Wirral as beautiful as you?"

Mia blushed; she knew very little about Sirod but was somehow drawn to him.

The following day Sirod was the first to awaken and with the morning came doubts over the plans they had made. Eitak had spent most of the night sitting against one of the stone walls and opened his eyes to find Awie's head, laying in his lap and beside her the map. He looked at the layout of the keep once more and went over their flimsy plan. When everyone had gathered their thoughts, Eitak stood up but didn't notice that his compass had risen to the top of his pocket and was now clinging to the edge, as he slammed the cell door shut, nobody heard as the compass then fell to the floor. Eitak then placed the keys onto the nail and led everyone up the stairs to the ground floor. From there they carried on up the stone, spiral steps to the top of the keep. Upon the roof, from behind the large stone parapets, they had a grand view of the market square to one side and the huge circular arena to the other and from the other two sides; they could only see the roofs of the other buildings bordering the market.

"We'll stay here and see what unfolds," Sirod suggested.

As the morning progressed, several similarly dressed men wearing the short chainmail vests of the rag-tag guards appeared in the market square and tethered the horses which pulled the wagons containing the Hasty Hagraals. The Hagraals were then led out of the square and around the corner to the ramp leading down into the Arena. Across the Arena, the door leading to the other keep opened and several metal soldiers emerged together with some more of the peasant guards; each of whom were armed with a short sword or pike and between the guards were the three prisoners from Monrith. The guards led the men down some steps between the rows of seats to the arena floor. Once there, one of the guards went across to the large arena doors and opened them, allowing seven wagons to enter. As the cages with snarling, salivating Hagraals were paraded around the outer edge of the stadium the, look of terror on the men's faces was obvious as Thaddeus and Felix fell to their knees, put their hands together and begged to the guards for mercy. The last of the wagons to enter the arena was empty and as it came to a stop, the men were forced inside to await their fate. A mixture of Golden Soldiers and guards then entered the arena and stood at intervals in aisles between the seats.

A little while later, people dressed in high society clothing entered the stadium through the main pedestrian entrances which were situated at ground level above and either side of the main arena doors. Once all of the seats were filled, trumpeters entered the upper seating area via the two fortified keeps and sounded a fanfare.

A trapdoor opened in the separate wooden gallery and up rose a tall and muscular man.

Arwie drew a gasp of breath. "The slave master," she said with fear entering her voice.

The Slave Master of Bagdoon walked forward from his 'Royal Box' and out onto the platform overhanging the Arena. This man, they had all heard so much about, was indeed very imposing. Aged in his 30s, he was over six feet tall and had a bald head with golden jewellery hanging from his ears. He was extremely muscular and wore a white cape over his wide shoulders which draped down the sides of his body, revealing the rippled muscles of his chest and around his waist, he wore a leather slatted battle skirt and had high laced sandals upon his feet.

The slave master outstretched his arms and raised his hands to the sky, there was a deafening roar as the crowd cheered before the master's majesty.

"Now," Sirod whispered, "this is our only chance."

Arwie raised her bow and looked over the parapet she drew back one of the blue tipped arrows and hesitated, she turned to Mia and said, "Do you remember the Umberjax back in Rampor, when It attacked us and I dropped my bow…Arwie held her hand to the scar on her face…How did you stop it?"

Mia looked at Arwie and then to the slave master standing on the platform. She saw Arwie touch her face and then remembered her own scar and lifted her own hand to her face too.

"I…I can't remember now…" she said defensively. "…Arwie, there's no time…"

Arwie handed Mia the bow and putting her on the spot said, "You were always so much better than me, you take the shot."

Mia tried to protest and pushed the bow back towards Arwie. "Please, just do it for me," Arwie insisted.

Mia took the bow and rather, awkwardly, raised her arms so that the arrow pointed at the slave master, she pulled her right hand back as far as she could and her arms began to tremble.

"Are you ready?" Sirod asked looking at Bones.

Bones took the orb from his pocket, breathed heavily upon the glass lens, polished it with the sleeve of his jacket and lifted it to his eye, "Ready," he replied.

"Citizens…" the slave master began…

"Now," Sirod shouted with urgency in his voice.

Mia let loose the arrow, all that was visible to the eye was the tiny glowing blue crystal as it accelerated away towards its target. Bones could now see the lock on the leading Hagraal's cage through the orb and he pressed the button just as the arrow struck.

The blue crystal missed the slave master and exploded on the arena floor next to one of the support struts supporting the platform. There was a large flash of light followed by a tremendous explosion and as the support was destroyed into splinters, the platform wobbled and began to slide down into the Arena. The slave master was taken completely off guard, lost his balance and fell to his knees.

Bonsai suddenly appeared, clinging to the Hagraal's wagon. With one hand holding onto the bars, he quickly unlocked the cage, the door swung open and Bonsai disappeared.

The front edge of the platform embedded itself into the arena floor whilst the back came to a rest against the surrounding wall. The Slave Master of Bagdoon rolled off the platform and fell face first into the sand where he picked himself up. As he looked around, he shouted furiously, "Guards!"

The Hagraal looked out of the open cage with saliva dripping from its mouth, it bared its dagger like teeth and then it was gone.

"Gua…" The slave master's bellow stopped in mid word by the massive Hagraal who appeared on top of him, pinning him to the floor with the claws of its massive paws embedded in his shoulders. And then with one bite, the slave master of Bagdoon was no more.

By now Bonsai had been 'transported' to all of the cages and had released every Hagraal. The Hasty Hagraals certainly lived up to their name. One moment they were in their cages and the next they had vanished only to reappear on top of, beside or behind the unsuspecting guards who had paraded them into the arena and in less than a second, the guards were dispatched to discuss their former lives with their maker.

Eitak's eyes widened in disbelief at the speed in which the Hagraals moved, it seemed to him that they had used the fallen platform as a means of escape as one moment, he saw one at the foot of the fallen structure and the next, it appeared in the seating area above. Chaos reigned all around as the Hagraals set about attacking anyone, who remotely resembled a guard or anyone who looked like they were assisting a guard. As hideous as the sight was, Eitak couldn't help but look and wondered if there was more to these creatures than met the eye. Just then, one of the metal soldiers moved in towards the Hagraal who was wearing the studded collar and lifted a large sword but as it got closer the red crystals around the Hagraal's neck, glowed brightly and at the same time, the blue crystal light behind the soldier's face guard dimmed. As its power faded, the metal warrior's actions slowed until it stopped, completely frozen and unable to move. The Hagraal turned to face the unmoving object and then disappeared. The same Hagraal then moved between all the other metal guards, its red crystal collar causing the blue lights in each one to dim and the clockwork soldiers to fall silent.

Within the first keep, one of the guards had run down the steps to the cells and was just about to check upon the prisoners when he heard the doctor cry out. Realising that he had somehow managed to lock himself in a cell, the guard removed the keys from the nail and unlocked the door.

"Thank you…thank you so much." The doctor snivelled. It was then that he caught sight of something shiny on the floor. He bent down to pick it up and saw that it was a compass. Examining the item, he quickly learned that the needle did not point north but pointed to the west. Realising that the compass was not broken, he dried his eyes and gleefully muttered, "A magic compass, how very fortunate." The compass was pointing along the corridor to the door leading to the Arena.

"What have you got there?" enquired the guard.

"Nothing, now why don't you run along upstairs," replied the doctor, not wanting to share in his precious find.

The 'doctor' took the keys from the guard and made his way to the end of the corridor, he unlocked the door and flung it open just as a Hagraal appeared on the other side and with lightning speed, the Hagraal opened its mouth and engulfed the doctor in one bite.

Having dispatched all of the guards and metal soldiers, the Hagraals jumped the low wall at the top of the stadium and ran into the streets of Bagdoon.

Sirod looked towards Bones and said, "You can release the prisoners now."

Bones transported Bonsai to the wagon, containing Thaddeus, Lucius and Felix, and once hanging from the bars of their cage, he duly unlocked the door with one of the keys. All three of the prisoners immediately jumped out and looked up to see their rescuers, waving down to them from the roof of the keep, they waved back and then ran up the makeshift ramp to the arena seats and to freedom beyond.

Once Bonsai was safely transported back, Sirod shouted, "Let's go." And the five friends jumped over the ramparts and onto the roofs of the houses surrounding the market.

Mia handed the bow back to Arwie who said, "That was fantastic. I could never have made a shot like that, I would have simply blown the whole platform to bits and that would have stopped the Hagraals escaping, I knew you would do a better job."

Mia shrugged her shoulders, her expression accepting Arwie's praise but tinged with penitence.

Around the perimeter of the slave market, several stalls had been set up selling various foods. The aroma of fresh baked bread, fine cheeses and cooked meat filled the air; however, the square was completely empty as news of the escaped Hagraals had spread.

"I'm hungry," announced Bones.

The group stopped running and came to a halt on top of a flat roof. Eitak looked down and suggested that he should be lowered so that he could collect some provisions, it had been a while since they had eaten and nobody knew how long it would be before they would eat again. Bones and Sirod lowered Eitak down over the side of the building so that his feet now stood on the canopy of a cake stall. Once he was satisfied that the canopy could take his weight Sirod and Bones let go. The moment his entire weight was back on his feet, the canopy gave way and Eitak fell through the fabric into several large sponge cakes below. Eitak hauled himself off the stall, brushed himself down and made his way across the market to a meat stand. As he helped himself to several large sausages, he caught a glimpse of something out of the corner of his eye. He turned to the market entrance and saw the crystal collared Hagraal looking towards him; in the blink of an eye, the Hagraal disappeared and re appeared directly in front of him. It was so close that he could have reached out and touched it. The Hagraal nodded its head and sniffed, Eitak stood there frozen to the spot with a sausage in his hand. The Hagraal nodded its head again and nudged Eitak with its large black moist nose and at that moment, Eitak realised that the Hagraal was not interested in eating him but wanted the sausage. He slowly extended his hand and the Hagraal gently took the delicacy from his fingers. It then tossed back its head and swallowed the sausage whole. The bear hound was enormous and could have eaten Eitak with one bite but now he could feel a bond forming and he turned to the meat stall and quickly began tossing as many sausages and joints of meat to the Hagraal as he could find. When half of the stall was empty and the Hagraal had eaten enough, it belched and its meaty breath invaded Eitak's nostrils. The Hagraal then moved its head closer and licked Eitak on the nose. It then bowed its head, turned and was gone.

Eitak stood there momentarily trying to comprehend what had just happened. When he came to his senses, he grabbed a large sack from behind the counter and set to work filling it with as much food as he could manage. At each stand, Eitak reached into his purse pulled out a coin and left it just in case the stall owner should return. He then ran back to the flat roofed building where Sirod and Bones hauled him back up.

"Did you see that?" asked Eitak.

"See it…I would have shot it, had it not have been for the fact that I would have blown you up too," Arwie replied.

"I'm glad you didn't…" Eitak responded. "…There is something about these creatures, there's definitely more to them than meets the eye."

Sirod suggested they continue to the city's southern wall before more of the guards arrived, fortunately the city had been built in such a way that it was easy to jump from roof to roof over the houses and before long, they could see the curve of the city wall ahead of them. As they got closer, the concentration of guards increased in the streets below and now several squads began to form up in readiness to take back the city. At the most inconvenient of places, the city planners had agreed to the construction of a three-storey establishment which was completely out of keeping with the other buildings in the street and this structure now stood directly in the way of the companion's escape.

The group of friends stopped in their tracks, unable to go any further, the only options were to go back or jump down to street level and go around. As they discussed their alternatives, one of the guards looked up from the street below.

"There's them we had earlier," said the same tall skinny man who had brought them to Bagdoon.

"Yeah," replied his portly comrade.

And within seconds, arrows and pikes began to whizz past the heads of the escapees.

"Duck!" Sirod shouted.

"This is no time to be passing out the food," Bones replied trying to make light of the situation and together with the others; he lay down on the roof where he tried to make himself as flat as possible.

"Arwie, can you take a shot?" Sirod asked, hoping that one of her crystal tipped arrows would solve their problem.

"Not without sitting up," she answered just as another volley of arrows whistled overhead.

Eitak managed to crawl to the edge of the roof and cautiously looked over the side. There in the street below were a dozen guards who were all looking up in his direction and those not engaged in the firing or throwing of missiles were shouting their orders to those that were. Totally engrossed in their single-minded aim, the guards failed to see the three Hasty Hagraals who had appeared further up the street.

"Aim…" shouted the skinny guard just as the three Hagraals appeared. Within seconds the guards were dead all except the tall skinny man who dropped his pike and backed away onto the doorstep of one of the buildings.

"There, there nice doggy," he said. "I won't taste good, too skinny not like my fat friend 'ere." He looked around and realised that he was now all alone. "Now look, I ain't a guard no more I'm a changed man." And as he said this, he reached slowly behind his back and removed a dagger from his belt. As he brought the rusty blade into view, the Hagraal ate him.

When the Hagraals had gone, Eitak climbed down a metal drainpipe to the street below followed soon after by the rest of the group. They stepped around the bodies of the guards and made their way towards the city wall and before long, in front of them loomed, the huge gate house and portcullis of the southern entrance to Bagdoon. Standing sentry at either side of the gate was a metal soldier armed with a golden pike and milling in front were several of the peasant guards.

Again, as with the access at the northern side, the gate house formed a part of the wall. Running all around the boundary was a cobbled path separating the huge barrier from the buildings of the main city. The road that the companions now found themselves standing in was directly opposite the gates and was the main southern route into the city. The only problem was that the guards were now stood between them and freedom.

"Quick, get against the wall," Sirod shouted and they tucked themselves in as tightly as they could to the building line. As they attempted to hide amongst the shadows, two further guards approached the gate house from the city behind them.

"'Ere is them over there?" called out one of the guards excitedly.

Eitak and the others huddled themselves further into the darkness that had been cast by the houses but it was too late; they had been discovered and there was no way of escape with guards, both to the front and to the rear.

The two guards rushed forward and grabbed Arwie and Mia who immediately began to struggle and screamed loudly. With their emotions running high and an overwhelming instinct to protect, Eitak and Sirod fought with all their strength to try and stop the men from taking the girls but within a few moments, they were joined by other guards who had run up from the 'gate house' and after a brief but determined struggle, the guards had won and the companions were led towards the gate house.

"So near, yet so far," Sirod quoted as they now stood on the cobbles in front of the portcullis. To one side of the gate Bones saw the end of a large pipe which terminated in an open gully, leading out through a hole in the wall. Looking through the hole, he could see a moat. Whilst the guards stood around, debating what they should do with the prisoners, Bones heard the sound of rushing water and he turned back just in time to see a surge of raw sewage rush from the pipe into the gulley and out of the wall where it cascaded down into the moat beyond.

"AAAGGGHHH!" Eitak looked up along the cobbled street which ran around the perimeter of the wall and there running towards him was a huge and angry crowd comprising of most of the freed villagers and slaves from the city. As the mob got closer, he could now see that they were being led by Thaddeus who was still wearing his night gown, boots and cap.

"I tell ya, I didn't sign up for this!" announced one of the guards as he dropped his pike on the cobbles and ran along the street in the opposite direction of the crowd. The crowd of ex slaves now numbered several hundred and realising the overwhelming odds against them, the rest of the guards threw their weapons on the ground and ran after their fleeing friend.

Once again there was a gurgling sound which preceded a surge of water as effluent gushed from the pipe. Seizing the opportunity, Bones shouted, "Follow me." And he ran over to the wide gutter and jumped into the flow of sewerage as it travelled at great speed towards the hole. He was immediately caught up in the fast-moving waste and was catapulted through the wall and into the moat.

Sirod turned just in time to see Bones who was now covered in sludge as he landed in the ditch.

"I'm not going in there," Arwie said as she looked through the hole and saw Bones waving his arms around delightedly.

The metal soldiers moved from their posts and began marching towards the rabble. As they raised their weapons, the mob engulfed them and threw them into the half pipe where a new tide of sewerage swept them along through the wall and into the moat where they promptly sank. The main part of the crowd then continued running along the inside of the wall in pursuit of the other guards. Thaddeus, Lucius and Felix, immediately recognised Eitak, Sirod and the others and stopped to thank them for saving them from certain death.

"I can't thank you enough, Eitak," Thaddeus said, truly gratefully. "If there is ever anything I can do…just ask."

"Well, you could open that gate." Sirod pointed at the portcullis preventing their exit from the city.

"It would be my pleasure." And moments later the windlass which wound the chains of the huge portcullis and drawbridge turned and the wall of Bagdoon opened to the lands beyond. Eitak and Arwie were the first to cross the moat and looked down at Bones who was pulling on various reeds and river plants as he hauled himself up and out of the water. Now dripping wet he stood before them, clean for the first time since the incident with the fish.

8. Canyon Land

The land to the south of Bagdoon was dry, arid and barren. The soil beneath their feet was hard and rock like and was covered with a yellow dust that was finer than sand. As far as the eye could see, this harsh wilderness stretched into the distance and was broken only by the odd cactus, succulent plant or boulder. With the city gates some distance behind, Eitak decided to look at the compass to ensure they were travelling in the right direction but as he put his hand in his pocket, he realised that it was no longer there. "I've lost the compass somewhere in Bagdoon," he announced.

*I bet that doctor has got it by now, either that or some Hagraal has found it and eaten it…*Bones mused.…*Anyway, I for one am not going back to look for it.* He then caught the smell of cooked sausage, emanating from Eitak's bag. "Anyone feeling hungry?"

Ahead was a series of huge rocks jutting out of the ground which had evolved in a semi-circular shape, facing away from the city, at the southern side of this formation, the winds had blown the ground smooth which made an ideal place to camp. Eitak handed out the cooked meat and some of the bread and cheese. "We will have to ration the food, we'll eat all of the meat now as that won't keep and save the cheese and bread for later. I also managed to find some fruit cake which should last us several days if not weeks," he suggested, trying to be organised.

"What are we going to drink?" Arwie asked, they had not managed to collect any drinking water from Bagdoon and now several days walk lay ahead of them without any prospect of rectifying the situation. Mia stood up and walked over to one of the succulent plants and snapped off the tip of a broad leaf. She pulled the damaged limb towards her and a white liquid began to drip from the fat and fleshy plant.

"This…" Mia answered. "…It's quite delicious." And she cupped her hands and drank the sweet sap.

Sirod sat back, leaning against one of the large rocks, the heat of the sun baked down on his brow and he began to perspire. He wiped his forehead on the back of his hand and noticed that the skin of his brow began to ripple and fold. Quickly hoping that the others hadn't noticed, he smoothed the skin back over his skull and then looked at the back of his hand, he was beginning to turn yellow and he knew that in this temperature, it wouldn't be long before he required a new host. "I hate this heat," he announced but the others were far too busy eating to pay any attention. After food and rest they left the sanctuary provided by the rocks and headed out into the vast space beyond. Towards the end of the day, the landscape had changed and turned from a flat wilderness to an inhospitable rocky terrain. Eitak looked at his map which now showed that they were entering Canyon land.

"We should find somewhere for the night soon," Sirod suggested, looking around for a suitable place to camp.

"How about over there?" Mia said pointing at another grouping of large rocks.

Eitak and Arwie went off to look for firewood and Bones played with Bonsai who found great delight in tormenting a small spider with a very old and dry stick whilst Mia and Sirod decided to stay around the rocks and talk. Sitting opposite each other, Mia couldn't help but notice that Sirod was looking distinctly yellow. "Are you OK?" she asked caringly. Sirod put his hands to his forehead and pulled the skin, stretching it over his skull once more. He then tugged gently at his ears, checking that they were in their usual place but to his horror, the tip of his right ear could no longer cope with the pressure and came away. Sirod immediately cupped his hand over his ear, hoping that Mia hadn't noticed.

"Your ear," she said startled and with obvious concern. "What happened to your ear?" And then a sudden wave of realisation and understanding washed over her.

"A Nagraal," Sirod replied quietly, answering Mia's next question. "I'm ashamed to say that yes, I am a Nagraal."

"Why are you ashamed?" Mia looked at Sirod and stared deep into his eyes, in past the flesh and into his soul. There was something very familiar about him and she felt that she knew him but then again, she had never met him before their encounter at Bagdoon. As Mia's thoughts subsided, she became conscious of the fact that Sirod was staring at her too. What was it about this man, she thought and why was he so familiar to her?

"I can't stand it anymore, you have to tell me…tell me your story…" she continued. "Who are you…no, who were you?"

"That is a long story…" Sirod replied. "…And it was a long time ago, 200 years ago, in fact…" He saw Mia's eyes widen, he saw her leaning forwards towards him trying to reach out, trying to speed the story along. He looked at her red hair, he looked at her soul and he knew or at least he wanted to believe that he knew her but no, how could that be possible. He was the Nagraal…Ember…the thought had been there all along. She looked so much like Ember, he wanted to ask…he needed to ask. His mouth was dry and his throat was parched and the word was on the end of his tongue…

"Ember……?"

"No…no, it can't be…Seth…is it…you?" Mia leapt up and ran over to him, she threw her arms around his shoulders and they held each other for the first time in what seemed like an eternity.

Their private moment was suddenly interrupted by Eitak and Arwie who returned with armfuls of old, white coloured dry wood.

"Have I missed something?" Eitak asked.

"Mia…?" Arwie added.

Sirod and Mia released their embrace. Mia looked directly at Arwie and spoke first, "There is something we need to tell you but it is best that everyone is together."

They called Bones who was pulling faces, trying to imitate Bonsai and Bonsai was responding by showing his teeth in a wide grin followed by high pitched laughter. Bones put Bonsai onto his shoulder and the group sat down in front of Mia and Sirod.

Mia began and retold the story of how she and Sirod had been lovers and how she was betrothed to Kalag, who was brutish and cruel. She told them how she had called Sirod on the night of her wedding and how she desperately wanted to leave. She relived the moment that the knife sank into her flesh and how she had been taken away. She turned to Sirod "…I was going to die…I remember the tears running down my face as I didn't want to leave you my love…and then Niastar came and told me that he could save me if I drank a potion. He told me my life would be different but he didn't tell me the true horrors of what I would become. I drank the concoction and became a Nagraal…"

Sirod watched the tears as they ran down her cheeks and found their way into the deep channel caused by her scar...of course, it all made sense to him now...how else could she have survived. Niastar was a Magistan after all and had at his disposal, all of the potions and elixirs known to man. Sirod knew what it was to be a Nagraal, the true horror of spending an eternity going from rotting corpse to rotting corpse looking for peace and an end to the madness.

"...I passed out and when I came to, I realised what I had become, my flesh no longer felt like my own, I knew that I would spend the rest of my days going from body to body and I believed that no one would want me ever again. I couldn't face you my love...I left my home and travelled. Until one day I met a merchant. He gave me an elixir and told me that when the time was right, if I drank from it, I would remain in the body of my current, choosing until the day of my natural death."

Sirod put his hand in his pocket and felt the small bottle that Malarog had given him in Illya.

"But ...what about Mia?" Arwie asked.

"In time I grew tired, I knew that Seth and all of my friends would be dead. My travels took me to the forests of Rampor and I saw for the first time the metal army. I found Mia's body at the edge of a stream. She had been shot in the back with an arrow. I looked at her and she reminded me so much of the body I once shared with Seth. My soul gently entered her and as I looked into the stream, I knew that it was the time to end this life of soul jumping and so I drank the merchant's potion and became whole for the first time in 200 years. I was now free to live my life to its natural end and was as close to my true self as was possible." Mia, now sobbing, turned to Arwie and said, "I am so sorry...I never meant to deceive you or to hurt you...please forgive me as I just couldn't tell you the truth."

Arwie with tears running down her face made her way over to Mia and put her arms around her. "It's all right, it's all going to be all right," she whispered and they held each other close.

Everyone was now crying, the only person unaffected was Bonsai who wiped a finger down Bones' face and sucked the salty liquid. After a while, Sirod went over to Mia and Arwie and put his arms around them both.

"What I want to know is, why did you both change your names and what should we call you now?" Bones asked as he dried his face.

"I felt so ashamed with myself for not being able to save Ember that I didn't want anyone to remember me and so I changed my name to Sirod Spa. I kind of like the name Sirod and have got used to it now."

Mia then spoke, "I didn't know Mia's name until I went to Rampor but I would rather go back to my old name of Ember…if that is OK with you, Arwie?" Mia then looked to Arwie for approval and Arwie nodded still with tears in her eyes.

"So, Sirod and Ember it is," Bones announced decidedly.

As darkness fell, night came as a welcome end to the roller coaster of emotions and intensity of the day. Arwie lay close to the fire watching the sparks rise into the darkness, her thoughts were of Mia and the good times they shared back in Rampor. Tears ran down her face as she came to terms with her grief. Eitak lay beside Arwie and held her hand, he really liked her and wanted desperately to hold her in his arms but felt that now was not the time and he also didn't know how she would react or if she felt the same way about him. As he pondered whether they were they just good friends or if their relationship could ever be more, the weight of the day took its toll and he fell asleep.

Ember lay on her back and looked up at the stars with Sirod asleep next to her. For the first time in two centuries, she was happy but now she was mortal and Sirod was still a Nagraal. She didn't know that in his pocket was the potion given to him by Malarog and she wondered what future lay in stall for the both of them.

Bones looked at his friends, snuggled up around the camp fire, he wrapped bonsai into his jacket and soon everyone was fast asleep.

With the morning came another beautiful day of sunshine and the hope of good things to come. Eitak began by looking at his map and found a route through the Rocky canyons and after a breakfast consisting of bread and cheese, they all set off.

The pass through the Rocky terrain rose with a steady incline over several days, huge rocks lined the path, which over time became a sheer cliff face rising high into the air either side of them. Each day the sun rose with increasing ferocity and the companions were grateful of the shadows cast by the high trench walls which afforded some protection against the unforgiving rays burning down upon them. Every so often they would come across a small cave formed within the sandstone rock. These hollows provided some sanctuary from the severe heat of the midday sun and a little comfort from the extreme cold of the night air. The food rations of meat, cheese and bread had now gone leaving only fruit cake and cactus milk as their staple diet. Eventually, the track became less of an incline and more of an arduous mountain ascent and with every step, the steep sides of the deep gorge became lower until they finally stood on top of a wide plateau.

The five travellers could go no further as now in front of them, as far as the eye could see was the widest, deepest and most awe-inspiring canyon that any of them could ever have imagined possible. As they looked down into the deepest crevice on Kennet, they couldn't help but marvel at its majesty but the realisation of the impossible task which lay ahead caused both their hearts to sink and their knees to buckle. At the edge of the precipice was a path, not even a path; it was more a series of rocks and jagged edges which jutted out into the canyons belly, precarious stepping stones which led down into the centre of the planet.

Sirod steadied himself and looked down at his hands. The baking sun had sped up the decomposition process and once again they were now speckled with black spots as his body began to rot. He touched his face and could feel how thin the skin had become and how it began to ripple and wrinkle over his cheeks. Also speckled with black spots, a small hole had appeared around his jaw exposing his teeth for all to see. "I can't go much further," he said as he looked in despair at the enormity of the journey ahead.

"If we can just get to the canyon floor my love..." Ember looked at Sirod and knew the helplessness of his situation.

"Well, one thing's for sure..." commented Bones. "Bonsai's going to enjoy himself." And there below them Bonsai had found himself an old dry tree root which poked out from the sheer cliff face into the canyon, which he was using to swing around in an arc totally oblivious of the dangers provided by the abyss below.

Suddenly all around, echoing off the canyon walls was a terrifying screech, deafening and shrill followed by the whooshing sound of air moving fast towards them, they looked over the edge of the canyon just as the enormous black leathery form of a huge Terror Soar, soared up from the depths of the chasm and landed on the rim just in front of them. The creature was enormous, totally black with leathery skin and had huge outstretched wings which were tipped with hideous claws. Both its head and neck were very long terminating in an elongated jaw filled with a complement of dagger like teeth.

There was no time to run, the Terror Soar was upon them and their lives would end here and now, just the speed of their deaths would be at the mercy of one of the most feared creatures in all of Kennet.

Arwie closed her eyes, there was no time to load her bow so she accepted her fate and awaited the end. Ember turned her head into Sirod, shielding her view from the inevitable. The creature reared up on its powerful legs, gave out one last screech…and then fell backwards over the edge of the canyon.

Arwie slowly opened her eyes and Ember emerged from Sirod's cape.

"What happened?" Bones asked with a slight quiver to his voice.

Sirod stepped forward and looked into the gorge. A short distance below on a ledge, lying on its back and unmoving was the Terror Soar.

"I think we'd better make a move…while we have the chance and before any more of those things come along," Eitak suggested.

They all agreed that it was no longer safe to stay where they were and that no matter how perilous the treacherous steps down were, they were still the better option for survival. Eitak went first, followed by Arwie, Bones, Ember and then Sirod, who brought up the rear. With each step came extreme danger, the stones were narrow and uneven and a fall would mean certain death to the canyon floor far below. Every so often, the smaller stones were interspaced with huge boulders which hung in large ledges, giving a welcome respite to the hazardous stairway. Eitak stepped out onto the first ledge which was the largest and looked behind as Arwie, Bones and Ember joined him.

"Where's Sirod…?" Eitak asked with panic in his voice. He knew that Sirod was struggling with his condition and looked over the edge of the platform. "…Did anyone see…?" he continued as he looked back up along the steps.

"Listen!" Arwie shouted, her voice echoing around the canyon.

As her voice dissipated into the rocks, the air around them changed and there was the faint sound of a gentle wind which blew and grew stronger. The silence of the entire landscape was then devastated by another deafening and lingering screech which caused the four climbers to cover their ears, shielding their senses from the sudden and intolerable onslaught of sound.

"Terror Soar!" Eitak shouted and the four friends threw themselves to the ledge and lay as flat as possible, in an attempt to hide from this new impending danger.

Bones couldn't resist and looked up just in time to see another huge Terror Soar land on the ledge with them. The massive creature just stood there, looking around and then it spoke, "It'ssss meee…Siiirod," it said in a serpent-like whisper.

"Sirod?" enquired Eitak, questioningly trying to grasp an understanding of what had just happened.

"Sirod, my love?" Ember added as she looked in amazement at the vast creature stood before them.

"Heaaart attaaack," hissed the Terror Soar. "It diiied of a heaaart attaaack."

Full realisation then swept over Ember. The Terror Soar they had seen fall over the precipice of the canyon, had clearly died of a heart attack and realising that his own body was failing, Sirod's soul had jumped into this magnificent yet terrifying creature.

"Oh, Sirod, my love, what is to become of you…" Ember said despairingly.

"It'sss temporary," Sirod answered, "buut noow we can flyyy."

Sirod lowered his enormous body and allowed his friends to climb up onto his back. Bonsai sat at the front, perched on top of Sirod's head and looked forward to the adventure ahead.

Sirod then turned around and the great Terror Soar, leapt from the precipice and into the void.

As with everyone else on Kennet, Sirod had never flown before and the Terror Soar now plummeted towards the ground at great speed as the wind rushed through the companion's hair. The forces created manipulated the skin on their pliable faces and contorted their expressions to the great amusement of Bonsai, who turned and smiled and allowed the air to force open his mouth so that his gums flapped uncontrollably.

"Aaaaah," screamed Arwie, Bones and Ember as the canyon floor loomed ever closer.

"Open your wings…open your wings…OPEN YOUR WINGS!" shouted Eitak desperately.

With that Sirod stretched open his vast leathery wings and the wind flowed over them, drawing him out of his uncontrolled dive. It was at the last possible moment when his massive bulk soared over the ground and rose upwards into the sky.

With the sun in their eyes and the ground at their backs, everyone found themselves rushing upwards at a speed equivalent to that when they had been plummeting down. Again Bonsai looked around and saw his friends pulling funny faces at him. With the ground now behind him and the canyon floor, a long way below, this really was the best fun he had ever had and he smiled with a broad grin.

"Turn your wings down slightly…turn your wings…DOWN A BIT," Eitak screamed more terrified than he had ever been in his entire life.

Sirod adjusted his great wings and soon the huge Terror Soar levelled off and the companions were able to relax slightly. They looked down and could see the canyon which still looked massive despite them being so high in the air. Ahead a long way in the distance, beyond the rocky landscape of canyon land and surrounded in a haze of heat, glistened the endless expanse of the Crystal Desert.

9. The Crystal Desert

After several hours of flying, the sprawling endless sea of sand that was the Crystal Desert flowed in vast dunes below them. The day was drawing to an end and from their high vantage point, they could see the curtain of darkness beginning to draw across the lands to the east. Now that daylight was fading, all across the desert floor glowing fluorescent specks of blue and red light were visible which had not been present during the day.

"We need to find somewhere to rest soon," Eitak shouted and Sirod began to descend slowly towards the sand. As it drew closer, the desert floor showed more detail and they could now see a small figure dressed in rags looking up at them. The figure showed no apparent fear at the sight of the huge Terror Soar but rather unharnessed, a huge bow from its back, set an arrow tipped with blue crystal into the string and fired. The missile whistled past Sirod, who instinctively lurched to the left, causing his passengers to lose their balance and grab a hold of any part of his body they could hang on to, all that was except Bonsai who was caught completely off balance and he fell from the Terror Soar and tumbled to the desert below. Bones saw Bonsai fall and in desperation, fumbled in his pocket for the orb. Hanging on with one hand, he grasped the orb between his fingers, pointed it at Sirod's head and pressed the button.

The figure on the ground had set another arrow in the bowstring and had drawn back its arm ready to release another arrow. Sirod desperately tried to regain control, hoping to rise once more into the air when Bonsai reappeared from thin air and landed across his left eye. Now completely distracted, Sirod lost all awareness of his surroundings and crashed to the ground heavily causing everyone to fall from his back and tumble into the sand.

Eitak picked himself up and looked around for the character intent upon their destruction, however, there was no longer any sign of him anywhere. "Where's the guy with the bow?" he asked in a slightly more than concerned voice.

Sirod slowly stood up on his powerful legs and there embedded in the sand was the body of the archer.

Ember looked at the figure lodged in the sand. "A Dust Dweller," she announced. "Look at his eyes." Sirod craned the Terror Soar's neck down and stared. The Dust Dweller was male, tall and was about 35 years of age. His clothes were more wrappings of cloth than tailored garments, his legs being covered in several long swathes of multi coloured bandages. On his body, he wore a loose fitting, sand coloured shirt over top of which was a tattered jacket of many colours torn in strips and tied at the waist with a long length of rope which encircled his waist several times. The Dust Dwellers features were mostly hidden by a long red and white coloured scarf and head dress. Ember pulled the drapes to one side to reveal a yellow and jaundiced looking face. The Dust Dwellers eyes were narrow slits and were bright yellow with slim black pupils and they were covered by two eyelids, an inner membrane and an outer lid. But most noticeable of all was the complete lack of any hair.

"I didn't mean to land on him," Sirod hissed remorsefully.

"It doesn't matter he would have killed us without so much as a thought," Ember replied with a degree of harshness to her voice.

Sirod took no comfort from her words and then added, "But hee waaass probably ssscaared ssstiff when hee sssaw mee flying towardsss him."

"Well, he's dead now and that's that...it's not as if we can bring him back."

Sirod thought about Ember's comment for a moment and then he lay down on the sand and reached out and touched the Dust Dweller with the tip of his wing. A few seconds later, the great Terror Soar lay still and the Dust Dweller slowly moved pulling himself up out of the sand.

Bones was now getting quite used to Sirod's ability to change body at will and joked, "Well, if we are going to be here for the night, you might as well slip into something a little more comfortable."

The others all laughed and Bonsai bared his teeth and screeched loudly unable to resist joining in.

"Never a truer word..." Sirod brushed the sand from his clothing and then suggested they try to find something to burn for a fire.

"I'll go with Arwie," Eitak said and handed Sirod his staff. "Hold it up high and wave it around from time to time and that way, we will know where our camp is." He and Arwie then walked off into the desert. They had only gone a short distance before he found a small blue Orilion crystal glowing brightly in the sand. He picked it up, looked at it and put it in his pocket. 20 or so paces further along, he found another and another. "You never know, these may come in useful," he suggested and before long his pockets were bulging. Dotted amongst the numerous blue crystals were several much larger sandstone boulders. Eitak grew bored of the fruitless task of looking for anything combustible and out of frustration upturned one of the rocks. As he overturned the rock, to his total horror, he was met face to face with a set of sharp fangs as a mouse like creature jumped up at him. The small ferocious rodent bit into his shirt and began to tear away at the fabric until the sleeve was nothing more than a tattered rag. Eitak grabbed down at the back of the animal's head and held it between his fingers, pulling it away from his shirt. It now hung in mid-air with its legs dangling beneath it and shreds of fabric held tightly in its jaws. "What is that?" Eitak asked, horrified at how much damage the rodent had caused in such a short space of time.

"I think that it's a Widget Hunter…" Arwie answered. "…They are quite dangerous or so I am led to believe."

"No kidding…my shirt's ruined, the question is what do we do with it now?"

"Well, we could either kill it or put it back under the rock and run," Arwie suggested.

"I vote for option two." Eitak chose not to kill the small Widget Hunter, just because it had ruined his shirt. And with that he put the rodent back where he had found it and replaced the rock. As soon as the rock was restored, he and Arwie ran. After several moments, Eitak looked back over his shoulder and to his amazement the Widget Hunter had chosen to stay where it was and was not in pursuit.

Eitak looked around trying to gain his bearings but now the night was upon them and the entire desert was in darkness. It was so dark that he could hardly see his hand in front of his face. As he scanned the horizon, he noticed just ahead of him was a glowing red crystal. He walked over, picked it up and examined it. It was just like the blue crystals except that this one was red and was the same as the red crystals studded in the Collar of the Hasty Hagraal back in Bagdoon. Eitak decided to keep the red crystal too and he put it in his pocket with the others. Before long, Eitak had found several more of the red crystals and he kept them all until he could carry no more.

"Are we lost?" Arwie enquired totally unable to see any sign of their 'camp'.

"I'm not really sure." He then pulled his map from amongst the crystals in his pocket and holding a glowing red crystal was amazed to see that the map had now changed and showed a detailed plan of the desert floor from where he stood...to their camp. "It's this way," he announced and off they set into the darkness. They had only travelled a couple of paces when Eitak stubbed his foot on something and using one of the red crystals for light he bent down to find several planks of wood bundled in a small pile in the sand. "Now that is odd!" he exclaimed but not wanting to look a gift horse in the mouth, he collected up several of the boards and then continued towards the camp.

When they eventually got back to the rest of the group, Eitak couldn't wait to show off his collection of crystals but first he needed to light the fire and so set to work, snapping the wooden planks into a more manageable size. Before long, they all sat down to the relaxing hissing and popping sounds of a warming and relaxing fire. Eitak put his hand in his pocket and took out three red crystals which were now glowing brilliantly and placed them on the sand. He then pulled out another red crystal and several...dull grey stones. Eitak looked at the rocks and frowned. "I don't understand," he said. "These were bright blue a moment ago..." The others, all looked on bemused, wondering what Eitak was talking about. "... These crystals, I found some red ones over there and some blue ones... Orillion stones, I put them all in my pocket and now the lights in the blue ones have gone out...dull...dead, I don't understand," Eitak continued, somewhat confused himself.

"But, look, the red ones are brighter..." Arwie commented. "... Find another blue one." Without hesitation, Eitak got up and ran back in the direction he had found the planks and there in the sand were several more brightly glowing blue crystals, he scooped them up into his hands and turned back to the camp. It was now easy for him to find his way as he homed in on the fire which acted as a beacon in the darkness. Moments later he was back and placed the crystals on the ground. The brilliant blue stones radiated light in all directions and stood in complete contrast to the dull grey ones next to them.

"Put one of the red ones next to a blue one," Arwie suggested. Eitak obliged and moved a red crystal closer; as he did so, everyone was amazed to see the red stone glow brighter as the blue one faded to grey. He repeated the same experiment several times until all of the blue gems were nothing more than clear dull rocks.

After several minutes, the red stones reverted to their natural state and although still radiant were no longer supercharged with light.

"That's amazing," said Bones. "I wonder if they still blow up."

"How about we leave that until the morning," Sirod said as he looked at Bones with one eyebrow raised, concerned that the entire camp was about to explode. Bonsai caught Sirod's 'look' and grinned baring his teeth.

"Where did you find the planks?" Sirod asked changing the subject.

"Over there, they were stacked up in the sand."

"Perhaps, someone was going to build a sand castle." Bones quipped and began to laugh at his own joke.

Bonsai was still staring at Sirod pulling faces and sticking out his tongue when he heard Bones laugh and decided to join in not wanting to miss out on any fun.

The morning brought with it hunger as the last inadequate ration of the fruit cake was shared out. "We really must find more food and water by tonight or we will never make another day, not with this heat." Eitak warned.

"I agree and the sooner we get going, the better. I suggest we fly to the hurricane's path and take the Dust Dweller with us; he may come in useful if we meet more of his kind and he is also a little less conspicuous."

Sirod touched the Terror Soar which moved its great head from the sand just as the Dust Dweller crumpled to the ground and lay alongside. Eitak, Arwie and Bones helped strap the body of the Dust Dweller to the Terror Soar's back and then everyone climbed aboard.

"Hoooold oooon," hissed Sirod as he outstretched his leathery wings and ran along the desert floor then with a powerful leap, he threw himself into the air. As he felt the warm currents of wind lifting him from the sands, he flapped his limbs with all of his strength until at last he was flying. The Crystal Desert seemed to go on forever as far as anyone could see and in all directions but in time, the flat sands gave rise to a sea of golden dunes which looked like the huge broiling waves of an angry sea.

From time to time Eitak looked at the map to ensure they were going in the right direction until at last they saw what they had been looking for. Ahead was an enormous ridge of sand which ran from east to the west without end. The northern side of the elevation was as steep as any mountain, whereas, the southern aspect slipped away in a gentle slope terminating in a vast, wide and totally flat expanse of tortured sand which looked blackened and burnt in places with long deep gouges running along its length.

Eitak pointed to the ground and Sirod swooped low over the crest of the ridge and followed the wide trench towards the east. The ravaged terrain was littered with wreckage and debris, ranging from old dead trees to the skeletons of several creatures unfortunate enough to have been caught up in the hurricane's angry winds. The clear blue skies of the Crystal desert gradually got darker; at first, a few fluffy white clouds floated by quite casually but in time their numbers grew and soon the sky was predominantly thick white cloud with a few specks of blue. The further east they flew, the darker the sky became until eventually it turned to a grey black colour and an enormous black cloud hung down in the shape of a gigantic anvil.

"The hurricane is coming," Eitak shouted and Sirod carefully came to rest on the ground and to his surprise, the terrain was firm, hard like rock with just a light covering of sand. The companions jumped from his back and untied the Dust Dweller as Sirod took over his body once more.

The great dark mother ship cloud grew larger as it advanced towards them. The air felt strange, calm and electrically charged. Just then Eitak realised a sudden flaw in their plan. "There is just one question…" he asked. "How are we going to enter the hurricane without dying?" As crazy as it seemed, no one had given any consideration to this question but the seriousness of the problem now affected them all. Bones put his hands to his head and rubbed his face. Ember and Arwie looked at each other and shook their heads whilst Sirod rubbed his hairless chin. The only one unaffected was Bonsai who jumped up and down on the spot. Thud, thud, thud. It was a very satisfying sound he thought, like the beating of a drum. Thud, thud, thud, he jumped again and again until the sound entered Sirod's consciousness. Sirod emerged from his thoughts and looked over to Bonsai who was having great fun leaping up and down. "The ground shouldn't make a noise like that," he said.

"Sorry?" enquired Eitak, not quite sure if he had heard properly.

"I said, the ground shouldn't make a noise like that." And he lifted his foot and brought it down on the ground. There was no noise at all except for that made by the light dusting of sand as it moved back into the small indentation that had been created by his foot. He then walked over to Bonsai and stamped his foot up and down, thud, thud, thud. Sirod bent down and excitedly brushed the sand aside with his hands. By now he had been joined by the others who were both inquisitive and excited at the possibility of having made a grand discovery. As the sand parted, it exposed a series of wooden boards lying beside one another in a rectangular shape. Once all of the sand had been cast away, it became obvious that this was not just a series of boards abandoned in the desert but rather a trap door for something below the ground.

The air had now turned from its calm pre-electrostatic state and a slight breeze began to blow.

"Help me open it," Sirod shouted excitedly but considered the possibilities of what might lie below. "On second thoughts, you stay here out of sight and let me open it." Sirod mustered his strength and slowly opened the wooden hatch. Underneath the cover was a rectangular pit with a wooden ladder strapped to the side, the walls of the pit were lined with wooden slats which kept the sand at bay. Sirod looked down and could see the bottom of the ladder which was a distance of around twice the height of the average man below. Sirod slowly climbed into the hole and disappeared into the shaft. As he reached the bottom of the ladder, he could see a narrow wood lined tunnel leading off into the distance. The underground passage was lit by several blue Orillion crystals, held to the walls by small clay cups. Sirod became aware of movement further into the tunnel and then into the light, he saw the face of a Dust Dweller. Sirod jumped, startled by this confrontation. The figure said nothing but brought together its hands and touched its fingertips and thumbs, making a triangular shape in front of it. Sirod thought this must be some form of greeting and copied the gesture. He then turned slowly, climbed back up the ladder and exited the shaft. Once back on the desert floor, Sirod looked to the east and saw that the hurricane was approaching fast. The prevailing wind was now blowing with great strength and the vast rotating mass of the hurricanes shape was now visible in the distance. The hurricane was unbelievably wide and tall and the anvil cloud that had heralded the great storm had been all but swallowed up and engulfed by its powerful, spiralling girth.

Sirod found that he now had to shout to make himself heard above the noise of the wind which grew louder by the second. "It's an underground tunnel and is our only hope of getting into the hurricanes eye, but there is a Dust Dweller in there and I don't suppose he will want to share."

"Do you mean to say that people hide down there?" Bones asked in disbelief.

"Yes…" Sirod shouted, "…but has anyone got any ideas how we get him out and quick?"

Eitak looked around and then something familiar caught his eye. "Sirod…there…follow me," he shouted and ran over to a large boulder which was stuck in the compacted sand. "Help me turn it over but we will have to be careful and very quick," he warned.

Sirod upturned the large rock and as he did so, a Widget Hunter jumped up at his throat with its claws outstretched and jaws open and its two front fangs ready to take a large chunk of flesh from his face. Eitak saw the rodent land on Sirod's jacket and was ready; he reached forward, grabbed it in both hands and held it at arm's length as the crazed vicious creature wriggled and thrashed about trying desperately to sink its teeth into anything that it could find. This hunter was a lot larger and stronger than the one he had met before and was the size of a very small dog, its teeth were sharp and yellow and its eyes glowed red. Eitak ran as fast as he could to the trapdoor and shouted for Bones to open the hatch. Once the door was open just a crack, he threw the Widget Hunter into the shaft and Bones dropped the lid.

The hurricane was almost upon them, the wind had an urgency that Eitak had never experienced before. The clouds swirled like a massive maelstrom, hail the size of large eggs now fell to the ground, pounding into the firm sand, lightning struck all around scorching the ravaged ground, debris, wooden planks, whole trees, wagons and creatures, large and small, swirled in huge circles caught up in the vortex and were catapulted with tremendous speed in all directions as the hurricane approached. The noise was deafening worse than 20 waterfalls and louder than a dozen avalanches.

Arwie and Ember huddled together, Bonsai clung to Bones and Eitak shouted to Sirod, however, his words were lost in the wind. As the sands were stripped from the floor in front of them, a trapdoor opened a short distance away and further to the east, from it ran the Dust Dweller who had been hiding in the underground passageway, his face caught in a silent scream as he was pursued towards the hurricane by the ferocious Widget Hunter. Eitak watched as he was grabbed by the invisible arm of the hurricane and was sucked up and into oblivion. The Widget Hunter turned in its tracks and darted to the nearest rock where it dug into the sand.

"Run," shouted Sirod as he opened the lid to the tunnel and the five companions jumped in. Once inside, Sirod looked up and saw two wooden hooks on the underside of the trapdoor. At the bottom of the ladder was a sturdy wooden beam. "Quick, throw me up that brace," he shouted. Bones grabbed the thick piece of wood and threw it up to Sirod who pushed it into the hooks and wedged it into the wooden planks, lining the shaft. The great storm was now directly over the trapdoor that was further down the tunnel. The one from which the Dust Dweller had escaped. This hatch was unfortunately now insecure, the wooden planks lifted slightly and then it was gone, torn from its hinges and smashed to splinters. The winds howled over the open shaft and created a tremendous suction which travelled down into the tunnel and pulled at everything not tied down and that…included the five companions who now held onto the ladder with all their might. The winds ravaged overhead. The one secure trapdoor above them rattled, clattered and lifted as if it wanted to go and join its former counterpart now broken and swirling within the winds.

The situation was desperate, Sirod was still stood at the top of the ladder just under the trapdoor and could feel the power of the winds as they clawed their way westwards. Eitak and Arwie had also climbed onto the ladder and were stood a couple of rungs below Sirod. They had linked their arms and held onto each other so tightly that they could feel the blood drain from their hands. Bones hid Bonsai in his jacket and sat on the floor linking both his arms and legs around the bottom of the ladder. Ember had been caught off guard by the sudden loss of pressure within the tunnel and had only just managed to grip the ladder with one hand, now the immense sucking power of the storm lifted her feet from the ground and tried to pull her up and out of the shaft. She screamed but there was nothing anyone could do, her fingers weakened and then she lost her grip. Bones saw her as she was torn from the ladder. Sirod shouted out powerless to do anything just as Bones instinctively raised his hands into the air and grabbed Ember by the wrist. The hurricane continued to pull and drag at her with all of its power, not wanting to let go of its new victim. Bones also had no intention of letting go and it became a battle of strength, the fisherman verses the storm. Bones' grip weakened his hands grew tired from holding onto Ember and his legs shook under the strain of gripping the ladder. Sirod could see the strain in his face as he battled the storm. "Don't let go…" Sirod shouted. "…Whatever you do, don't let go." Bones had given his all and had no more to give, his resolve was broken and he was on the verge of giving up…and then the winds stopped.

Sirod put his ear to the trapdoor, the ear-splitting roar above was fading away into the distance. "Quick…" he shouted. "…It's now or never." And he opened the wooden cover.

He could still hear the noise of the great storm all around him, but that was now greatly muffled and had been replaced by the sound of drums. He poked his head up out of the shaft and took a moment to take in what he saw. Heading towards him, some distance away was the most awesome sight he had ever seen, a vision that paled into insignificance the majesty and power of the great storm, for there on the largest wagon he could ever have imagined possible and being pulled by creatures, he had only every heard of but had never actually seen, was an immense cage and siting inside was an enormous giant.

The wagon rolled steadily towards him and was being pulled by six Rhinamoths. Huge, hairy, extremely powerful elephant like creatures but instead of a trunk, in the centre of their forehead was a large horn and either side of their mouth was a long white tusk. Each Rhinamoth was harnessed to the massive wooden wagon by a series of thick ropes linked to a carriage. The wagon itself was supported by a series of very large wheels which ran along its length, together with the firm nature of the ground within the trench, they prevented it from sinking and becoming stuck. Driving the carriage and sat at the front were two Dust Dwellers, one was beating a large drum and the other held a long whip. As impressive as the spectacle was, Sirod's eyes kept going back to the enormous cage, constructed from metal bars, the size of gigantic Alder trees, the bars reached high into the sky and were spaced around the huge cage which was at least twice the size of the fortified keeps in Bagdoon. In the cage, sitting cross legged was a huge giant, his head was bent over and in his hands, he held a massive hammer which he was using to bend and fashion various sheets of metal. The giant looked sad, miserable and despondent; his great eyes betrayed his inner thoughts. Sirod thought that he appeared quite young, not that he knew how long giants lived but the giant appeared to be in his early 20s and had dark curly hair, he wore fine clothes, a shirt and trousers and a black leather waistcoat.

Sirod glanced beyond the cage and saw a smaller covered wagon trailing along behind, this was pulled by a double team of Rhinamoths and was driven by a further two Dust Dwellers.

"What can you see?" Bones called up from the bottom of the ladder.

"You wouldn't believe me if I told you…" Sirod replied, himself finding it hard to take in what his eyes had seen.

"What are we waiting for?" Ember asked, getting impatient and wanting to get out of the tunnel before the hurricane returned.

"Trust me, we have got to time this just right or it will be a disaster."

Sirod looked back at the giant's wagon just as the first Rhinamoth came alongside the shaft, its huge feet pounding the ground causing the tunnel to shake.

"What in Kennet's name is that?" Bones shouted.

Sirod had no time to explain and yelled into the tunnel, "Wait there until I call you." And he scrambled out of the hole. The air was cool and calm, surrounded by dense grey and black clouds in every direction, the Rhinamoths now passed by so close that he could smell them and they smelled awful, a sweet musty stench. The Dust Dwellers looked down at Sirod and put their hands together forming another triangle in greeting and recognition, Sirod copied their actions and as the procession continued on its journey to the west, he found himself stood alongside the enormous cage as the large wheels of the wagon rumbled past. Hanging from the side of the platform between the wheels was a wooden access ladder.

"Now," Sirod shouted and Eitak and Arwie poked their heads up from the shaft and stood totally motionless, amazed and open mouthed at the sight before them. "Quick, there's no time," Sirod shouted with desperation in his voice and they climbed out to join him at the side of the wagon. Ember and Bones were next and as with the others, Ember stood stunned for a few moments before she jumped out of the pit and joined Sirod as the wagon continued to roll past. Bones was the last to emerge from the hole and was so interested in keeping Bonsai inside of his jacket that he barely noticed what was going on until he too stood at the side of the wagon looking up.

"Climb up there," Sirod shouted over the din of the wheels and pointed to the ladder leading up to the giant's cage.

"Are you mad?" Bones answered in disbelief at Sirod's request.

"No, I'm quite serious…now if you don't get going, we're all doomed."

"And if we do…he might eat us," Bones added.

Eitak went first followed by Arwie, Ember and Bones whilst Sirod brought up the rear. Fortunately, the processions pace was slow and matched the progress of the hurricane as it travelled across Kennet, the wheels were not moving fast enough to cause any great danger or threat…that came from the uncertainty of how the giant would react. As Eitak's head presented itself above the parapet of the trailer bed, the giant lifted his gaze towards him.

In a deep low questioning voice, the giant spoke, "Hmmm?" he said.

Still holding onto the top of the ladder, Eitak held one of his hands up in front of the giant and said, "Friend." He then slowly climbed onto the platform and stood just outside of the cage next to the giant's enormous boot. When Arwie climbed up onto the platform the giant's eyes widened in surprise and in a slightly higher pitched and approving tone said, "Hmmm."

As Ember appeared, the giant was now paying a great deal of attention and moved slightly which caused the cage to shift. Bones was already stood on the trailer when one of the Dust Dwellers stood up and looked towards the back of the wagon. The four friends quickly moved between the bars of the cage and blocked themselves from view. Sirod was now at the top of the ladder, the drummer acknowledged his presence with the familiar hand symbol; however, Sirod could only nod in recognition. The drummer satisfied that nothing untoward was taking place, sat back down and faced the front.

"Friends?" the giant boomed with a powerful and thunderous voice.

Startled by the level of sound and concerned that they would be discovered, Eitak patted the air in front of him with outstretched hands and said, "Shhhh." And then he pointed towards the Dust Dwellers at the front. The giant nodded understandingly and then Sirod appeared.

The giant immediately shouted in fear and moved to the far corner of his cage, terrified by the small figure in front of him. "Noooo," he boomed.

Eitak waved frantically for Sirod to get back down onto the ladder and then looked at the giant and pointing back at Sirod said, "Friend…he's just wearing a disguise."

The giant slowly emerged from the corner and looked towards Sirod's head, now just poking above the ladder. "Friend?" he boomed questioningly.

"Yes friend…all friends." And he waved his hand in an arc presenting the five companions. "I am Eitak and this is Arwie, Ember, Bones and…" Eitak pointed to the face looking up from the ladder. "…and that is Sirod, he is a Nagraal."

The giant looked towards the Dust Dweller now climbing up to join the others and laughed loudly. "A Nagraal," he thundered, seeming to understand the implications of Sirod's condition.

Once again Eitak patted the air in front of him, worried that the giant's enthusiasm would give the game away. "We've come to rescue you."

"Can't," the giant replied in a low deep voice as he pointed to a large lock attached to the bars at the back of the trailer. Eitak took a moment to look at the mechanism which was halfway up the cage and out of reach, from what he could see the entire back of the cage was an enormous hinged gate that was secured by the lock which as large as it was, only had a very small keyhole.

"Where is the key?" Eitak asked.

"There," replied the giant and he pointed to the wagon bringing up the rear.

Eitak looked to the canvas covered wagon and saw that the two Dust Dwellers driving were drinking heavily from a large glass demijohn, which they passed between each other as they swayed in drunken merriment at the front.

"We must think of a plan," he said turning to the others.

Sirod took a moment to look in the cage, in one corner piled high were assorted cogs, wheels, springs ratchets, gears and pinions whist in another were sheets of golden metal, cut and fashioned into various shapes resembling parts of armour. To one side was a huge anvil and scattered around were numerous hand tools designed for the cutting and shaping of metal. On the floor in front of the giant was an almost completed soldier from the Golden Army.

"Then it is true," Sirod said, "you have been making the army." The giant turned to him and screwed up his face with great regret at what he had done.

"I am Klum," he said in a low voice and patted his great chest. "I am ashamed...I was tricked into this cage..."

Just then the Drummer leading the wagon stood up and turned back towards the cage. Once again, the companions hid behind the bars whilst Sirod acknowledged his gaze and the Dust Dweller sat back down.

"We must do something about them," Eitak said and apologised for interrupting the giant's story. "Sirod, you are the only one who can get close enough, so it's down to you to do something."

Sirod realised that it would only be a matter of time before they would get caught and so he slowly made his way to the front of the cart and climbed up onto the platform where 'his fellow' Dust Dwellers sat. Fortunately, they were sat side by side and close together and only turned at the last moment to acknowledge his presence. As they did, he quickly put one hand either side of their heads and cracked their skulls together with a thud. The two 'drivers' immediately fell back in their seats unconscious. The huge Rhinamoths didn't even notice, they continued their rhythmic pace towards the moving clouds in front of them, oblivious to the fact that anything had changed. Sirod beckoned to the others who joined him and between them, they dragged the sleeping bodies back to the cage and pulled them in through the bars, Klum looked at the sleeping guards, grabbed a sheet of metal and wrapped it around each one imprisoning them in gold.

"So how did you end up in here?" Arwie asked.

The giant looked at Arwie and smiled, "Pretty…" he said and then turned to look at Ember with her fire red hair. "…Very pretty," he said approvingly before continuing with his story. "… Sometime ago, I walked by the Thunder Mountains when I heard someone call for help…from the caves, I went in and before my eyes could see in the dark, the gate closed behind…and I was trapped in this cage. The cage was pulled up onto this wagon by Rhinamoths and it was taken to the vast Plains of Ishtar. There it was left until the full moon, when we giants enter our dormant sleep of stone. When I awoke with the dawn, I found that I was inside the hurricane with no means of escape. The dwellers came and told me that they had others of my kind and that they would kill them if I didn't build an army of gold. I asked them if they had taken my wife, Min, and every day since they have tortured me and told me that she cries out in pain and calls for me constantly."

"How do they get the finished soldiers out of the cage?" Eitak asked wondering how anyone could enter the cage without Klum escaping.

"They come with the full moon when I turn to stone. It can be a curse but sometimes it can be of great benefit for when the moon is full, nothing can harm me. That is when they open the cage but it is only once every week."

Bones then piped up, "We can't wait here another week, we'll starve before then."

All six of them sat down and debated long and hard about what they should do next.

"We cannot take too long as soon we will approach another pit and the guard will change," Klum warned.

Within an hour, they had come to a decision, a plan that relied heavily on Sirod's ability to fool the drivers of the cart that followed. Sirod climbed down from the trailer and walked slowly towards the wagon. The Rhinamoths ignored him and they walked ponderously past, he found a ladder leading up to the driver's platform and climbed up. The two Dust Dwellers had by now drunk so much alcohol that they were completely senseless and were on the verge of unconsciousness. Sirod joined them and sat down on the bench beside the one who held in his hand the empty glass demijohn. Sirod slowly shifted his position on the seat, forcing the two Dust Dwellers further along and to the edge of the bench and then with an almighty shove, he pushed them both off the bench and over the side of the wagon. Sirod looked down, hoping that the sudden fall had not brought them to their senses but to his delight, they both lay perfectly still on the ground asleep; he then sat back in the bench and waved for the others to join him.

Eitak, Arwie, Ember and Bones climbed aboard whilst Sirod jumped down and went around the back of the wagon where he slowly parted the curtains. Inside the canvas covering, it was a cluttered and jumbled mess of disorganisation and at the entrance abandoned here and there were various sacks and barrels piled high which touched the roof. Towards the back, behind the disarray of items, Sirod saw a short, thin man sitting down in the process of placing a blue Orillion crystal into the head of a golden soldier. Distracted by the sudden increase in light and draught caused by the parting of the curtains, the man stopped what he was doing, got up and walked towards Sirod.

The man was a small weasel of a character, aged in his 40s with thin pointed features and greasy black hair, slicked back over his angular head. He had narrow, beady, untrustworthy eyes and a small thin mouth.

The man spoke with a high pitched, nasal and whining voice, "What do you want?" he asked in a clipped and curt manner.

Sirod was caught off guard, he had given some thought as to what he might find in the wagon but hadn't really expected this rather small and extremely brusque man. "Erm…I just thought that I would check to see that you are OK," he said.

The man had now reached the curtains, forcing Sirod to take a step back and as he held the canvas apart, he looked out annoyed at Sirod's intrusion and said, "And why shouldn't I be OK?"

"Erm…well, I just thought…that I would er…make sure," Sirod replied indecisively, making up the excuse as he went along. Just then something caught the small man's attention, something unusual, not quite right or as it should be. There a little way into the distance were two Dust Dwellers, picking themselves off the ground and staggering to their feet, the man looked at Sirod and then back at the dazed and confused figures beyond. Not sure what the man had seen, Sirod turned around just in time to see the stunned Dust Dwellers come to their senses but it was too late. The hurricane had caught up with them and they were torn from their feet sucked into the great swirling winds and were gone. Sirod looked back at the man and for a moment their gaze met, a brief moment in time before realisation of a situation and then Sirod lunged, the man threw the curtains closed and could be heard stumbling and falling into objects as he made his way hurriedly to the back of the wagon. "Guards!" he shouted. Sirod rushed forward, parted the canvas and there coming towards him was a fully assembled golden soldier. Horrified, he stepped back as the metal guard jumped out of the wagon and began its pursuit.

Bones jumped down from the front wagon and made his way to the back and was opposite Sirod who was now being chased by the golden machine. Eitak and Ember also joined in but ran towards Sirod, hoping to distract the guard who held no weapon but advanced tirelessly upon him. This left Arwie on the platform at the front.

Bones had reached the back of the wagon and looked in. Stood in the far corner, he saw the thin faced man who was now holding a large knife and hanging on a hook from his belt were a set of keys.

"If you come any closer, I'll cut you to ribbons," the man threatened in a whining voice and screwed up his face, causing the skin on his nose to lift and wrinkle accentuating his shrew like features. Bones didn't like the idea of tackling an armed man in a confined space and looked to Bonsai who was sat on his shoulder, he twisted his hand and wrist in front of him as if opening an imaginary lock and Bonsai bared his teeth and grinned in acknowledgement and understanding of what was required.

Arwie climbed up and onto the carriage and leant over the front edge of the driver's platform. Holding onto the wooden rim, which surrounded the floor, she reached down between the back legs of the huge Rhinamoths and grabbed a large metal pin which held the harnessed creatures to the carriage.

Eitak, Sirod and Ember fanned out and each time the soldier came close to one, the others shouted and waved their arms frantically in an attempt to divert the metal guard's attention. Eitak suddenly remembered the red crystals and patted his empty jacket. He cursed himself as he recalled leaving the stones by the camp fire the night before; how useful they would have been right now in defeating this unstoppable menace.

Bones had taken the orb out of his pocket and pointed it at the small but mean looking man, he pushed the button and almost immediately Bonsai appeared clinging to the man's belt. With a look of sheer disgust, the man swung the knife around in front of his body, aiming to sink it into Bonsai's back. Bonsai grabbed the keys from the hook just as the knife plunged. Bones pressed the button once more and Bonsai re appeared on his shoulder with the keys in his hand, the knife bit deep into the man's left leg who immediately cried out at the sudden and unexpected pain.

Arwie struggled to pull the heavy pin from the carriage's towing eye, although not moving fast, there was not much room between the huge Rhinamoths on either side of the harness. With her arm, shoulders and head now alongside their powerful legs, she tugged at the pin with all of her might, her fingers began to lose grip on the platform and she now clung to the rim supporting her weight by her fingertips. The gait of the enormous Rhinamoths caused first one and then the other to ponderously collide with the central beam separating them and with each heavy bump, the carriage jolted and forced Arwie to move her body dangerously close to the creature on the opposing side. She gave one last almighty heave just as the hind quarters of both Rhinamoths swayed towards the central harness together, the pin moved and then it came free, Arwie pulled her body back towards the platform just as the creatures squashed against each other and then parted. The large pin was extremely heavy and Arwie dropped it to the ground and climbed back onto the platform. The great Rhinamoths continued their steady pace westwards as their carriage separated from their burden and the wagon slowly came to a stop.

Bones pointed the orb at the catch on Klum's cage which was now pulling ahead of the covered wagon. Bonsai clung to the large mechanism, put the small key into the massive lock and turned.

The hurricane was now catching up with the stationary carriage. The golden soldier advanced on its three tormentors but then changed strategy and honed in on one target, ignoring the cries of the others. Ember was the closest and now found herself backed into a corner between the front of the covered wagon and the end of the harness beam which now sat embedded into the ground. The metal soldier stretched out its hands and extended a small knife from its limb.

The huge gate swung open and for the first time in a very long while, Klum placed his first step onto solid ground. He climbed from the cage, rose to his feet and stretched the immense powerful muscles in his back; he looked towards the other wagon just as his metal creation was about to thrust the knife into the pretty girl with the red hair.

"Nooo…" Klum bellowed, his voice echoing around the circular cloud base like thunder itself. He leapt into the air and with one huge jump brought his enormous hammer down on top of the metal soldier, pounding it into the earth with a single tremendous blow. Wheels and cogs flew everywhere and springs now protruded from the twisted metal figure, squashed into the ground at Ember's feet.

The trailing wagon was now perilously close to the hurricane, its winds catching up fast from the east. From inside, Eitak could hear the clanking and whirring sounds of a clockwork mechanism coming to life and everyone ran back towards Klum's cage which was still moving steadily into the distance. The curtains parted and out popped the long-pointed nose of the thin, mean and creepy looking man which was followed closely behind by the all too familiar blue glow of another golden guard. As his head poked out from the wagon, the storm grabbed the cart and began to turn it into the winds, he tried to climb from the carriage but it was all too late as the hurricane seized the wagon and pulled it high into the sky. The formidable power of the storm ripped the wood and canvas apart and scattered its contents across the horizon. Small explosions of blue light flashed like powerful fireworks in the air as Orillion crystals from the wagon collided with various other missiles caught up in the winds. All this added with the intermittent lightning strikes of the storm came together to form a wondrous display against the backdrop of the grey and black cloud.

Ember was in severe shock; the tremendous impact of the massive hammer had shaken her very soul and she worried that the trauma to her body would turn her back into being a Nagraal. Sirod went over and put his arms around her, holding her tight as they continued to walk at a steady pace following the great cage. Klum walked slightly ahead of the group and since he had become free, no one had really noticed just how big he was. Eitak now walked alongside of him and the tip of his head only just reached to the top of Klum's calf length boot. The great Rhinamoths, which now roamed free from the covered wagon were also huge, but even they only came up to Klum's waist.

"That just leaves the Dust Dwellers on the other cart," Eitak said pointing ahead.

"I don't really think that is going to be too much of a problem." Bones chuckled as he watched the two Dust Dwellers scramble from their platform. They had seen the escaped Klum and now ran to the next wooden trapdoor which had just entered the safety of the hurricane's eye. As they got to the lid, it opened and up popped the head of two more of their kind. The two panicked wagon drivers waved their arms around frantically and then jumped into the pit closing the lid tightly shut.

"What shall we do with them?" Eitak asked.

"I say we kill them and be done with it," Ember snapped.

"No," said Klum calmly. "That would be bad, they are no threat anymore..."

It was getting late and the clear sky above the centre of the hurricane was starting to turn dark.

"I trusted you..." Klum said in a booming voice. "...And now it is time for you to trust me, you must do as I say but we don't have much time." He then walked over to the huge cage and pulled on the bars with all of his strength, slowly it began to slide from the back of the wagon and then fell to the floor with a resounding thump. The cage now sat in the middle of the trench and the Rhinamoths continued their ponderous pace, pulling the huge and now empty wagon to the west. Klum moved quickly, he grabbed the two stray Rhinamoths, broke the straps of their harnesses and led them to the cage, he opened the door and then guided the huge creatures inside. Once safe in their new home, he closed the gate behind them. Klum then ran over to the other Rhinamoth, bent down between them and removed the pin, separating them from their burden. Once free, he led them over to the cage and when they were separated from their harnesses, he pushed them one by one into the cage to join the others. Although quite cramped, the Rhinamoths made no fuss of their new predicament and accepted their fate in a calm manner. Klum then sat down in the middle of the trench by the huge cage with his back to the storm as it advanced from the east. He crossed his great legs in front of him and sat still with his back slightly hunched and his head bowed. He called to the others, "Quick, there is not much time now. Just remember, trust me. I am your friend too." He scooped up the companions one by one and placed them carefully between his huge legs so that they were now surrounded on all sides.

As the sky above turned dark out of that darkness shone the full moon. The great storm was now upon them and the winds began to increase around the huge giant. Once everyone was huddled between his legs, he bent forward and folded his huge arms across the top of his lap and as the moonlight shone through the eye of the storm, Klum turned to stone.

At first, there was a cracking noise which began at his feet and then moved up his legs and spread to his whole body as he quickly became rock. A broad smile set had upon his face, hewn into the stone as he sat motionless like a huge statue.

The violent storm blew all around, howling and tugging at everything in its path. Dreadful winds whistled over Klum's huge arms but inside their rock tomb, the five companions were safe and in the dark, Eitak's staff glowed blue giving enough light to see.

"The legends are true then, giants do turn to stone…" Sirod confirmed as he tapped the knuckle of his index finger on Klum's boot. "Funny how the clothes turn to stone too," he continued as he ran his hand along Klum's boot.

"So, what do you think, my love?" Ember enquired. "…can we trust him?"

"Well, we have a good basis for a relationship, we saved him and now he has saved us."

"So far, my love, so far…"

"Well, I say if he was going to do us in then he would have done so by now…" Bones interrupted. "…What's more important though is the fact we have no food."

The five friends agreed that they were all hungry with no prospect of anything to eat but realising there was nothing that they could do about it, being stuck between Klum's legs they decided to sleep.

The morning came around much sooner than it was welcome and with the first light of dawn, Klum reverted back to flesh and bone; with his first breath of the day, he stretched his arms above his head and kicked out his huge legs.

"What in Kennet's name…" Bones shouted, having been awoken most rudely from a particularly pleasant dream.

Klum looked down with sudden realisation that he was no longer in the cage and was instead harbouring his new friends. "Sorry," he roared, upset with himself for nearly squashing them all to death.

Klum stood slowly, the day was going to be another glorious one and the red sun rose up into the sky, turning the horizon the most amazing shades of red, pink and orange. The storm had now passed and the only trace that it had ever been was the tell-tale sign of destruction it had left in its wake.

Klum looked around at the debris. Strewn about there were parts of the covered wagon and its contents including several sacks and barrels, most of these had either split apart or had burst under the immense pressures within the hurricane but there were one or two whole ones which had become firmly embedded in the ground. Klum went over to the first barrel and found that it contained oil which was not much use to him or anyone else when food was the most important commodity; the next barrel contained salt and the third held thousands of pure gold coins which were ready to be melted down in order to make the golden soldiers. Klum threw the barrels aside, frustrated at not being able to find any food they, hit the ground and split open their contents spewing onto the hardened sand. Ember's eyes caught sight of the glistening coins. "You have got to be joking...the soldiers...I didn't think they were made of real gold..."

"They are not, only the more intricate parts are made from gold," Klum answered being somewhat of an expert on their construction and then he found another barrel slightly smaller than the others. He picked it up and pulled off the top and inside was...'Water'. Klum hollered with such excitement that everyone covered their ears from acoustic shock. He rushed over to the group and everyone gulped down great mouthfuls of the barrel of clear liquid which was so much more valuable than a hundred barrels of gold. Klum continued his search of the sands and soon returned with more and more precious finds. He found a sack full of salted ham, another of dried bread, some dried fruit including dates, prunes and apricots and...a barrel of beer. They all sat down to breakfast and feasted like it was their last supper and now with bellies full of food, Klum went over to the cage and set free the Rhinamoths. Once everyone had eaten their fill and had ensured that they had reserves of water, the gentle giant took the barrel over to the beasts and allowed them to quench their thirst.

"You must come to Kidder Doon with me so that I can find out who else has been taken hostage...only there can we truly plan to stop this nightmare that I have created...that reminds me where is my hammer, you never know when something like that might come in useful."

"Are they all as friendly as you in Kidder Doon?" Bones enquired.

"Mostly...I would say." Klum looked towards the great Rhinamoths. "Now that they have been watered, you should ride the beasts while I walk; that way, we will cover more ground," Klum suggested.

Soon they had all packed as much of the scavenged food as they could carry and chose a ride, Arwie approached her mount which bowed its head, allowing her to stand on one of its large curved tusks. Clinging to the huge ivory, she was lifted into the air and acrobatically leapt onto the creatures back where she sat tall looking down on the rest of the group.

Bones watched, astounded by her athleticism. "You must be joking if you think I can do that."

Klum laughed, walked over to Bones and lifted him onto the Rhinamoth's back dumping him behind the creature's ears in a rather undignified manner. Bonsai saw Bones, raise his eyebrows to the sky and copied following up his impersonation with a broad grin.

Once everyone was safely seated on their respective rides, Klum set the pace and they marched off across the desert towards the Plains of Ishtar. Klum's stride was so long that the Rhinamoths had trouble keeping up but the huge beasts were renowned for their endurance and tirelessly marched, following Klum north eastwards towards the Thunder Mountains and onto Kidder Doon.

As the day came to a close and the sun began to set, the travellers still found themselves in the Crystal Desert. Klum stopped and looked around as if he found the stark terrain familiar. "We will rest here for the night."

Dotted all over the sand, the bright glow of the numerous blue and red crystals returned with the failing light, Eitak looked at the small brilliant gems and turned to Klum. "What do you know about these stones?" he enquired.

"We first discovered the true qualities of the stones centuries ago, since then and from time to time, we come to the desert to harvest them for the great power they hold. In Kidder Doon, we use the blue crystals to power the machines we create. We soon realised that the red stones take power from the blue ones when they are close to each other but the power of the red stones is unstable and cannot be harvested. It is the blue ones that were used to make the Golden Army. It was only a few rotations ago that we first became aware of this Golden Army. Soldiers appeared beyond the Thunder Mountains and asked if we would combine our strength and build a force strong enough to take over all of Kennet; in return, we were promised the lands to the east. We have no quarrel with the people who share this world with us and we declined the offer…soon after that I was taken. Now I have to undo what I have done and it would be best for us to collect as many of the red crystals as possible…they will be very useful in the future for defeating the golden soldiers."

"How many soldiers are there?" Eitak continued.

"That is the problem," Klum answered as he put his head in one of his large hands. "Some of the machines I created are able to build more of their own kind, there could be thousands, even tens of thousands, I really don't know."

"Tens of thousands?" Bones repeated Klum's words out loud. "There is not a force on Kennet, capable of defeating any army of that size."

Sirod joined in the conversation. "I suggest we eat now before it is dark and then go about filling the empty food sacks with as many of the red stones as possible."

Eitak said nothing as he looked at Sirod and noticed that he was showing the first signs of decay as dark patches now appeared all over his face.

After a satisfying meal of salted meat, dry bread and water, Eitak and Arwie set about collecting as many of the red crystals as they could carry.

Klum lay down on the sand, closed his eyes and fell asleep and with the second day of the full moon, once again he turned to stone.

The five friends decided to keep some distance between themselves and the huge giant so as to avoid a repeat of the mornings near death experience when Klum awoke.

As the heat of the desert escaped into the clear night's sky, a biting chill like winter fell upon the companions. When morning came, everyone was awoken by a loud and somewhat familiar cracking sound but before Klum moved, he looked around to find his five new friends huddled together between his huge body and outstretched arm.

"Don't move," Bones shouted in a panicked voice.

"Ha-ha, I remembered today," Klum roared and he waited for his friends to move before he stretched his body and stood ready for the day.

After a quick breakfast, everyone mounted up and followed Klum as their second day of travel began. Before long, Bones grew bored of the journey and pointed his orb at the other Rhinamoth. The sudden shock of Bonsai's appearance in front of each of his friends caused them to jump violently and provided both Bones and Bonsai with great amusement as they laughed amongst themselves hysterically.

The heat of the second day baked down upon Sirod, exacerbating his condition and by midday, the skin on his face was black and cracked. "I can't last much longer," he announced looking down at his withered hands.

Klum looked back, knowing Sirod's fate. "We are almost at the plains but there will be no host suitable in Kidder Doon," he announced.

Bones scratched his head and thought hard. "We could divert across to Illya if Klum can help us over the wall, I know a nice little take away body shop there," he said thinking of the undertakers and trying to make light of the situation.

"That is not as bad an idea as it sounds," Eitak agreed. "We could split up; one half could go to Illya whist the others could go on to Kidder Doon."

"I'll go with you, my love…" Ember confirmed. "…After all, I can't marry a Dust Dweller, now can I?"

"Marry? Did I hear right?" Sirod asked, shocked and stunned but extremely pleased at the proposal.

"Of course, my love, you don't think I'm going to lose you again, do you?" Ember then endorsed her statement with a kiss which she blew across from her Rhinamoth to his.

"Then I accept, of course, I accept. This is indeed cause for a celebration and what better way celebrate than with a new body."

By late afternoon, they had reached the eastern end of the Great Wall where it joined the thunder mountains, this being the remotest stretch of the fortifications, it was left unguarded and the only obstacle over being its sheer size. Klum stood against the wall, stretched his arms up and jumped, his fingertips only just reached the top of the ramparts and he hauled himself up. Klum now stood on top of the wall, the companions craned their necks and looked skyward as Klum's head seemed to reach up and into the very heavens.

"Over, under or through?" he bellowed.

"Did he say through?" Bones shouted, trying to hear himself over Klum's bellowing voice.

"Through," Klum confirmed with a thunderous cry and he jumped down on the other side of the wall. A few moments later, there was an almighty thud, followed by another and another, Boulders, rocks, stones and splintered shards came flying out of the wall where the companions stood and showered down like a meteor storm that forced them to take cover by clinging as close to the wall as they possibly could. The immense blows kept coming from the other side as the group cowered beneath the rock fall from above. The ground shook from the constant pounding rhythm and then an enormous section of the fortifications cracked and began to fall.

"Run!" screamed Eitak and the five friends ran in all directions just as half of the wall collapsed to the floor where they had stood.

Klum's head and shoulders appeared through the huge gaping gap and he waved his enormous hammer in his hand. "I told you this might come in handy," he announced admiring his handy work.

"So how was 'under' ever going to work out then?" Bones enquired.

Only Sirod and Ember needed passage through the barrier and now the pile of rubble to the southern side of the wall provided the ideal platform for their great Rhinamoths to step up onto as they passed through the gaping cavity.

Eitak handed Sirod his staff. "Take this, you may find a better use for it than providing light, after all Malarog said that a crystal this size has great power." He then turned to Ember and gave her a handful of red crystals.

Sirod took the rod and Ember accepted the crystals and once at the makeshift entrance, Klum helped them through the wall to the other side where they sat astride their beasts and rode off towards Illya.

"I miss them already," Eitak admitted as he sadly watched them go. Having received no response, he turned around to see Arwie and Bones holding hands and sobbing as they waved goodbye to their friends who now faded into the distance.

10. Passage to Thunder Pass

The journey to Illya was uneventful and took just two days, thanks to the relentless pace of the great Rhinamoths. In the distance, they saw that the city gates were now patrolled by two of the rag-tag guards who checked the details of everyone entering and leaving Illya. Sirod guessed that word of the incident at Bagdoon had spread and that the guards were most likely looking for the five fugitives, however, he considered it unlikely that they would be suspicious of a Dust Dweller and his prisoner.

"Just take my lead," Sirod said as he grabbed Ember by the arm and led her towards the guards. "This is one of the prisoners we have been looking for, I am taking her to the market to claim my bounty," he announced.

The two guards were different to the ones in Bagdoon and were unfortunately slightly more educated and, therefore, less likely to be duped. One was short and aged in his 30s whilst the other was a tall teenager who had attempted to look more mature by growing a wispy beard and moustache of fine blonde downy hair.

"Ooo do you think you are? We have to er…you know," began the younger guard trying to assert his authority and then he looked to his older and slightly more learned colleague to help finish his sentence.

"What ee's tryin ta be all fancy about is that all noo prisoners enterin Illya, 'ave ta be booked in fru the new slave master," the shorter man interjected.

"I am a personal friend of the slave master general and he is expecting me, now if you don't let me through, I can assure you a posting to the icy wastelands of Sivestol within a month," Sirod demanded forcefully.

"General? Look 'ere, I don't care ooo you fink yoo are…" the younger man persisted, puffing out his chest and pouting his lips. "…An anyhow, what happened to yer face?"

"Right, that's it…" Sirod snapped, "…Not only are you refusing me entry, you have also insulted a personal friend of the slave master general. Now what are your names?"

"Now 'ang about…'ang about, there ain't no need to be 'asty like. I'm sure we can overlook it this time," interrupted the older man as he kicked his young associate in the shin.

"What yoo kicked me for…" snapped the younger guard. The older man gave him a glaring look and then sudden understanding of the situation came to the young man.

"…Er…yeah, that's right, we can overlook it, this once nah get goin." And he waved Sirod and Ember through the gates and into Illya.

A sense of normality had returned to the streets since their previous visit and the Hagraals assisted escape but although calm, there was a sense of impending doom. It could have been the sight of Sirod's face that caused everyone to drop their heads as they passed him by or it could just have been the fact that he was a Dust Dweller escorting a fugitive prize; either way, there was a hidden feeling of unease about the place. After several minutes of walking along the narrow cobbled streets, they reached the market square. Spaced around the perimeter were several golden soldiers and here and there huddled in groups were members of the rag-tag army. Both Sirod and Ember bowed their heads so as to seem less conspicuous and they made their way across to the sign that read 'Undertaker'.

Sirod had given Ember instructions of what to do and he laid down on the wooden decking in front of the building as Ember went in.

"I have been sent here by the slave master general; one of his close friends has taken a turn for the worse and died. I had him brought over here and he's outside," Ember announced.

The undertaker looked through the glass panelled door and saw the Dust Dweller lying on the deck. "Why is it you people always come at lunchtime? Look just put him out the back, I'm off." And with that the undertaker walked out leaving Ember to help herself.

After several moments, she opened the front door and called to Sirod. "Pssst, it's clear," she whispered and Sirod slowly rose to his feet and crept in. "I'll wait here," Ember suggested and she went outside and stood watch in the street whilst Sirod went 'out the back'.

One of the guards had taken a great interest in Sirod's charade and approached Ember along with one of the golden soldiers.

Sirod made his way to the rear of the building and lifted a sheet which covered the only available body on the undertaker's slabs. To his complete surprise, the body was that of a very handsome looking young man. Sirod lay on the table and transferred his soul to the new host and then made his way back to the front of the shop. He was about to leave when he heard a conversation taking place outside. Looking through the glass panelled door, he saw Ember talking to the guards in a very loud voice. "I'm sorry, I can't hear you properly," she announced and slapped her right ear with the palm of her hand. "…You say that you want to know what I'm doing here… I'm waiting for my friend," she continued.

The rag-tag guard was very suspicious and although he had no reason to make any connection between Bagdoon and the current situation, he was still inquisitive enough to pursue his enquiries.

"You wait 'ere, wiv 'er while I go in 'ere," he instructed the clockwork soldier and off he went into the undertaker's shop.

"Can I help you?" enquired the young man behind the counter.

The guard looked the 'undertaker' up and down. In front of him stood a very handsome young man with an olive-coloured complexion. He was aged in his late teens to early 20s, was tall, slim and athletic with a fine mop of jet-black hair which was slicked back over his head and tied in a ponytail. He wore a red coloured shirt which had puffed sleeves and flamboyant cuffs and upon his legs, he wore black trousers which were held up by a belt with a small silver buckle. His boots were short, ankle length and pointed.

"Bit young for an undertaker, ain't cha?" asked the guard.

"I've only just started…" replied Sirod truthfully. "…It's a bit of a dead-end job and I don't think I will stick it out much longer to be honest."

"There ain't much work out there for a young 'un, especially a fancy job like this, I reckon you should give it a go," the guard suggested helpfully, having totally missed Sirod's joke. "…Anyhow, enough of the jibber jabber, now show me out back."

Sirod looked down at the desk in front of him, sitting on the side was a very heavy looking metal tray, holding a single mug of cold tea.

"After you, sir, it's through there, I was just going that way to make a cup of tea…Do you fancy one?" And with that, Sirod picked up the heavy tray and followed after the guard.

The Golden soldier stood next to his detained female, scanning the market place for any signs of trouble. Ember tried to appear as casual and natural as possible and leaning on one hip, she placed her hands into her pockets and tossed her hair so that it glistened in the sun. This distraction technique had always worked in the past, having the ability to mesmerise most men and cause them to forget what they were about to ask or do but unfortunately, for Ember, this guard was metal, uncaring, incorruptible and devoid of any emotion. Nonchalantly, she looked around the market square, timing the moment when she would strike and then it came. In the far corner of the market square, a disturbance had broken out between a slave trader and a disgruntled customer who was unhappy with his recent purchase. Every guard in the market turned to look at this new source of entertainment including Ember's Golden watchman. Instantly, Ember took one of the red gems from her pocket and thrust into the face guard of the machine. The red stone glowed bright red as the blue crystal power gem faded to a dull grey and the golden soldier's legs buckled beneath it as it sank to the ground lifeless.

The rag-tag guard looked across at the marble slab upon which lay the Dust Dwellers lifeless body. "What 'appened to him?" The guard asked, not quite understanding.

Sirod approached the man from behind lifted the heavy metal tray and brought it down on the back of the guard's head. "Something heavy landed on him," Sirod replied and he dropped the tray to the floor and ran from the undertakers.

Once outside, he found Ember still standing next to the golden soldier trying to look inconspicuous. "What happened to him?" Sirod asked looking to the hunkered down and totally inert pile of metal.

"Stoned to death," Ember quipped. She turned and found herself facing the most handsome man she had ever seen, she couldn't hide the immediate chemistry; in that moment, her eyes widened and her pulse raced and she just knew that she wouldn't be able to control her feelings. "You are Sirod, I take it?" she enquired as her face flushed red.

"Well, I should hope so by the way you are looking at me..." Sirod affirmed. He looked across the square and saw that whatever commotion had taken the guards attention had managed to sort itself out as now they began to look around at the other areas of the market place. "...We need to find a way out of Illya and quick," he urged.

As they left the market place, the unconscious rag-tag guard had come to and discovered the golden solider now deprived of both strength and power. Whistles began to blow all over the square, the sound carried on the breeze and soon all of Illya was engulfed in the high-pitched noise as guards ran around from here to there, looking for any sign of who could have committed such an act.

"Now we really are in trouble…" Sirod warned. "…We must find refuge as soon as possible and wait for the panic to die down."

The two fugitives made their way across the city and hid amongst the shadows, whenever a guard ran past and before long, they came to the large hill leading up to the Grand Observatory. "Of course, in all the excitement I didn't think to bother Malarog," Sirod declared as he slapped his forehead with an open palm, slightly annoyed for being so remiss. They ran up the hill to the large oak doors. Sirod ran his hand over the carved inscription and smirked, "Heaven's gate," he mumbled.

"Sorry, my love?" enquired Ember.

"Oh, it's nothing. I was just thinking of Eitak and wondered how the others are getting along."

With the Great Wall, two days behind them, Eitak, Arwie, Klum, Bones and Bonsai found themselves at the base of a steep escarpment leading up to the Thunder Mountains. Although just as high as the Mountains of Light to the west, the Thunder Mountains had no snowfall and began with a gentle elevation at the base which then rose to become a perilous and sheer rock face further up towards the summit. Bones looked up to the top of the mountain and protested, "We are not going over that, surely."

"We just need to climb to where the slipped land meets the mountain's body," Klum announced.

"What then?" Bones enquired sarcastically. "I suppose we just go through it?"

"Exactly," Klum boomed.

From the top of the hill, Sirod could see the rag-tag guards and the metal soldiers scurrying around, looking for the duplicitous renegades. It would only be a matter of time before they came hammering at the doors of the grand observatory.

Sirod dropped the heavy metal ring, surrounding the black planet door knocker and waited.

A few moments later, the door opened and there stood Malarog with a golden monkey just like Bonsai sitting on his shoulder and as with Bonsai, this monkey also wore a collar with a blue crystal stone.

"What do you want? Can't you see I'm busy?" protested the short stout Magistan.

"Do we really have to go through this, every time...It's me, Sirod."

Malarog looked at the two figures stood before him, just then something caught his eye and he looked over Sirod's shoulder to the base of the hill and there beginning their ascent were two golden soldiers.

"Sirod!" Malarog shouted excitedly. "Come in, come in, did you bring that other fellow with you? The one with the staff?"

"No..." Sirod replied, "...why? is there a problem?"

Malarog's shoulders slumped as a look of disappointment swept over him. "No, I just needed his staff for an experiment."

Sirod reached behind him and took the staff which was secured on his belt and produced it to his old friend. Malarog's eyes widened, his shoulders straightened and his face lit up with a broad smile as he looked slightly mesmerised by the bright blue crystal staff.

"Wonderful, that's wonderful," he proclaimed as he snatched the staff and scurried off into the observatory.

Sirod and Ember looked at each other quizzically and entered the building. They had trouble keeping up with Malarog who had rushed up the spiral staircase and quickly disappeared out of sight. Sirod followed the sounds of the building as the heavy observatory doors slammed shut; once upstairs, he opened the doors to the viewing room and found Malarog at the large table in the corner.

"Now where is it? Where is it?" Malarog muttered to himself.

"Where is what?" Sirod asked.

"The orb...the orb and the new collar," he replied in a frenzied state.

The small golden monkey swung down from Malarog's shoulder and lowered itself to the floor in one flowing movement and as Ember approached the bench, it jumped up and down and grinning, pointed to something rolling around underneath.

Ember looked under the table and there hiding in the corner of the room was another orb, exactly the same as the one that Malarog had given to Bones.

"Is this what you are looking for?" she enquired as she emerged from under the table.

"Wonderful, yes, that's wonderful." Malarog smiled and snatched the orb from Ember and threw it into the air like a child with a new ball.

Sirod hadn't seen his old friend, this animated for a very long time. "What's all the excitement about?" he asked.

"Eh, what...oh, sorry." Having found what he was looking for, Malarog slowed down. "After you left the last time...I got to thinking about the transporter and realised that the reason it wouldn't work on anything bigger than Bonsai was probably because it didn't have enough power."

"Is that it?" Sirod groaned, not considering the experiment worthy of this level of enthusiasm.

'Thump, thump, thump'. The sound reverberated from the front door, up the spiral staircase and filled the observatory room.

"The guards..." Malarog stated. "...I didn't want to alarm you but I saw them coming up the hill when you called. Now help me find the new collar I made while I get the telescope ready..." With that, Malarog grabbed a long pair of wooden steps and took them together with the small orb over to the huge telescope. Once in place, he climbed the rickety steps to the top and began fiddling around with the eyepiece.

'Thump, Thump, Thump', the knocking was now somewhat louder than before and it was clear that even the patience of the clockwork army had its limits.

"Throw me up that tape!" Malarog shouted as he pointed back down to the table. The small golden monkey jumped onto the workbench and picked up a large reel of brown coloured sticking tape. He then swung back down to the floor and ran over to the steps on his hind legs, holding the tape high in the air with his outstretched arms. Once at the steps, he scrambled up the rungs and handed Malarog the item before sitting on top of the telescope.

"How is that other fellow anyway, the one with Bonsai, and for that matter, how is that little scamp?" Malarog enquired.

"Bones you mean? Oh, they are both fine, they should be at the Thunder Mountains by now."

"The Thunder Mountains, then we should be able to see them from here," Malarog remarked excitedly, still perched rather precariously at the top of the rickety steps.

"Is this the collar?" Ember asked, holding up a large leather strap with a metal ring attached to the clasp.

"Yes, that's it. Now hold on a minute and I'll be down." Malarog strapped the small golden orb to the telescope's eyepiece, wrapping the tape around and around until it didn't move and then climbed back down the ladder. "Now hand me the collar," he instructed. Malarog took both the collar and Sirod's staff over to the table.

'Thud, thud, bang', sounded the noise from downstairs as the heavy oak doors of the observatory burst open.

"Damn, Usurpus and his army," Malarog snapped, annoyed by the swiftness with which the soldiers had breached the observatory's sanctuary.

Ember turned where she stood to face Malarog. "Usurpus?" she sputtered. "What has he got to do with all this?"

"Didn't Sirod tell you? He's the one behind all of this mess…do you know of him my dear?" Malarog enquired.

"You could say that if it wasn't for me then he might never have been," Ember added cryptically.

Working quickly, Malarog lifted the staff and brought the crystal down heavily on the table, 'crack' the large Orillion stone, snapped away from the shaft and rolled onto the table.

"You want to be careful with those things," Sirod warned. "They have a nasty habit of blowing up."

"I'm sure that a stone of this size can take quite a bit of punishment," Malarog replied confidently and using some old wire fixed the large blue stone to the metal ring within the collar.

'Klank, Klank, Klang!' the sound of the metal soldiers walking up the marble staircase, reverberated around the observatory.

"We really don't have much time," Malarog warned and he scrambled back up the stepladder, taking with him a long length of rope. When the got to the top, he threw the rope over the telescope so that the two ends of the rope fell to the ground. He then wrapped his foot around one of the lengths and called down to Sirod, "OK, if you can just hold onto the ends of the rope and Ember if you turn those wheels at the side of the mechanism until I say stop, we should be about there." And he put his right eye to the orb.

Ember saw two small brass hand wheels at the side of the telescope. She grabbed a hold of one and turned wildly. The telescope swung in an arc within the wide-open observatory dome, taking Malarog with it. The Magistan clung desperately to the eyepiece with both hands whilst one foot held his weight in the makeshift stirrup. Sirod was caught off guard by the sudden increase in weight as Malarog was swept from the ladder and flung around in the same arc as he followed the telescope.

"Perhaps a little slower," Sirod suggested.

"There's no time for that…" Malarog shouted. "Quick as you can, girl." And Ember turned the wheel as fast as she could until at last Malarog shouted, "Stop."

Ember then turned the second wheel and the huge tube, nodded its great eye towards the ground as Malarog shot up into the air. Again Sirod was caught off guard and was lifted upwards, still holding onto both ends of the rope. Keeping the tension tight, Sirod allowed the rope to slip between his hands until he was safely down on the ground. "Stop," shouted Malarog and he removed his foot from the stirrup and slipped down the rope.

'Klang, Klang, crash' the soldiers had reached the observatory room.

"Bring the collar," Malarog demanded urgently. Ember grabbed the modified leather strap and handed it to Malarog who quickly put it around his neck. "If I'm right, this should work…Now hold hands."

"Should work? What do you mean…should work? And more importantly…what should work?" Ember enquired now that she had a moment to question what they had just spent the last few minutes doing.

The metal soldiers entered the room and marched over to claim their captives.

The three friends held hands and Malarog looked up to the golden monkey and shouted, "Jangles, now!"

Jangles ran along the large tube to the eyepiece and pressed the button on the orb.

Eitak, Arwie, Klum, Bones and Bonsai had dismounted from the Rhinamoths who had followed along up the steep slope behind them with great loyalty. The sheer granite rock face of the Thunder Mountains loomed ahead as an impregnable barrier reaching to the heavens.

"We are nearly there." Klum announced reassuringly.

Now exhausted Bones looked at the Granite wall. "Nearly where? All I can see is no way through," he complained.

Klum reached out and rubbed his huge hands across the stone. *I'm sure that it's here somewhere*…he pondered, …*but it has been a while.*

From the top of the escarpment, Eitak had a really good view of the surrounding countryside, across to the west, he could see the Mountains of Light and to the north, he could just about make out the hill top observatory of Illya. I wonder how Sirod and Ember are getting along, he thought to himself.

"Found it," Klum boomed excitedly and he pressed a small section of rock. A terrible cracking noise filled the air followed by the scraping of rock on rock as half the mountain seemed to give way and a huge doorway opened up leading into the Thunder Mountains.

"The Thunder Pass," Klum bellowed delightedly, the sound of his voice reverberated and echoed into the darkened tunnel leading through the granite.

Bones looked into the hole. "There is just one thing Klum…won't you turn to stone if you go in there?"

Klum laughed and then answered, "Do you see a full moon? There won't be another here for a few days, so we'll be fine."

By now the Rhinamoths had caught up and had reached the Thunder pass just as the five friends were about to enter. All of a sudden, there was a strange fizzing noise which filled the air and then, Sirod, Ember, Malarog and Jangles appeared.

Malarog's eyes focused on Klum and panic set in. "A giant…" he screamed. "…Run for your lives!"

Klum turned to face the small strange man with fluffy white tufts of hair and frowned. He then saw Ember and a broad smile spread across his face. "Ember," he bellowed. The sound of his voice echoed and magnified in the gaping maw which was now fully open through the mountainside and was so loud that everyone threw their hands over their ears and grimaced.

As soon as the noise had died down and his senses returned, Eitak looked around and recognised Ember but it took him just a moment to register that the handsome young man stood before him was Sirod in his new body. "Malarog…" he shouted, realising the Magistan was now running as fast as his short legs would carry him down the steep slope. "…It's all right…it's me Eitak, Klum's a friend."

Malarog slowed to a stop and turned to see everyone standing by the mountain laughing down at him. "Well, how did I know…" he muttered under his breath. "I thought giants were supposed to eat people." And soon he had climbed back up the escarpment and joined his friends both old and new.

Arwie hugged Ember, Eitak hugged Sirod, Malarog and Klum looked at each other and raised a hand whilst Bones shook his head as he watched Bonsai and Jangles jump up and down as they embraced each other and grinned.

With the introductions over Arwie turned to Ember. "So how did you get here then?" she enquired.

"By telescope." Ember looked northwards and could just about make out the observatory building high on its hill, she didn't have a clue as to how she had arrived at the Thunder Mountains but what she did know was that she was happy that she was no longer in Illya.

Klum led the way into the mountain. As they stepped through the huge granite doorway, Malarog marvelled at the intricate contrivance of cogs and pulleys which held back the huge slab of rock and couldn't help but notice the bright blue glowing Orillion crystal at the heart of the mechanism. "Who designed and built this?" he enquired with curiosity getting the better of him.

"My people! They made this tunnel a long time ago, long before you or even I stood on this planet. It was after the discovery of the power gems that it was built as a way to travel from the Crystal Desert to Kidder Doon," Klum divulged with great pride.

"We could do with another torch in here," Bones suggested. "...The only light we have is from that rock around Malarog's neck and the small stone at the door and I doubt that they provide much brilliance for long, Sirod have you still got Eitak's staff?"

Malarog looked at the large stone still hanging from his collar and then confessed, "I'm sorry to say that this is all that is left of Eitak's staff...we needed to make some...alterations...for the transportation."

Eitak looked at Malarog's necklace. "That's all right," he conceded, "it's probably more use that size because to be honest, it was getting in the way a little and anyway Bones, we have plenty of these red stones left for light." And he set to work, handing out several of the red stones that he had collected from the Crystal Desert.

Ember couldn't resist bringing up the subject of Usurpus with Sirod. "You know that all of this is my fault, if it wasn't for me, if I had just married Kalag and had done with it then Usurpus would never have been born." Tears that were hidden in the darkness began to run down her cheeks. "It is, it's all my fault," Ember repeated, sobbing.

Sirod put his arm around Ember and held her tight. "Of course, it isn't your fault, how could you have known that this would happen, after all it wasn't you who held the knife that day and why shouldn't you be able to choose who you marry...none of this is your fault, if anyone is to blame, it is Usurpus himself."

After some time, the companions had led the Rhinamoths through the tunnel to the other side and to everyone's surprise, piled high by the opposing door mechanism was an abandoned pile of glowing blue crystal gems.

Klum pressed a section of rock and once again a huge slab of granite shifted as cogs and wheels opened the mountainside to reveal...

To their absolute horror, from their vantage point on the eastern face of the mountain, the seven companions had a clear view of the entire Plain of Ishtar and there amassed on the flat grasslands were some 10,000 soldiers of the Golden Army. The army comprised mainly of clockwork soldiers but amongst them were at least 1,000 of the rag-tag guards dressed in leather armour and ready for battle. The plains now stood between the travellers and the foothills of Kidder Doon beyond.

"Seriously..." Eitak questioned with defeat in his voice, "...how do you expect us to get past that lot? We might just as well turn back now."

"We need a diversion," Sirod announced. "We just need to think of a way to distract them to the south whilst we slip past and keep a low profile in the longer grasses up here to the north." And he pointed out his plan using his finger like a military commander planning a battle strategy.

"That's all very well and good..." Bones agreed, "...but who's volunteering to make the diversion?"

Klum looked at Malarog and then back into the tunnel entrance. "That may not be necessary," he whispered trying to keep his voice down as low as possible. "Pass me as many of those blue crystal stones as you can carry."

Before long, a small pile of the blue crystals had collected at the giant's feet. "Now get ready because we won't have long," Klum ordered and with that he picked up a crystal in his hand, pulled back his arm and threw it as hard as he could, high into the air and towards the south. The companions looked and held their breath. The Golden Army below them were totally oblivious to the catastrophic event which was just about to take place. Klum picked up another stone then another and another and launched them high into the sky so that they followed the same path as the first. When the first gem landed, a blinding flash of blue light lit up the southern horizon, this was followed closely by another and another until before long, the entire southern end of the great plain burned with bright blue light from the many explosions taking place. The Golden Army reacted as planned, the mechanical soldiers slowly made their way towards the attacking front, leaving behind them a light guard which included several members of the rag-tag army.

"Now," Klum roared and his voice rolled around the mountain like thunder as the companions quickly climbed up onto the Rhinamoths and raced as fast as the enormous creatures would carry them, down the slope leading to the Grasslands below.

Klum led. His huge strides meant that he reached the plain ahead of the others. Eitak followed and rode with Arwie, Bones rode with Malarog and Bonsai and Jangles whilst Sirod and Ember brought up the rear. Running at full speed, the huge Rhinamoths kicked up stones and dust which rolled down the hillside and the sound of falling rock mixed with the tremendous sound of pounding feet created the illusion of a great storm brewing to the west.

The golden soldiers who had been left behind turned to face, this new enemy, they raised their weapons and marched towards Klum who was now running at full speed across the plains towards them. The first soldier raised its sword and Klum raised his giant hammer. The force of the impact created by Klum bringing the hammer down hard combined with the speed with which he ran caused the metal guard to fly into the air with tremendous speed. Another soldier appeared in Klum's path and once again Klum mashed his hammer into the ground, this time directly on top of the metal guard's head. The soldier immediately vanished, having been pummelled into the firm grassy ground. The huge giant was by now more than three quarters of the way across the plain and then with a clatter and a crash, the first metal guard landed by his feet and smashed into pieces.

A golden soldier marched towards Eitak and Arwie as their Rhinamoth thundered along behind Klum. Arwie drew back her bow and let loose one of the blue crystal arrows, the blue stone tip entered through the metal cage of its faceguard and struck the power gem, an almighty explosion took place and pieces of metal, cogs springs and pistons flew everywhere. The detonation was so loud that the entire northern end of the Golden Army turned back and began to march on the new battlefront. As the army returned, Arwie let loose another arrow and a further explosion destroyed several more of the metal guard.

"Faster…Faster," Eitak screamed as he watched the army closing in on his right flank.

Klum stood still and waved his hammer around in a great arc, scattering the small metal men in all directions but even he was vulnerable as waves of arrows now filled the sky and rained down upon him, Klum was forced to retreat and looked back across the field to his friends as the army closed in.

Bones and Malarog were having problems, their short legs had trouble clinging to the creature's wide flanks and even though they grabbed onto the beast's long hair, they still bobbed up and down uncontrollably. As they passed by the golden soldier, who had been mashed into the ground, Bones muttered, "I hope that's not his idea of 'under'."

"Pardon?" replied Malarog, unable to hear over the thunderous noise created by the charging Rhinamoths.

"Nothing…" Bones answered, "…you needed to be there, really."

Bonsai and Jangles on the other hand were having a whale of a time. They had managed to collect a handful of tiny blue Orillion crystal pebbles from the Thunder Mountain and now, with their feet gripped into the Rhinamoth long fur, they stood up and threw the small gems at the advancing soldiers. With each stone came a small explosion and with each explosion Bonsai and Jangles looked at each other, bared their teeth and gave a broad grin.

Each time a golden guard made its way into the Rhinamoth's path, the great beasts bowed their heads and butted them aside, using their long tusks and horns. Sirod and Ember charged forward, however, their way ahead was now greatly hindered by the many returned soldiers and although their great beast was able to cut a swathe through their ranks, the numbers were now overwhelming. Ember saw Bonsai and Jangles up ahead and decided to throw one or two of the red crystals she had been given by Eitak. She let go of the Rhinamoth's hair, fumbled in her pocket, retrieved a stone and pulled back her arm. As she threw the first gem, her Rhinamoth bowed its head as it brushed a few more of the metal men to one side, the sudden lurch caused Ember to lose balance and she fell from her ride and into the long grass. Within seconds, she was overwhelmed. Sirod hadn't noticed her fall and together with the others, his beast charged at full speed across the plain until it reached the safety of the treeline on the other side. It was only then that he turned around to find that Ember was no longer behind him.

"Woah, stop," he shouted in desperation but his great beast carried on running deeper into the woods until at last it came to a clearing, where the others stood having managed to gain some control. Sirod's Rhinamoth slowed to a stop and pulled up alongside Eitak.

"We've got to go back…Ember, she fell…we have to save her," Sirod cried with blind panic having set in.

"Ember?" Klum bellowed and he immediately ran back towards the plain.

The entire Golden Army had now amassed at the northern end of the plain and had fanned out to form an eastern and a western flank. The western side of the army now stood bows, pikes and swords at the ready, facing the tree line where the companions had gone. Klum ran from the woods and into the firing line as a volley of 1,000 tiny fire splinters rained down upon him. His skin burned as the arrows bit into his flesh, forcing him to retreat back behind the trees.

Sirod stood next to him and peered out from the safety of the wood. In the middle of the plain, a central column of rag-tag guards had seized Ember and now dragged her backwards across the grasslands towards the south.

"I will save you Ember…I will save you and wreak my revenge," Sirod swore emphatically as tears rolled down his face.

"I will help you…this I promise," Klum declared as he plucked the tiny wooden splinters from his arm.

With the image of Ember disappearing into the distance etched into their minds, the companions made their way back to the clearing where the Rhinamoths were busy eating grass and tree shoots.

The journey through the woodland to Kidder Doon was a silent one as everyone was consumed by their own thoughts but by evening, they had reached the foothills leading up to the largest volcano on Kennet.

The hills around the volcano were heavily wooded and it was difficult to see the route through, but Klum marched ever onward ahead of the others with huge tireless strides. The Rhinamoths appeared spritely and Eitak put this down to the fact they had just eaten but even they could not keep pace with Klum.

"I could do with a decent meal," Eitak shouted ahead, loud enough for Klum to hear.

"We will soon be home," Klum confirmed and he waved in encouragement for the others to keep up.

As they got closer to the volcano, Eitak was aware of a presence, watching him from the woods, he had this feeling for some time now and he strained to look into the darkness between the trees. Out of the gloom, Eitak could make out several sets of glowing green, yellow and red coloured eyes.

"We are being watched," he whispered.

11. The Giants of Kidder Doon

Sirod turned his head just in time to see a pack of Hasty Hagraals appear, who immediately fanned out and surrounded the group. The Rhinamoths froze, even they seemed to realise that running was not an option. Better to meet this enemy head on and take your chances as slim as they now seemed.

As the Hagraals lowered their huge heads and sniffed the ground, Eitak noticed something quite strange, for around the neck of each one was a thick leather collar studded with bright glowing red crystal gems. The Hagraals and the Rhinamoths stood facing each other when suddenly, ahead of Klum, a large Hagraal with a white flash of fur on its head, crashed through the trees and bounded up to the huge giant. Eitak immediately recognised the Hagraal as being the same one, he had saved both in Illya and Bagdoon.

"Hunter!" Klum exclaimed with great excitement and held open his huge arms and embraced the over enthusiastic Hagraal who licked him all over his face.

Klum turned around to see the standoff further down the hill. "Down," he roared and the pack of Hagraals did as Klum commanded and lay on their bellies with their hind legs under them.

"So I see that you have met my hunting dogs," Klum roared and he raced back down the hill and made a huge fuss of the pets he had not seen in such a long time.

"I knew it…" Eitak announced. "…I knew there was something about these Hagraals."

"Now that's what I call a dog…" Bones added. "…And you mean to say that you actually hunt with these things?" he continued.

"Of course…" Klum replied, "…they have a lovely nature once you get to know them." And he sat on the ground whilst the Hagraal pack rolled on their backs in submission and Klum rubbed their bellies with his huge hands. The giant then pointed to each of the Hagraals in turn.

"Let me introduce you, this is Sprinter, then we have Dasher, Rusher and Whoosher." Klum finally pointed to the Hagraal with the white flash of fur on its forehead. "…And this one is Hunter, he is my favourite and the most loyal of all."

"We've already met," Eitak declared and he proceeded to tell Klum of his adventures in Illya and Bagdoon. Having listened to the tale, Klum smiled in approval.

"Thank you…" he acknowledged. "I could give you a hug…if you weren't so small."

Eitak climbed down from his Rhinamoth and slowly approached Hunter. The huge Hagraal sniffed the air and recognising Eitak's scent, moved forward so that he was now nose to nose with the man who had freed him twice, he then extended his oversized tongue and washed Eitak's face with one giant lick.

"That's gross," Eitak professed as he wiped the slobber from his cheek. Hunter nudged Eitak with his snout who responded by extending his hand and scratching the Hagraal behind his right ear.

Jangles slowly emerged from his hiding place behind Bonsai and peering over his shoulder, looked at the Hagraal pack. Realising that they were no longer a threat, he put his arm around Bonsai and grinned.

"Well, I think that I should introduce you to my family and get something to eat," Klum suggested.

"That's the best idea you've had yet," confirmed Bones approvingly and the seven companions, two monkeys, eight Rhinamoths and four Hagraals walked towards the volcano.

The volcano towered above them and reached high into the sky, its girth curved around to both the east and the west and joined with an arm of the Thunder Mountains. There was no easy way over the sheer granite face and everyone wondered how they were going to scale the mountain before tea.

Klum approached the volcano and pressed a section of stone. A loud cracking noise filled the air and a massive section of rock began to slip to one side.

"I might have guessed…" Malarog smirked as he touched his forehead and then raised his hand in the air.

Once the volcano had opened, the companions stepped into a long tunnel and made their way through the mountain to the other side. Eitak was the first to emerge from the passage and found that he was now stood on the edge of a village. Behind him, the inner wall of the volcano and the northern face of the

Thunder Mountain rose to the sky, whilst ahead of him and opposite to where he stood, there was no opposing side to the volcano at all; in fact, the whole thing appeared to be a pretence, a facade with no substance other than the entrance, they had just walked through. Eitak looked out into the village which stretched as far as his eye could see. It was just like any other village only everything was many times bigger.

"Welcome to Kidder Doon," Klum announced.

"The secret land of the giants!" Arwie exclaimed, "…a place of legend and a realm that no one has ever visited until today."

Klum turned to the others. "You might want to cover your ears for a moment," he suggested and then shouted as loud as he could: "MIN!"

Even with their hands over their ears, the noise was deafening and caused the very ground to shake but a few moments later as the sound of Klum's voice subsided, the ground continued to shake.

"The volcano's erupting," Bones cried and fell to his knees, putting his hands over his head.

Thud, thud, thud, a new noise invaded their ears and increased as it got closer until in the dusty path ahead, Eitak could see a group of huge giants running at full speed towards him.

With his arms stretched wide, Klum ran forwards until halfway along the street he was met by an enormous female giant who threw herself at him in a warm and lasting embrace. Klum enthusiastically spun the huge woman around and to Eitak's amazement, he saw that she was a mirror image of Ember, slim and athletic, albeit a lot larger. Her hair was the same, deep burnt orange colour of fire but was wild and untamed. She had Ember's high cheekbones, hazel-coloured eyes and a very full bust. All the other giants surrounded Klum and hugged and squeezed him tightly but then he remembered his companions. "Let me introduce you to my friends," he announced and pointed to the five tired travellers. The giants stood still, frozen to the spot as they looked upon Klum's 'friends' in total amazement.

The large female who first greeted Klum was the first to speak. "Little people? Here? What are you thinking of Klum?" she said.

Klum ignored the comment and continued, "This is Eitak and Arwie. Then we have Sirod, Bones and Malarog. The two tiny ones are Bonsai and Jangles." As he spoke, the two monkeys raised themselves to their hind legs, stretched their arms high into the air and grinned at the audience of giants.

"They are the only reason I am here…" Klum added. "…If it wasn't for them, I would either still be a prisoner or possibly even be dead."

The giants looked at each other and mumbled amongst themselves for a few moments and then nodded their heads. The female giant looked towards the companions and announced, "Then you are our guests and you may stay as long as you wish, if Klum says you are his friends, then you are our friends too."

"Let me introduce you to my beautiful wife, Min," Klum declared and he lifted the female giant's hand and kissed it gently. Min blushed and then lifted the hem of her pretty green coloured dress and curtsied to the group.

"This other lot are my friends and neighbours," Klum continued as he pointed to the giants one by one. "Here we have the boys, Kram and Tum and next to them are the ladies, Nim, who is Min's sister and then the twins, Luj and Noj."

The three other female giants tittered amongst themselves and blushed at Klum's reference to ladies. Bones couldn't help himself, he stared thankfully, open mouthed and speechless for the first time since his meeting with Eitak on the shores of Monrith. Nim was one of the most attractive women, giant or not, that he had ever seen, she was truly beautiful with long golden coloured hair which cascaded down her back, she was slim and very athletic looking and had piercing blue eyes and the prettiest of any smile. On the other hand, he looked at Luj and Noj who were two of the ugliest females he had ever laid eyes upon. They each had short, thick, unkempt, dark brown, bristle like hair, very short fat noses, buck teeth and were grossly overweight. They both wore matching dresses, albeit Luj was in yellow and Noj in orange, the dresses were so tight that it caused their oversized bosoms to spill over the top of the low cut and square necklines.

"I think I'm in love," Bones finally announced.

Luj and Noj looked at the short fisherman and giggled. Malarog raised an eyebrow as he saw the interaction between Bones and the giant twins. "Well, it takes all sorts to make a world," he muttered, considering his friend's taste in women to be a little bazaar.

"Come, we will have a feast to celebrate," Klum suggested and led the companions through the village. Each of the massive buildings was single story, made of stone and mortar and was finished off with a thatched roof and chimney. Smoke slowly rose from the rooftops and as Eitak looked in through several of the open doors, he could see huge lit hearths with roaring fires; each the size of the beach bonfire in front of the house of the midday moon.

The northern end of the village opened onto a large grassy field and in the middle was the largest bonfire any of the travellers had ever seen.

"We like to keep a small fire going," Klum said as he looked upon the roaring flames, he led his friends to several logs scattered around at some distance from the immense heat of the fire and sat down. The companions chose one of the smallest arranged tree trunks and dangled their legs over the side. Several minutes later, other giants entered the field and sat down followed soon after by several more and several more after that. Before long, the entire field was abuzz with the deep hum of giant conversation. After some time, a few of the female giants came over and handed out huge plates, the size of tables which were piled high with cooked meats, warm bread and various fruits and vegetables. One of the girls dragged a massive tree root over to where Eitak sat and placed the plate on top.

"This is the finest banquet that I can ever remember," Bones confirmed as he tucked into a huge rack of ribs.

Eitak wanted to know more about the village and called to Klum. "Tell me about the volcano and how is it that you ended up here," he asked.

"Well, Kidder Doon has always been our home, the old volcano erupted centuries ago and the explosion took with it half of the mountain. It is the ideal home for us as it provides an impenetrable barrier to the south and combined with the Mountains to the east and west and the insuperable Cylesian Cliffs to the north, we are protected from all sides. No one bothers us and we bother no one and that is how we like it, the races of Kennet either look upon us as a nuisance or as monsters and that is fine with us as we can quite easily just live without them."

"That is such as shame," Eitak replied. "I have only known your friends a few hours but they have made me feel as if Kidder Doon is my second home."

Music rang around the field and Eitak looked over and saw Tum playing a large U-shaped stringed instrument similar to a lyre but a lot larger. The music was mesmerising and as he watched the giants dance around the bonfire, combined with the lullaby sounds of the lyre and the feeling of a full belly of food he soon fell asleep.

Sirod had cried himself to sleep but awoke with a new determination and went looking for Klum. Bones awoke and pulled Bonsai and Jangles from his chest and stretched; the morning air was cool, still and filled with the last trails of smoke from the huge bonfire which had burnt to ember in the middle of the field. He rubbed his face in his hands and picked several traces of sleep from the corners of his eyes when he heard the sound of two women squabbling.

"I saw him first, he's mine," one bellowed.

"No, I did and he fancies me, he don't like you coz your nose is bigger than mine," argued the other.

As he blinked his eyes in an attempt to focus, Bones saw Luj and Noj walking towards him, pushing and shoving each other as they went.

"I tell ya, he was lookin' at me and he's got such a cute little smile," Luj retorted as she shoved Noj on the left shoulder.

"Whatchoo gonna do wiv him, anyways? It's not like you would know what to do wiv him or nuffin," Noj replied and returned a shove into Luj's left arm.

Bones shook himself awake. Malarog got up having been woken by the argument and stood next to him. "Well, it looks like your two fancy women have got a crush on you," he warned.

Bones eyes widened, he turned to Malarog as it suddenly became clear to him that the two girls must have thought he was talking about them, when they met the previous evening.

"I'd say that you are in a spot of bother there my, friend." Malarog sniggered.

The two girls had by now pushed and shoved their way over to Bones and towered over him. He looked at them and considered they must be around 30 years of age if giant years were the same as human ones, although they could quite easily have been a lot older. Noj spoke first. "Well, which one is it?" she demanded. "…Do you like me best or is it her." And once more, she shoved her sister on the shoulder.

"It's me, isn't it? Go on, tell her," Luj retorted.

Malarog looked at Bones and whispered some advice, "I should be very careful how you answer that one if I were you."

"Oh, thank you, that's just so helpful," Bones replied sarcastically. He took a moment and looked between the two giants. They had quite clearly spent some time beautifying themselves as both 'girls' had plaited their hair into pig tails to make themselves appear younger and they now wore several layers of thick make up including bright red lipstick which looked as if it had been applied during the heat of a furious argument and with only the partial use of a mirror.

"Do you know, ladies, I just can't choose…" Bones decided not wanting to hurt either of their feelings. "…You are clearly both as lovely as one another." The two women looked at each other, sniggered and then ran off across the field and back towards the village.

"Great," Malarog quipped, "now instead of one woman after you, you've got two."

Bones looked towards Bonsai and Jangles for support but the two monkeys looked up at him and each put a hand over their eyes in a gesture of despair.

Sirod found Klum splashing water over his face from a huge barrel which stood outside one of the houses. As soon as he saw Sirod, he smiled. "Did you sleep well?" he enquired.

"Of a fashion," Sirod replied and then came straight to the point. "I was just wondering if you meant what you said when you offered your help to defeat the Golden Army." Klum looked at his little friend and could see that he was only just managing to hold it together. He put down the huge towel he was using to dry his face and considered his answer.

"Of course, I will help you…" he agreed, "…but I need to convince the others as we cannot do it alone, the Golden Army are too many in number."

"What do you think they will do with Ember?" As painful as it was, Sirod had to know what was likely to have happened to the only person he had ever truly loved.

"It is most likely that they will take her to the marshlands where this Usurpus lives, Malarog tells me that he is behind all of this and I should think that having captured her, he will want some answers, especially, as by now, he will know that it is because of her that I am free."

Arwie awoke on the village green next to Eitak and as she looked at him, she wondered if he felt the same way about her as she now felt about him. She felt awkward about their situation, sure he had saved her from the market and sure she thought he was very handsome and yes, they had been on an adventure together but he had never made his feelings truly known and now she wondered if he just considered her to be a friend or even a sister or if there was something more. As she considered her options, several giants began to congregate on the field and Eitak awoke. "I wonder what's going on," she asked.

The sun rose into the morning sky and the village green filled with all the giants from the village. A huge wooden 'throne' was carried which was placed just in front of the exhausted bonfire. Sirod and Klum entered and together with Bones, Malarog, Bonsai and Jangles, they came to stand next to Eitak and Arwie.

A fanfare of two huge trumpet horns sounded as the Giant King walked across the field to the throne and sat down. The king was as tall as any other giant but was slightly overweight with a round face and rosy cheeks, he appeared to be around 50 years of age by human standards and had the overall appearance of being rather jolly. He wore fine clothes, befitting of a king, a flamboyant shirt embroidered in gold, a jacket of crimson cloth, golden tights and a cape of soft white fur. Upon his head he wore a simple golden crown.

"Welcome to our friends and guests," the king announced. "I am Gom, king of the giants, Klum has told me about the Golden Army now massed on the Plains of Ishtar. The army is a threat to all the races of Kennet and it will not be long before they come knocking at our door and I don't think they will want to make friends. Now is the time to put a stop to this nonsense, we need to meet them on the grasslands whilst they are all together and defeat them once and for all, for too long has this army seized our hunting dogs, for too long have they threatened our people and I say we avenge Klum and help our new friends to rescue Ember."

A great roar and cheer echoed around the mountains as the giants raised their arms in approval. Luj and Noj waved as they looked across the field and caught Bones staring at them.

The giant king continued his speech, "We must plan. Kram, you are the finest blacksmith in all of Kennet, you will make weapons and armour. Tum, you are to ready the Hagraals and everyone else prepare for battle, the giants are going to war."

Another cheer erupted around the field and then silence fell as an immaculately dressed female giant walked across the field. She walked over to the king and stood behind him. "Well, what are we all waiting for?" she announced and the field began to empty as the giants busied themselves in preparation.

The five companions remained where they were until the female giant beckoned them over. "I am Num, Queen of the giants," she declared. The companions looked at the queen, she was around the same age and build as Gom but had an air of superiority about her, it was quite obvious that in her day, she had been rather beautiful but time and good food had taken its toll and now although immaculate in appearance, she no longer had the looks of her youth.

"Klum has told me all about you…" the queen continued, "but what I really want to know is what do you intend with my daughters?" and she looked directly at Bones.

"What? What? Erm…nothing, I mean I really like them, but…" Bones spluttered, unable to speak or think, having been put in a position which was not of his own making.

"Just as I thought," snapped the queen. "Another time waster, I tell you Gom, we will never be rid of those two." The queen looked down and into the centre of Gom's crown as the sun shone brightly above. "Ear…" Nom continued, "…you're going a bit thin up top, my love." And with that she marched off across the field towards the village, mumbling under her breath.

Gom raised his eyes to the sky and shook his head. "That's all I've heard all night long from both Luj and Noj, all about you, young man." And the king pointed to Bones. "How you told them that you love them both, I really don't mind you know, you can have them both for all I care, just a bit of peace and quiet would be nice."

"There must be some sort of mistake…" Bones began but Sirod kicked him in the shin before he could go any further.

"What do you mean a mistake? Don't you like them?" the king demanded.

"No, no, no, it's not like that at all. Of course, I like them," Bones replied nervously, not knowing how to get out of this situation.

"Well, that's settled then. I will arrange the marriage after the battle." And the king marched off to tell his wife and daughters the good news.

"That should be a really good do," Malarog joked.

Eitak, Arwie and Sirod walked off into the village to help the war, effort leaving Bones, Malarog, Bonsai and Jangles alone in the field. "So, that will make you Prince of the giants then." Malarog pointed out.

Arwie found Tum tending to the Hagraals. "Is there anything I can do?" she asked.

"I don't know," Tum replied. "What can you do?"

"Well, I'm a trained archer."

"Really? In that case, come with me." And Tum led Arwie back to the village green just as several of the giants were setting up some huge targets at the far end of the field. "Perhaps you can teach this lot how to shoot properly then," he suggested.

Arwie approached the giants who looked at the pretty blonde girl and smirked. "Would you like me to teach you?" she enquired.

"What would you know about archery?" one of the giants asked as he looked at his friends and sniggered.

Arwie removed her bow from her shoulder and placed a blue tipped arrow into the string. She pulled back her arm and let go of the feather fletching. The arrow flew into the air in a great arc and landed right in the centre of the recently placed target. A bright blue explosion erupted across the field and where the target once stood, there was now nothing but a pile of burning straw.

"I know a bit," Arwie replied casually.

Eitak bumped into Tum on his way back from the Field. "I was meaning to ask you about the Hagraal's collars. Who had the idea to stud them with the red gemstones?" he asked inquisitively.

"Well, we started to lose several of our Hagraals a while ago," Tum relayed. "...We heard that the Golden Army were catching them to sell at the slave markets, they make good money for fighting in the arenas. I think it's dreadful because I like to know what they're eating; anyway, I had the idea of studding their collars with the red stones and for a while, the Hagraals were safe, that was until they changed tactic and began to trap them using the rag-tag army, as you call them, damn nuisance is what I call them."

"Well, I think it was a brilliant idea. I saw Hunter using his to great effect in Bagdoon," Eitak added approvingly.

Malarog walked around the village and found Kram at the forge making huge armour plates. "Who are these for?" he asked.

"The Rhinamoths," Kram replied. "We can't have them coming to harm now, can we?" Kram put down his huge hammer and showed Malarog around. In his workshop, there were several machines designed for the pressing, cutting and shaping of metal including a large lathe. Each of the machines utilised a blue crystal gem as its power source.

"This is fantastic," Malarog acknowledged. "You really must show me how to utilise these stones for my observatory." And he tagged along with Kram for the rest of the day.

That night the entire village including their guests attended a huge banquet set up on the village green. A vast table had been laid with specially modified chairs for those not quite large enough to reach. A huge side of meat turned on a spit close by and on the table were vast slices of cooked meats, cheeses, vegetables fruit and bread, there was wine and fruit juices a feast fit for an army and that's just what it was.

The giants marched into the field two by two, dressed in heavy leather and shining armour plate. The sound of their feet pounding the ground mixed with the clanking of metal on metal, made the hair on the companion's necks stand on end.

"Where is Arwie?" Malarog asked. "I haven't seen her all day."

"You'll see, just keep watching," Eitak replied.

Arwie entered the field being carried aloft by two enormous giants, dressed in light armour, slung over their shoulders they carried huge curved bows and quivers containing many heavy-duty arrows. In her hands, Arwie held a new bow carved from the finest alder wood, she was dressed in a tailor-made leather tunic with matching trousers and light silver-plated armour which shone in the light of the newly lit bonfire in the middle of the clearing.

As the archers entered the field, the village folk erupted in a round of cheers, especially having caught sight of the new and very talented archery teacher.

Music began to play and before long the food and wine flowed.

"This really is the best time I have ever had," Bones agreed, not realising that Noj and Luj were standing close enough to hear. Now after a little wine, they scooped the fisherman off his seat and facing each other, held him between their ample breasts.

After the initial shock, Bones realised where he was and looked up at the two sisters. To his amazement, he thought they looked a little less ugly than when he had first met them or was it just the wine? Either way he snuggled back and announced, "Actually, I could get quite used to this."

The morning was heralded by the sound of the trumpet horns, Klum woke the companions who had been given the use of a huge bed within his home and after a hearty breakfast, everyone made their final preparations for war.

Malarog went off to find Kram and after a while they returned with gifts of light armour.

"I'm going to stay here and keep the machines running," Malarog announced. "I'm far too old for this sort of thing and will just be a nuisance. Kram and I made the armour yesterday and he's coming with you instead."

Sirod agreed that this was the best idea, Malarog was 'getting on a bit' and didn't have the reflexes of his youth and they couldn't afford for anything to happen to him as that would also mean taking up valuable battlefield resources.

Tum was stood in full battle dress and as with everyone else, he now wore a suit of light armour and a heavy fur cape. "Where are the Hagraals?" Eitak asked wondering where the hunting dogs had got to.

"They are off playing." Tum replied. "I'll call them." And he picked up a large horn and blew hard. As the reverberating note dissolved into the surrounding mountains, the Hagraals appeared. One moment they were gone and the next they were there. Each Hagraal wore a red gem studied collar and had a suit of armour which covered their bodies and tapered down to a point over their huge heads.

"I don't think I'll ever get use to their speed," Eitak remarked.

"I've found something which I think might belong to you," Tum confessed and in his huge hand, he held the magical compass which Eitak had lost in Bagdoon. "Passed right through Sprinter this morning..." Tum continued. "...I showed it to Malarog and he told me that it's yours, so you best have it back." Eitak gave the compass a quick 'sniff' and then looked at the needle which was now pointing towards the Plains of Ishtar in the east.

Following the blowing of the horn, a steady pounding sound could be heard coming from the far end of the village and soon the great Rhinamoths lumbered down the dusty streets also dressed in full battle armour. The entire village gathered at the entrance to the volcano, the king was there distinguishable from everyone else by his golden armour and everyone said their farewells to Malarog and the women folk.

Noj and Luj picked Bones off the ground and held him between their bosoms; he looked up at them and frowned. They really were looking distinctly more attractive he thought.

"Take care, my love," Noj whispered.

"Come back to us safely," Luj added and they gently placed him astride one of the battle ready Rhinamoths.

Everyone carried a weapon, some of the giants held massive two-handed war hammers whilst others held shorter and single-handed versions, a contingent of giants stood alongside Arwie with huge bows slung over their shoulders, their arrows were now tipped with large blue Orillion crystals. Some of the giants carried huge axes whilst others carried simple slingshots. Kram pulled a huge wagon piled high with blue and red Orillion stones. The stones separated from each other by a heavy metal divider. This prevented the red ones from draining the power from the blue ones. As Kram pulled the wagon, Tum walked with the Hagraals who drooled and salivated in expectation of the hunt.

King Gom placed his golden helmet upon his head. "Let's go to war," he bellowed and at his command, the volcano opened and the Giants marched into the gloom.

12. Battle

The giants moved cautiously towards the Plains of Ishtar, Klum had warned them about the flank of soldiers with their archers trained upon the woods. Gom looked out from the tree line and to his surprise, found that the Golden Army had moved further down the plain to the south. Their western flank had been replaced by several hundred villagers who stood facing them with nothing more than a collection of farm implements and acquired weapons. Eitak shuffled alongside Gom and viewed the men who clearly appeared determined to achieve their own destruction. At the front of the group, Eitak recognised Thaddeus the butcher, Lucius. the blacksmith and Felix, the baker from Monrith.

"I know them…" Eitak announced to Gom, "…and perhaps it will suit us to join forces and even up the odds a little."

The Giants spoke briefly amongst themselves and then having come to a decision, Gom stepped out onto the plains. Thaddeus looked at the Giant as he emerged from the woods. His men stood their ground and presented their pitch forks and weapons of various origins towards Him. Eitak urged his Rhinamoth forward and removing his battle helmet stopped in front of the butcher.

"Lower your weapons, the giant is with me," Eitak shouted.

Thaddeus threw down his weapon and opened his arms wide. "Eitak…so we meet again…" he beamed, delighted to see his young customer from Monrith.

Eitak looked at the butcher who was now wearing a pair of black boots, loose fitting brown coloured trousers and a white shirt unbuttoned to the waist.

"It's nice to see you dressed in something a little more fitting," Eitak said jokingly. "… I would like you to meet Gom, the King of the Giants." And Eitak waved his arm around in an arc presenting his massive new ally.

"I can't top that," Thaddeus confessed, "but these are all the villagers I could muster. The whole planet is infested with these mechanical things and when I heard that they were massing here. I got together as many men as I could. Our will is strong it's just our numbers that are weak."

"Well, hopefully, I can remedy that," Gom boomed and he beckoned for the rest of the colossal men from the village to join him on the battlefield. The ground began to shake as 40 giants in full battle armour marched across the plain and stood next to the 300 villagers and four metal clad Rhinamoths and their companion riders.

"Now I am impressed," Thaddeus admitted, nodding his head in approval.

"I thought you told me that you didn't know anything about fighting," Eitak said to Thaddeus thinking back to Bagdoon.

"Well, I got to thinking that there really isn't that much difference between fighting and being a butcher, just one is dealing with the dead and the other is dealing with what is about to become dead…besides, I'm a fast learner."

The entire Golden Army moved up the field to face their new enemy and stood in columns, arranged in squares of 50 guards wide by 50 guards deep. The columns continued south as far as the eye could see. There were 10,000 soldiers ready for battle and that included 1,000 of the rag-tag army who, having seen the giants cowardly slunk their way back through the metal guards to take up a position at the southern end of the field.

"Is someone going to start this battle?" questioned the king. "Or are we just going to stand around looking at each other all day?" Gom had just finished his sentence when a trail of high speed, blue light soared over the tree line from the direction of Kidder Doon.

The streak of light travelled through the sky to the southern end of the plains where it plummeted down amongst the rag-tag guards. Several very large explosions immediately erupted in flashes of blinding blue light and the peasant army scattered in all directions away from the savage heat of the resultant fires. Eitak looked back towards the treeline as several more blue streaks made their way across the battlefield where they exploded amongst the human contingent of the Golden Army. Chaos ensued and half the rag-tag, soldiers lost all cohesion as their ranks fell apart, whatever enthusiasm, they once had all but left them and they threw down their weapons and ran from the battlefield.

Only the most evil and determined of the rag-tag guards and the metal army remained.

Within the mountains of Kidder Doon Malarog had discovered a relic from the past, a huge crystal powered catapult and together with the women from the village, he had busied himself by loading the mechanism and launching Orillion crystals to the southern end of the plains. "Well," said Malarog, "I reckon that's got the party started."

At the northern end of the field, the golden soldiers raised their swords, axes and pole arms and marched on their enemy.

"Now this is more like it," said Gom and he ran down the battlefield towards the advancing army. The other giants let out a roaring battle cry and thundered after their king.

Gom smashed his hammer into the first rank of soldiers who flew into the air like skittles and disintegrated under the immense force. Small explosions like fireworks erupted in the air as their Orillion crystals burst and showered the ground with burning junk. Arwie sat astride her Rhinamoth and organised the giant archers as they drew back their huge arrows that were twice the size of a man. Volley after volley of Orillion tipped arrows slammed into the army decimating their eastern flank and opening up a passage to the southern end of the field.

Tum blew his horn and the Hasty Hagraals disappeared, within the time it took to blink Hunter, Sprinter, Dasher and Whoosher reappeared right in the thick of the rag-tag guards. Having seen the danger, The Golden Army to the south turned and moved swiftly towards the giant hunting dogs. The ferocity of the Hagraals made quick work of the human guards and those that could, fled from the battle as broken men. The Golden Army closed in and threatened to overrun the Hagraals but the red gems of their collars began to glow and one by one, the metal soldiers fell lifeless at their feet. Once the last of the peasant guards had been neutralised, Tum blew his horn and the Hagraals returned to his side, unharmed.

Whilst Gom and several of the giants seemed to be having a fantastic time smashing and pummelling the metal machines through their centre lines, Kram and the other members of his village held a position deep in the heart of the western flank where they swung their double handed war hammers in a huge arc, destroying anything that got in the way.

Thaddeus and the other men from the villages threw down their feeble weapons and collected up great armfuls of the red crystal gems from Klum's wagon. As they entered the battle, most of the golden soldiers now lay on the ground smashed or damaged in some way or another but Thaddeus and his men threw their stones into the face guards of those that showed the remotest signs of life, rendering them immediately and permanently inert.

The Golden Army that remained fired arrow after arrow at the giants and Rhinamoths and all to no avail, they thrust their swords, pikes and spears but despite their relentless enthusiasm, their weapons were no match for the giants' armour plate. The giants had called their armour lightweight and it probably was to them but to any of the other races of Kennet, it was made from the thickest metal they had ever seen.

Eitak turned to Bones and shouted, "It's now or never." And patted his armoured Rhinamoth as it carried him into the enemy's weakened eastern flank. The great beast swung its head from side to side, tossing the metal men high into the air whilst Eitak threw a combination of blue and red crystals amongst them from a large wicker basket tied to the Rhinamoth's nape. Miniature suns of blue light flashed as the power gems exploded and then faded away as the red stones drained what power was left. Bones followed behind with Bonsai and Jangles, who stood on top of their basket, and hurled their gems with extraordinary accuracy, always managing to hit the power gem within the faceguard of each soldier they aimed at. Everything was going exceptionally well...

Eitak's Rhinamoth charged forward, cutting a swathe through the army's ranks to the southern end of the field but then a terrible thing happened, one of the rag-tag guards who had been left for dead lay on the ground directly in front of Eitak, the huge Rhinamoth did not consider him to be any threat and ignored him as its ponderous feet landed on the ground either side. The man picked up his spear and thrust it upwards beneath the beast's underbelly and struck one of the thick leather straps holding its armour in place. The Rhinamoth didn't feel a thing or even notice and it carried on to the end of the enemy lines. Bones followed and again his huge ride ran over the top of the now stationary rag-tag guard. As it thundered above him, the guard thrust his spear once more. Bones' Rhinamoth immediately locked its front legs in front of it and slid to a stop. Although not fatal, the creature was taken off guard and was surprised at the sudden feeling of pain from the right side of its belly and reared up. Bonsai and Jangles clung to their basket and held on tight as they desperately tried to keep the remaining crystals in the basket. Bones lost his grip and tumbled head over heels backwards as he fell to the ground. The Rhinamoth realising that it was not going to die brought its front legs back down onto firm ground and thundered at twice its original pace headlong into the remaining ranks of the southern contingent of the metal soldiers. It was furious and trampled everything underfoot and using its enormous horn and tusks it butted and speared at everything, tearing the very metal of the soldier's bodies apart and leaving a trail of debris and destruction in its wake.

Bones lay on his back and wiggled his toes and fingers and once he realised that nothing was broken, he afforded himself a smile and opened his eyes. Standing above him with his spear raised in his hand was the rag-tag guard.

Tum sounded his horn.

Klum had seen the incident too and ran across the field with several of the other giants. The rag-tag man brought down his spear and it pierced through Bones' metal armour plate and bit into his flesh underneath. The armour slowed the spear down but it was much thinner than the giants had wanted but unfortunately, it was all that humans were capable of carrying. Bones' mind wandered in his delusional state, he saw a river and his own reflection looking back up at him. He was no work of art and who was he to have judged the looks of Luj and Noj, they were two of the kindest people he had ever known, the images in his mind swirled and he saw Luj and Noj looking at him, waving for him to go to them, they were the only two women ever to have taken any interest in him at all and now he knew, albeit too late that he loved them as much as they did him. "I love you," he mumbled and then the world went dark.

Hunter was the first to arrive and as he appeared, so the rag-tag guard disappeared in two separate pieces.

Bones closed his eyes just as Klum arrived and on seeing his friend's motionless body, the giant went berserk. Tirelessly and without end, he brought his hammer down upon his creations, smashing and mashing every trace of the metal army. He was now without control and had lost all awareness of everything. Single-mindedly, he pummelled the enemy mercilessly until nothing of the eastern flank remained. Retreat or surrender was not a word that the army understood and for every soldier that fell, another replaced it and for every replacement, a hammer blow awaited.

Eitak had now made his way back through the enemy's decimated southern lines and slid down the right flank of his Rhinamoth and held Bones in his arms. The spear had snapped off at the handle and the tip remained firmly embedded under the armour, blood seeped from under the breastplate and Bones remained unmoving. Tum arrived with the Hagraal pack who fanned out to face what little of the enemy remained. Drooling and salivating, every so often, one of the huge hunting dogs would disappear and then re appear having just rushed out to meet and neutralise any of the metal guards stupid enough to approach.

"I will take him back to Kidder Doon," Tum suggested. "Only there will he stand any chance of life."

Eitak agreed and Tum gently scooped Bones motionless body off the ground and marched towards the woods, holding him in his huge hands. As he got to the tree line, Tum blew his horn and The Hasty Hagraals vanished from the battlefield only to reappear moments later next to him. Eitak waved as the fate of his friend now lay in the hands of the Giants.

By evening the battle was silent. Every last one of the golden soldiers had been smashed to pieces and now lay across the great field in tatters. The long grass had been replaced by craters and dunes caused by the exploding crystals. Nuts, bolts, washers, cogs, wheels and pieces of unidentifiable metal lay strewn across the landscape. The giants looked exhausted; Klum held his shoulders hunched low as he dragged his massive hammer behind him and joined the rest of the group at the northern end of the field.

"How many did we lose?" Eitak asked Gom and Thaddeus.

Gom removed his helmet and gauntlets and wiped his great brow with his hand, he looked at Eitak and shook his head. "Battle always begins with expectations of a great glory but inevitably ends with suffering and misery; our coin of luck has two sides this day, the glory of our victory and the misery of our defeat. We have all lost a dear friend in Bones. The happiness he brought my daughters in the short time that I knew him will remain with me for an eternity. I have no other casualties this day but I will grieve for the one we have for a very long time to come."

Eitak turned to Thaddeus who added, "I have eight injured, none serious, Gom is right in everything he says but it seems to me that if you are evil, power hungry and overcome with greed and envy then you go looking for war, but if you are good and just try to live your life peacefully, then war will come to you, there is no escaping it, this day was always going to come."

"So what do we do now?" Eitak asked as he looked at the destruction before him.

Sirod spoke next, he had listened to everything that had been said and saw that this was a turning point for the planet. "I say we finish what has been started and cleanse Kennet once and for all, we could encourage all the races of Kennet to unite, Giants, Wirrall, Nagraal and even the Dust Dwellers. I am sure there are those amongst them who would like to be included in a unified new world."

Everyone agreed Arwie of the Wirral, Gom King of the Giants and Thaddeus, representative of the humans, all shook hands with Sirod the Nagraal and so by the end of that day, a new one was ready to dawn.

The unified races of Kennet stayed on the plains that night, they lit a huge fire and shared some of the combined foods they had brought with them. However, there was an overriding air of despair at the loss of Bones. Whenever a blue glow was sighted on the field, someone would rush forward and extinguish it using the neutralising power of the red power gems and by morning there was not one trace of blue light anywhere.

Gom picked up his helmet and addressed the group: "I must return to Kidder Doon, I will take with me ten of my kind. Of the other 30, 20 will go on to Illya with Thaddeus and his men, to free the city and remove the last traces of slavery from our planet. The remaining ten will guide Eitak, Sirod and Arwie to the edge of the Marshlands where they must face Usurpus alone."

Bonsai and Jangles just jumped up and down screeching.

Gom looked at the two monkeys and added, "I suggest Bonsai and Jumbles tag along with Eitak." Jangles looked at Gom lowered his brow and scowled. Bonsai thought the king's mistake was hilarious and with a look between them, the two monkeys grinned widely.

Deep in the heart of Kidder Doon, Bones briefly opened his fevered, watering eyes to find that he was lying on a huge bed and sitting at the end were two of the most beautiful women he had ever seen. He struggled to look but the fever grasped him once more and he slid back into the dark world of unconsciousness.

After a brief farewell, Eitak, Arwie and Sirod climbed onto their Rhinamoths and rode alongside Klum and his men, as they headed off across the plains to face Usurpus.

13. Usurpus

Usurpus Sly looked into his jet-black eyes in the mirror. Everything he and his sister had ever wanted had been provided for them by their mother but since her untimely death, he had become consumed by anger and envy. On her death bed, his mother had told him of how his family had come to be banished to the marshlands, she spoke of Kalag and how those loyal to him had built castle Sly out of the mists. How many of them had walked unwittingly into the marshes where they sank to their deaths and how it took them an age to realise that it was the Wisp Warblers who had corrupted their souls. In time and after many lives were lost, Castle Sly stood as an imposing fortress in the east and today as with every other day of his life, the windows remained sealed against the Wisps who threatened to invade at any opportunity. The only way to the castle was through the mists and only those wearing special masks survived the journey. His mother blamed a man named Sirod Spa for his family's banishment. She told him how his great, great grandfather, Kalag, had been cheated out a life of riches and with it his birth right, a chance to rule Illya or even all of Kennet. She told him how Kalag had only really loved one woman and how she had betrayed his love and how this Sirod had caused her death. Usurpus was always his mother's favourite and when she lay dying, he vowed to avenge his family's shame and punish the world for their lack of compassion and understanding. Since then his sister, Syagonus, moved to the icy wastelands of Sivestol where she announced herself as queen of all that is white.

Usurpus looked at his reflection and thanked his mother for his exceptional good looks; now aged 29, he was in his athletic prime, tall and slim with a good head of black hair which was parted to one side he was very handsome, the only mar on his otherwise perfect face were his soulless and colourless deep black eyes. Being of Magistanian descent, he was born with a special ability as with all Magistans, that ability changed from generation to generation and no two Magistans were the same. Usurpus had the gift of insight, a rare gift amongst his kind and one that had not been seen for hundreds of years. He need only touch the face of any person or creature to know of their entire existence, everything they had seen or done, everyone they knew or had known, their wishes, their dreams, their thoughts of the past and plans for the future were his to know, a rape of the mind, a rare gift indeed and one which was very useful, especially for someone planning on taking over the planet.

It was Usurpus who had thought up the plan to capture the giant, his Golden Army now stood on the Plains of Ishtar, ready to take back all he was owed. Once more his family would be able to walk tall amongst the peoples of Kennet who he would force to bow and grovel at his feet. His plans were going all too well until some Dust Dwellers came to Castle Sly and told him how the giant had been freed by three men, two women and a monkey.

Today he awoke with the news that one of the women responsible had been captured and now languished in the castle dungeons. Usurpus threw on his finest green velvet cloak and looked at himself once more in the mirror before he rushed out of his dressing room and made his way to the cells with his cloak flowing behind him as he went.

The dingy corridors of Castle Sly were lined with thick stone walls which were lit periodically with oil burners. Usurpus made his way through these corridors to one of the castles two towers and from there, he walked down the stone steps to the dungeons below ground.

Two very fat, bald gaolers, who looked like twins and who were dressed in filthy, food, blood and sweat stained vests, which at some stage in their creation had been white, stood guard to three large, damp and dark cells.

"She's in 'ere, me lord," said one of the rough and blunt speaking men as he pointed to the cell behind him. "She ain't said much tho' and I don't think you'll be able to persuade her otherwise either."

"We shall soon see about that, now bring her to me," demanded Usurpus confidently.

The two gaolers entered the cell and seized the wretched figure who was cowering in the corner of the room. As she was dragged forwards out of the cell, Ember lifted her head and could see a handsome man wearing a green cape standing in front of her.

"Leave her," Usurpus commanded and the two guards dropped Ember to the floor where she stayed on her knees with her head bowed low. Usurpus looked down upon the woman hunched before him, her burnt orange hair fell either side of her face which made it impossible to see any of her features. "Look at me," Usurpus demanded. Exhausted and deprived of food and water, Ember remained motionless on the floor with her head resting upon her knees.

"Guards bring her to her feet," Usurpus shouted having lost what very little patience he had.

Each of the sweaty and disgusting guards placed an arm under Ember's shoulders and once she was lifted to her feet, they each used their free hand to pull her hair back lifting her face towards their master. Ember looked drained, bedraggled and exhausted and only managed to open one eye, just a crack in order to see.

"It really needn't be like this, you know, just tell me who the others are and it will all be over," Usurpus said in a calm soft and reassuring voice.

"I will tell you nothing," Ember snapped.

"Hold her head tight," Usurpus replied venomously and the gaolers held Ember's hair tightly back reducing any movement of her head. Usurpus held out his right hand and touched his fingers by the side of her left temple. Within a moment, Ember's entire life flashed before her eyes, The Plains of Ishtar, the Rhinamoth, the Thunder pass, the Great Wall, the Crystal Desert, Klum, Bagdoon, the Forests of Rampor, Mia, Nagraal, Ember Firestorm, Kalag…Sirod Spa.

Usurpus pulled his hand away quickly. "So, Ember Firestorm…the love of my great, great grandfather's life…my day has just improved so much more than you could ever have imagined," he announced in a slow, evil and fiendish manner.

For Eitak, Arwie and Sirod, the journey to the Marshlands had been somewhat uneventful due primarily to their heavily armoured Giant escort; but now, just two days later, they stood on the edge of the low-lying wetlands. Ahead of them the firm ground gave way to a floating bog land path with a low-lying lake either side which spread into the distance as far at the eye could see.

Klum looked at the path and spoke, "I dare not go any further, the ground can no longer support my weight."

Eitak jumped down from his Rhinamoth and placed one foot onto the floating bog, the matted, grassy ground rippled like standing on a cluster of loosely tied logs on a river. "Will it even take mine is the next question?" he replied, concerned that he would fall right through the mat of grass and sink into the waters below.

"I should remove your armour just in case," Klum replied.

Eitak, Arwie and Sirod removed their armour as Klum had suggested and Eitak looked through the provisions they had brought with them, until he came across the black velvet jacket, he had found in the wagon on the road to Bagdoon. After a brief farewell, the three companions together with Bonsai and Jangles stepped out onto the floating carpet. They very soon discovered that walking together caused the ground not only to ripple but twist from side to side due to the uneven dispersal of weight between two people walking alongside one another and that the only way that this was ever going to work was for them to walk in single file and several steps apart. Eitak went first, followed by Sirod and then Arwie and for every step that they took, the ground rippled like the waves on the sea. Bonsai and Jangles brought up the rear and holding hands, they grinned at each other as they jumped the rippled ground as it came towards them.

After a long and arduous walk, the ground began to rise and became a little firmer. Although there was no longer a danger of sinking beneath the grasses, eerie looking marsh mists began to twist up out of the lake on either side.

"I don't like the look of that much," Arwie commented as she viewed the mists with some trepidation and concern. "There's something about mist that gives me the creeps."

"And sometimes with good reason..." Sirod replied with caution in his voice. "...For those are not normal marsh mists, oh, no, not normal marsh mists at all...they are whisp warblers."

"Whisp warblers!" Arwie exclaimed with panic setting into her voice. "Like the ones in Illya? I saw what they did to the slave master and I don't want to end up like him."

The whisp warblers had now grown considerably in number and intensity and swirled around like dancing snakes in front of those who had intruded into their watery land.

"It's far too late to worry now, just clear your mind of all evil thoughts and it should be OK," Sirod said as a line of mist entered through his nose.

Arwie began to panic and tried to bat the mists aside with her hands but every time she struck out at one of the columns of vapour, it simply reformed itself. The mist came closer and closer, Arwie tried holding her breath but even her athletic lungs were not capable of lasting without oxygen for ever and as she gasped for breath, so a Wisp Warbler entered her body.

Eitak too had succumbed to the mists and now all three of the companions stood motionless as their eyes glazed over.

The only ones totally unaffected by the Warblers were Bonsai and Jangles, who playfully danced around, trying to grab at the mists as they passed right over them without entering their bodies at all.

After a moment, a cold feeling came over Eitak and a voice began to whisper in his mind. "We know you, Eitak Ladoog." it said. "We can hear your thoughts and we know your mind, we can see what you have done and what you intend, your spirit is pure and is not corrupted, you are welcome to pass through our realm. Farewell." Slowly the mists left through Eitak's nose and gradually his mind became his own once more.

The same cold feeling came to Arwie as the whisp warblers invaded her thoughts. "We know you, Arwie Willowbreeze of the Wirral. We can see what you have done and what you intend, your spirit too is uncorrupted and you are welcome to pass through our realm."

Sirod's eyes remained clouded as a second whisp warbler entered his mind. "We know you Sirod Spa. There is guilt in your soul for events long ago. Ember Firestorm, you feel that it is you who once caused her death. But no, she did not die…she is here in the Castle beyond…and you want to set her free. Ahead of you lies a great evil, Usurpus invaded our land long ago and pollutes our waters with the bodies of those he has slain, you must be careful or it is you who will require rescue or worse…you will join us in the lake as with your friends, you too are free to pass through our realm…farewell."

"I could feel them," Arwie shouted excitedly as Sirod came too. "They are not evil at all, they hate evil and that is clearly why the slave master had such a problem with them."

Bonsai and Jangles jumped trying to grab the last of the whisps as they left the path and went to settle over the lake.

Once they had regained their senses, the group of travellers continued on their way until, eventually, the path turned to cobbled stone and there ahead of them built on an island in the middle of the marsh lake and rising out of the mist was Castle Sly. The cobbled path led up to a fortified gatehouse and portcullis, leading off from this and circling around the castle was a high wall which was interspaced by several large stone turrets. Within the outer wall, the main castle comprised of a large stone apex roofed house, built on huge boulders which rose out of the lake. The building had several large windows which faced towards the gate and on either side of the main house, connected to it were two huge towers which rose high into the sky.

Eitak, Arwie, Sirod, Bonsai and Jangles approached the gate.

"And just how are we going to get in there?" Arwie asked with a feeling of defeat as she looked up at the imposing castle wall.

As Sirod and Eitak contemplated their next move, a rough and ready voice shouted from behind the portcullis, "Oi, you, stay where you are."

Sirod peered between the iron latticework of the large drop gate and saw one of the rag-tag guards approaching. The guard was wearing the same light leather armour as all the other guards that he had encountered except that this one had a scarf tied up over his nose. The guard put his pike to one side and fiddled with the gate mechanism until creaking and groaning the windlass turned and the portcullis was raised.

"Quick, run!" Arwie shouted to everyone. Upon her suggestion and seizing any opportunity for adventure, Bonsai and Jangles scrambled up the castle wall until they sat on the top and looked down on the events unfolding below.

"Wait," Sirod replied and everyone stood still. That is apart from the two monkeys who looked at each other, raised their upturned paws and grinned. "…This could be our only chance of getting in," he continued. "…Let's just go along with it for now and see if the guards take us to Ember."

The rag-tag guard was now joined by three of his masked rag-tag friends. "This way," he demanded and set off across the inner courtyard towards a thick wooden door which led into one of the large towers. The other guards lightly jabbed their pikes into the companion's backs and forced them to follow. Once through the tower door, an empty suit of armour greeted them before the three prisoners were forced to walk down the stone steps to the dungeons below.

Once in the dungeon corridor, the rag-tag guards handed their prisoners over to the gaolers who had the worst body odour that Eitak had ever smelt. "Elp us search 'em," one of the gaolers said to the rag-tag guards. Each of the men looked at Arwie.

"I'll do 'er," one announced.

"You can keep yer mits off, that's dessert, that is and I read somewhere that it's a gaoler's privilege," one of the gaolers replied.

Arwie's eyes widened. "I told you we should have run," she said sweating and trembling with fear from what was about to take place.

"Stick her over there, she don't look like she's got much on er but it'll be fun checkin," the second gaoler suggested, agreeing with his learned friend.

Eitak and Sirod removed their clothes down to their under garments and stood bare chested in the cold damp corridor as the gaolers went through the clothing they had removed. It wasn't long before one of the gaolers found the small glass bottle which contained the glowing green liquid that Malarog had given Sirod back in Illya, his fat fingers fumbled with the stopper which eventually came away in his hand. He put the potion up to his nose and sniffed. Immediately, he screwed up his face and turned sharply away from the pungent odour that was emitted from the bottle.

"Is it any good?" asked the gaoler's twin looking brother.

"Nah, probably kill ya if ya drunk it." And the first man replaced the stopper and put the bottle down on a heavy wooden table.

At that moment, a clattering sound came from higher up the tower.

"You better go an' check on that," one of the gaolers suggested to the rag-tag guards and after looking towards Arwie and sighing, the three guards headed off up the stairs.

The gaolers then patted down Eitak's jacket and there in the lining they found something that Eitak had long forgotten, the lapis handled dagger he had found on the road to Bagdoon.

Having torn the knife from the lining, one of the gaolers held it up to the dim light and turned it in his hand. "Nice," said the gaoler approvingly as he looked towards Eitak. The surprised expression on Eitak's face must have said it all as the gaoler continued, "Oh, forgotten it had ya, well, the young master'll like this."

The two gaolers then turned to Arwie, they were both identical in their appearance with their double chins, black teeth and crooked smiles. "Ear…right pretty you are," one of them said, salivating and drooling saliva from the corner of his mouth as he addressed her. The two men were just about to grab for their 'dessert' when there was an almighty crash and clatter from the ground floor as the sound of metal falling down stone steps, reverberated around the dungeon corridor. Startled the guards looked towards the stairs as the full faced helmet of the suit of armour from the ground floor rolled over to their feet.

On the ground floor, Bonsai and Jangles stood at the top of the steps and slapped their hands together. They were most pleased with the satisfying noise they had managed to create and once they had watched all of the armour

144

disappear down to the dungeon corridor, they scurried off into the shadows ready for the next opportunity for creating any mischief that might arise.

"Quick, stick em in a cell," one of the gaolers instructed the other.

"What 'bout our treat?" the other complained.

"I lost me appetite; now help me stick 'em in there."

And the two gaolers pushed Eitak, Arwie and Sirod into a cell and threw their clothes in after them. Once the door was closed, they stomped off up the stairs to investigate the cause of the problem.

The cell was fairly large with natural stone walls all around which constantly dripped water. Slimy green algae grew where the water flowed down to a drainage gulley which ran around the edge. Although dimly lit some light filtered into the room from the corridor torches and this allowed the companions to see around their cell and partly into the cell next door which was divided from theirs by a metal grate. Hunched in the corner of the next cell, Sirod could make out a figure. "Ember," he shouted. "Ember, it's me, Sirod." Slowly the figure unfolded itself from the ground and rose to its feet and then still slightly bent over, Ember shuffled to the dividing grate.

"Ember…what have they done to you?" Sirod asked at first, only being able to recognise her from her burnt orange coloured hair. As she drew closer, he thrust his arms through the grate and held her hands tightly in his. "Are you all right, my love? I can't believe what they must have put you through."

"What are you doing here?" Ember replied with tears in her eyes, concerned that her rescuers had been captured. "Usurpus is here…" she continued with panic now setting into her voice. "He is somewhere in this castle and he knows everything, he knows who I am, he knows about you and Eitak and everyone, I didn't tell him he just touched me and then…he knew." Ember began to sob, tears streamed down her face as relief seeped into her soul, she was no longer alone and that felt good.

After a while of just touching Sirod, Ember began to feel better and for the first time in two days, she managed to stand tall and as night fell, even the beginnings of a smile spread over her face.

Usurpus sat in the Great Hall. Spread out in front of him atop an extremely long table was a vast spread of fine food. Roast meats lay on platters surrounded by apples and grapes. The steam from tureens of soup and vegetables rose aromatically into the air. Blancmanges and jellies wobbled on plates and uncorked bottles of wine sat breathing, waiting to be poured and savoured by the guest lucky enough to have been invited to this magnificent feast. But as usual, the only guest was Usurpus and he sat in his arm chair at the head of the table picking grapes from around a roasted pig's head.

Knock, knock, knock…the sound came from the long room's double doors which faced Usurpus' chair. Usurpus hated intrusions at the best of times but to disturb him during dinner was the worst. This inconvenient interruption had better be good news or something so totally important that it couldn't wait or there were likely to be serious repercussions for the person doing the knocking.

Knock, knock, knock. "What is it?" Usurpus shouted demanding to know who had the audacity to knock with three knocks on two separate occasions. The door opened and in walked one of the rag-tag guards from the courtyard and standing behind him with his head bowed and metal helmet in his hand was another peasant guard; only this one had just come from the Plains of Ishtar.

"Well…" demanded Usurpus, "…this had better be worth it."

The peasant soldier stepped forward. "Can I 'ave a drink me, lud?" he asked graciously.

"No. Now what is it?" Usurpus replied impatiently.

"Well, it's like this really, you know your Golden Army, well, it ain't quite so big as it was, is the thing."

"What!" Usurpus yelled. "Not quite so big, what do you mean by that…Well?" Usurpus continued almost beside himself with anticipation and a brewing rage.

"Well, there were these giants…an' lots of 'ammers and flashes of light…oh, and some dogs, big 'uns…and now you ain't got no army, no army at all, really." The guard fiddled with his helmet which he held in his hands and with his head still bowed low, he raised his eyes and looked up at Usurpus who was now on the verge of erupting.

"…An' what's more; funny thing is, there's this stone statue of a giant at the end of the marshes. 'Ad to walk round it, I did," the rag-tag guard continued.

"Get out, get out, get out," Usurpus screamed and he threw platters and plates around the room, smashing crockery and flinging food against the walls and floor.

The two rag-tag guards beat a hasty retreat and left the room.

Usurpus looked through the closed dining room window and saw the full moon rising into the sky and screamed uncontrollably.

The following morning, the two gaolers returned with a bucket of white slop and cold stale tea. They were both dressed in exactly the same stained vest tops they had worn the previous day. One of the men stirred the slops with a ladle and then raising a spoonful to his mouth, he extended his yellow crusty tongue and licked the contents. "Licious," he announced as he replaced the saliva coated spoon back into the bucket. "You better get it while you got a chance, the master wants to see you soon." And with that, he opened the cell door and kicked the bucket into the room. As he passed by Ember's cell, he gave a wry smile and announced, "There ain't nuffin for you again, so you best get used to it." The two gaolers laughed and walked back up the stairs to the ground floor.

"If I get the chance, I swear I will…" Sirod began furiously with his teeth clenched.

"It's OK, my love," Ember interrupted, "I don't need anything, not now that you are here."

There was no way that any of the companions were going to eat any of the disgusting gruel and Eitak kicked the bucket over into the channel at the back of the room.

Before long the gaolers returned and on seeing the empty bucket, one said, "That's it, good for you that is, spat in it good and proper I did." Eitak almost retched as he looked at the white glutinous mass, festering in the gulley. The two fat men then went over to Ember's cell, opened the door and dragged her out. "You got a date with the master, again you have, must like you I reckon." And as Ember struggled against the gaolers, Sirod began to shout from his cell.

"I'll kill you, I swear I will kill you if you touch just one hair on her head, I promise you'll pay."

"What, like this you mean." And one of the men pulled a clump of hair from Ember's head. Ember screamed out in pain and Sirod shook the rusty bars of his cell with all his strength until his hands began to bleed.

Usurpus paced up and down the vast expanse of the Great Hall. He listened to his footfalls as they echoed around the high lofted ceiling and contemplated what he should do with Ember Firestorm. Not only had she broken his great, great, grandfather's heart and been the cause of his family's banishment to the east and helped to free his metal working giant, now he discovered that she may well have had some involvement in the destruction of his entire Golden Army and with that went his only chance of rising out of the cursed marshes and the conquest of all Kennet. Death would be too easy; he needed to think of a lasting punishment, something that would torture her mind for the rest of her days.

Knock, Knock, Knock, Usurpus hated people knocking, in fact, he hated most people full stop but people knocking usually resulted in bad news. "What is it?" he shouted.

"We've brought the prisoner, sire," one of the gaolers announced and he thrust Ember forward into the room.

"Ah, yes, of course…now leave us," Usurpus replied as he viewed Ember with a certain look of disgust. "Ember Firestorm," he continued, speaking slowly with venom in his voice. "I should kill you where you stand for all the trouble you have caused me. In fact, I may do that yet." Usurpus approached Ember and casually flicked her orange hair with the tip of his finger. "You disgust me, I don't know what my family ever saw in you…mind you, you have probably changed a bit since then, being a Nagraal and all…so tell me this, what is it like to be immortal."

Usurpus had not researched Ember's mind enough to know that she was no longer a Nagraal, having taken the elixir which had fused her soul to Mia's body. He walked around her with his nose in the air, trying to intimidate but she was stronger now, Sirod was downstairs and she knew that Usurpus could never take her love for him away, no matter how much he tortured or tormented her. As he walked around, Usurpus studied Ember looking for any weakness that he could exploit and the more he looked, the more he realised that she was in fact quite pretty. In fact, she was very pretty indeed, he reached out and touched her face and as he did so, his mind was bombarded by a rush of thoughts and feelings, emotions and experiences as Ember's life invaded his consciousness. Eitak…Arwie…Sirod…the cells. Usurpus pulled his hand away from Ember.

"So, Sirod is still alive…and is here," he hissed almost drunk with emotion. "Guards!"

No sooner had Usurpus completed the word when two of the rag-tag guards entered the room.

"Why was I not informed when the new prisoners arrived," Usurpus bellowed.

The two guards bowed their heads. "Well, it's like this…" one of them began.

"I'm not interested in your excuses, just bring them to me now," Usurpus hissed furiously both at the guards and for the fact that Sirod had the gall to show his face in Castle Sly.

The guards left the room and before long, the Gaolers brought Eitak, Arwie and Sirod to the Great Hall.

Knock, Knock, Knock…

"ENTER!" shouted Usurpus, incandescent with rage. "Must you always knock like that, I hate knocking," he shouted venomously.

The two gaolers pushed the three companions into the room and placed the bottle of glowing green liquid and the Lapis handled knife on the long table and then retired to stand by the door. But in the time that it took them to turn around, two small creatures slipped in and hid amongst the shadows.

Usurpus was so utterly consumed by his anger and rage that he visibly began to display signs of his extreme stress and a condition that had long since been kept under control surfaced from deep within and manifested itself in repeated and unconscious head and neck movements. Usurpus stuck out his lower chin and lengthened his neck and then in a circular motion, he rolled his head around in an arc from left to right. He slowly became aware of his actions and picked up a small silver handled mirror which was lying on the long table amongst the leftover food from the night before. He looked at his image in the mirror. Mother had always told him not to become over stressed but it was that stress which had spurned him on and allowed him to scheme and plot his rise to power, yet now on the very eve of the greatest day of his life, his army lay in tatters on the Plains of Ishtar and in front of him stood the single person who was responsible for ruining his plans.

Usurpus walked around the table and looked out of the window, the cursed mists had returned once more and began to swirl at the windows looking for a way in. "Damn you, Sirod Spa." Usurpus' voice broke to a venom enriched grumbling mumble and he threw the mirror across the room. The mirror passed between Sirod and Eitak and hit the wooden door between the two guards, where it smashed into pieces. "I was wrong," he continued, looking at Sirod as he rolled his head once more. "I thought it was Ember who had ruined my life but no, it's not, it's you. If it wasn't for you then Ember wouldn't have strayed from my great, great, grandfather, and I'm just willing to bet that it was you who freed my giant and broke my beautiful golden soldiers. Sure, she probably played her part but it is so obvious to me now and I've got just the punishment, a punishment fitting for you both, I'm just so glad that you managed to stay alive all this time Nagraal, so that now I can kill you myself, permanently." Usurpus stretched his neck again and rolled his head around in a circle before he walked over to the long table and looked at the items that the gaolers had placed there.

The shadows began to move as Bonsai and Jangles sneaked around the edge of the room. Together they grabbed hold of one of the long curtains, which had been gathered at the side of one of the large windows and quietly they climbed up past the low window sill and still hanging onto the curtains they peered out from behind the drapes.

"So, what do we have here? A magic potion," Usurpus continued talking to himself more than anyone else. "Gaolers…" he bellowed, changing the tone of his voice from quiet and soft to overly aggressive and shouting. "…Tell me who had the potion?"

The two gaolers looked between each other. "Erm, that'll be 'im." One replied pointing at Sirod.

"So, Nagraal," Usurpus added in a condescending manner as he waved the bottle under Sirod's nose. "…You thought that you would keep this from me, did you? Didn't think that I would know what this bottle contains. Well, that's where you are wrong. I know more about the old potions than you realise, my mother told me stories about you Sirod Spa. She told me that a potion was given to you by Kalag's father, Niastar and that it was he who made you a Nagraal. I had no reason to believe that you would still be alive and oh, what a bonus it was to me when I found you…both. How old must you be now, what is it 200 years or more, immortality shall be mine. You both seem to be doing very nicely on it, sure you have to find the odd body now and then but that is not a problem for me for I have an endless supply of bodies, just waiting for their owners to step aside as it were." Usurpus waved the potion between Sirod and Ember and looked over to the guards who both swallowed heavily. "You were going to keep this all to yourself," Usurpus continued as he held the small bottle of glowing green liquid up to the light. "Well, my mother told me always to share." And with that, he removed the stopper and sniffed the contents. The foul smell of the liquid was so strong that Usurpus recoiled and gagged but not to be put off he lifted the bottle to his lips.

"No," Sirod shouted, knowing that the potion was the only chance he might ever have of leading a normal life with Ember.

"I know you, Sirod Spa, you are selfish and always want everything just for yourself. Well, you are not going to ruin this." And Usurpus threw the liquid from the bottle to the back of his throat and swallowed.

Bonsai and Jangles looked out of the window and could see the marsh mists gathering outside, what fun they'd had playing with them earlier they thought...

A moment passed during which Usurpus stretched his neck nervously forwards and then realising that he felt no different than before, he said, "See, now I am as immortal as the rest of you except we shall see how that works out if you have no body to pass on to." Usurpus threw the small bottle to the floor and reached for Eitak's lapis handled knife. "So, this I presume is yours," he said waving the knife under Eitak's nose. He then looked at the item carefully and scrutinised the craftsmanship. "This is quite beautiful," he announced, "but I feel it would look better in red. Now who should I kill...you..." and he pointed to Ember, "or you?" and he pointed the blade at Sirod.

Bonsai reached across with one hand and pulled on the window catch which was very stiff, having not been opened since it was first put in. He looked at Jangles and bared his teeth in a broad grin. Jangles seemed to understand and swung across from his curtain and helped to heave on the small lever.

Eitak, Arwie, Ember and Sirod looked between each other and then around the room. Behind them stood the gaolers, who although overweight, looked very powerful and were quite capable of handling themselves if needed and in front of them stood a despotic mad man who was totally consumed by his own greed and power and he held a very sharp knife. Eitak's eyes wandered over to the long window and he saw Bonsai and Jangles pulling at the catch.

"I have decided," Usurpus announced as he quickly drew back his arm. Sirod saw the blade, he knew he had less than a second to react, the blade was thrust forward towards Ember's chest and Sirod threw himself between the blade and the woman he had always loved. The blade bit deep and sank into Sirod's chest.

The window opened, just a crack and in rushed the whisp warblers twisting, spiralling and swirling around the room, curling like snakes in the air, they found Usurpus who still had a hold of the knife.

Bonsai and Jangles swiped at the mists as they entered in through the window but like before, they simply disintegrated and reformed around their small hands.

"No," Usurpus shouted, cheated out of his moment of revenge. "I wanted you to suffer and see what it must be like to have someone you love taken from you."

The mists coiled back, ready for the attack and then they struck. The whisps rushed into Usurpus' mouth and nose and were gone. As he threw his head backwards and stood totally motionless and transfixed, more of the mists rushed in through the window and found their way over to the gaolers. One of the men realised what was coming and rushed from the room slamming the door firmly shut behind him. The other was less fortunate and frantically tried to bat the whisps away but it was useless and within a moment the whisps had invaded his body and taken over his evil mind.

Sirod slumped to the floor with the knife still embedded deep in his chest. Blood began to seep around the blade which made a dark damp patch on his red shirt.

Usurpus slowly began to walk across the room whilst Eitak, Arwie and Ember knelt beside their dying friend. Usurpus was now totally under the control of the whisps and was unable to resist their will. In his trance-like state, he made his way over to the long window where Bonsai and Jangles were still fiddling with the locks and catches. As Usurpus' knees collided with the low sill, the windows flew open and unable to save himself, he tumbled head-first to the courtyard below.

Ember lifted Sirod's head and held him in her lap and stroked his cheeks gently. "My love…" she said with tears in her eyes, "it was never meant to end like this." As she listened to the last gurgling gasps of his breath, Ember's mind drifted, was there anything she could do to save him? Sure Sirod was a Nagraal but even they could die. Niastar had told her a long time ago that once a Nagraal has taken over a body, they become as mortal as anyone else…unless…they can find another host. Ember looked over towards the helpless and motionless guard, could she bring herself to take a defenceless life to save that of another? She carried on scanning the room, there was something missing, now what was it? She wondered and then it came to her, where was Usurpus? No one had seen him fall as they had all been concentrating on Sirod. As her gaze met the window, she saw Bonsai and Jangles peering over the window ledge at something on the ground. Ember lowered Sirod's head slowly and rushed over to the window. Looking down she saw the lifeless body of Usurpus on the courtyard floor. Ember then rushed back to Sirod who was now struggling for his last breaths.

"Quick, help me take him outside," Ember announced excitedly. Gently she supported Sirod's head whilst Eitak and Arwie lifted him to his feet and supported his weight by stretching his arms out around their shoulders. As quickly as they could, they shuffled out of the room to the stone steps, allowing Sirod's feet to drag along the floor behind him. Once downstairs, they opened the wooden door and shuffled out into the courtyard.

"This way!" Ember shouted as she ran over to Usurpus' body which lay motionless below the open window whilst whisps swirled and rushed around overhead.

Having swiped at the last of the marsh mists, Bonsai and Jangles peered down from the dining room and decided to climb out of the window to join their friends in the courtyard below.

"Put him there," Ember instructed and once Eitak and Arwie had placed Sirod on the ground next to Usurpus, she stretched out his left hand and touched it against Usurpus' head and then it dawned upon Eitak what Ember was proposing to do.

"Surely you can't be thinking..." he began but just then Sirod breathed his last gasp of life and in that moment, Usurpus' chest slowly began to rise and fall and as it did so the whisps within him left.

Sirod slowly opened his eyes and saw his old body lying on the ground next to him and then he saw Ember and smiled. "Ember, my love, you are still alive..." and then a sudden realisation came to him, he remembered Usurpus and the knife, he remembered the pain in his chest and in the last moments of his consciousness, he saw the mists and the open window, he looked up at the dining room above and touched his face with his hands before he continued, "...But my love, what have you done?"

Eitak looked at Sirod's old body, lying on the ground next to Usurpus. "Why can't you just go back into your old body, I mean it's definitely dead?"

"It doesn't work like that," Sirod replied. "Once we have used a body, we cannot re-enter it, it's just the way that it is."

"So you're stuck like this, for how long?" Eitak asked feeling slightly uneasy at seeing his best friend in his worst enemy's body.

Sirod remembered Malarog's green potion that Usurpus had drunk before falling from the window and then realising the significance of that one event announced, "Forever."

The fat gaoler who had been in the dining room rushed from the tower under the control of the whisps and out through the main gate to the marsh road beyond, Eitak followed him as he ran straight into the lake and sank beneath the misty waters to the depths below.

Sirod lifted himself to his feet. "I think we should go, after all we don't know how many guards this place holds and once word gets out, there's no telling what might happen." As he finished his last word, a group of masked guards ran from the second tower and assembled on the cobbles in front of the companions. Sirod composed himself and shouted at the rag-tag company of men, "What took you so long?" he looked down at his old body and then up at the dining room. "This man has fallen from the window, now take him back inside and take those masks off, the whisps are…on our side now." Sirod looked at Eitak and winked.

The rag-tag soldiers did as they were commanded and removed their masks. Within the time it took to breathe the whisps had engulfed them and just for a brief moment, the men stood still, transfixed but then a madness took a hold and they ran from the courtyard into the marsh lakes where they were never to be seen again.

The gaoler who had escaped from the dining room looked across the courtyard from his hiding place amongst the shadows, he had seen what had happened to his master in the dining room and how the mists had taken him and there was no way that he was going to suffer the same fate. Now wearing a mask which covered his mouth and nose, he saw Usurpus rise from the ground, helped by the other prisoners and watched as they walked across the courtyard and left through the main gate.

Eitak, Arwie and Ember looked Sirod up and down and to their surprise, he had very little signs of any injury, the only indication that he had fallen from the window was a small cut on his forehead.

"Anything broken?" Eitak enquired.

"There doesn't seem to be," Sirod replied as he patted himself all over. "…It's almost as if he died from the shock of the fall rather than the impact…strange."

The companions made their way to the spongy path and once again walked in single file to limit the twisting effect of the floating grasses. The marsh mists swirled in the air around them and gathered ahead. Eitak, who was leading, stopped and everyone backed up behind him. A single line of mist coiled in front of him and slowly entered his body as he breathed, no longer scared, Eitak allowed the intrusion without hesitation and within moments he stood perfectly still and transfixed.

"We know you, Eitak Ladoog. Your spirit is pure and you are welcome wherever you may find us, now go and be safe for I sense that your journey is by no means at an end." The whisps slowly left Eitak and together with the rest of the mists, they slowly sank to the marsh lakes and were gone.

The homeward journey along the bog path seemed a lot quicker and once again the companions walked in a line with Bonsai and Jangles bringing up the rear jumping, the grassy waves as the ground rippled underfoot. Eventually, Eitak saw a tiny speck on the horizon and although he couldn't make out any features at this distance, he knew that it was Klum who had been waiting patiently all this time.

Before long the familiar outline of Klum grew a little larger until eventually, everyone could make out that their huge giant friend was waving to them. Eitak smiled and waved back but then he realised that Klum's arm movements seemed a little too frantic to be a gesture of greeting and he turned to look behind him. A short distance away and catching up fast was the masked gaoler from Castle Sly. He was running at full pelt, causing the already unstable path to twist and dip under his weight. The ground sank into the lake with each footstep. Eitak could now hear the splashing and sploshing sound as he approached. The companions were unarmed, they had taken nothing with them for the journey across the marshes, what little they did have had been removed by the very same man who was now running towards them.... and that very same man was now holding a sharp looking metal pike in his hands.

"Run," said Eitak as panic set in. The companions had no time to react, the gaoler was already under full steam and was almost upon them when all of a sudden, an enormous hammer fell from the sky, hit the gaoler in mid stride and with immense speed plummeted through the grass and into the lake, taking the gaoler down with it. Eitak looked at the grass path where the gaoler once stood as the grasses reformed covering the hole which had been punched through the path and then he turned towards Klum who was now waving joyously still some distance away.

"I'm glad he's a good shot with that thing is all I can say," Arwie said stunned by what had just happened.

"Or he was just lucky," Sirod replied. "Either way I'm glad, we will soon be back on dry land."

Before long the marsh road came to an end and Eitak put his first foot on firm ground. Klum knelt down and stretched out one of his huge hands, one by one the companions patted his palm, overjoyed to see their old friend once more.

"Who is this?" Klum asked looking at Sirod.

"That, my friend, is a long story," Eitak replied. "I don't suppose you have anything left to eat by chance?"

14. The Journey Home

Klum unpacked what provisions he had and as they all sat down to their first proper meal in two days, they told Klum of their adventures at Castle Sly and the encounter with Usurpus.

"So let me get this right," Klum asked Sirod, trying to get his head around what he had just heard. "Usurpus was in love with Ember and she was in love with you, I mean you...as Sirod...and now Usurpus is dead and you...Sirod, have taken over his body and are stuck with it forever, is that right?"

Sirod looked at Ember, feeling very awkward and wondering if she still loved him. *I mean how could she? How could she love a relative of the very man she tried to escape 200 years ago?* Sirod touched his face and he realised it wasn't just that, for not only had Usurpus' great, great, grandfather tried to kill Ember all that time ago, now Sirod found himself residing in the skin of the same man who tried to stab her earlier today.

"What I want to know is where the other giants are?" Eitak asked changing the subject.

"They returned to the village, there were no more soldiers and so they went back but I decided to stay and just as well I did...the thing is though, I was getting rather attached to that hammer." Klum sighed.

After a welcomed meal, the companions jumped up onto their armoured Rhinamoths and together with Klum they set off back to Kidder Doon.

As night fell, they had reached the halfway mark of their return journey and the companions made a small camp fire and lay huddled around listening to the crackling and popping sounds of the flames as they danced upwards into the night sky. Eitak and Arwie lay close to each other and were soon asleep, Klum lay on his back and before long, the rhythmic sound of his snoring gave the impression that they were camped at the edge of a large waterfall, whilst Bonsai and Jangles lay huddled closest to the warm fire. Sirod lay on his back, staring up at the starry sky with tears rolling down his face, Ember was next to him and they held hands.

"Do you still love me?" Sirod asked tearfully.

"More than ever," Ember replied.

"Despite what I have become?"

"I made that choice, not you."

"But now you will see me as Usurpus every day and for the rest of our lives."

"I made that choice because I love you, Sirod, I have always loved you and I cannot bear to be without you."

"But Usurpus, he tried to stab you."

"I know that and I know that you reacted instinctively all those years ago when his great, great grandfather did the same thing. I know that then you didn't save yourself at my expense consciously. But let's not forget today when Usurpus stabbed you instead of me…and that was a conscious act. I love you no matter what you look like. It is what is inside that counts; with all the body changes, I have made during the time that I was a Nagraal, the most important thing that I learnt that was that in time all our looks fade, we all become withered and wrinkled but it is our soul that matters, that never changes; we are always the same person, maybe wiser in some cases but always the same. I am not so shallow that I cannot see beyond all that…anyway, I thought Usurpus was quite good looking."

Sirod felt a lot better, he adored Ember and always had. He never wanted anything to come between them. "Was quite good looking?" he asked, emphasising the 'was' and fishing for compliments.

"Is," she replied correcting herself and they both snuggled up in each other's arms and fell asleep.

With the morning came the final leg of the journey to Kidder Doon and by evening, they had reached the Plains of Ishtar. The companions stood at the southern end of the plain and took a moment to take in the scene before them, for now scattered on the field across the entire plain and as far as the eye could see were the broken remains of the metal army. Everywhere they looked, the smashed metal bodies and mechanical remnants of the battle glistened in the evening sun. Having crossed the plains, they continued through the woods to the north and on towards the giants' village beyond the volcano.

"I wonder how Bones is doing," Eitak said thinking aloud.

Hearing Eitak's words, Sirod felt guilty. He had been so self-absorbed with his own thoughts that he hadn't given any time to consider Bones. "I'm sure he will be fine," he replied hoping that his words of confidence would make it seem as if he had given the matter some prior consideration.

"Well, we will soon find out," Klum replied. "We are almost there."

As the volcano of Kidder Doon came into view, Sirod became aware of movement in the trees, he stared into the wood and then blinked and as his eyelids lifted, Sprinter, Dasher, Rusher, Whoosher and Hunter stood before them. Klum knelt down and spread his great arms as the Hagraal pack licked and washed him all over his face. Eitak slid down from his Rhinamoth mount and stood on the woodland path. Hunter had smelled him from way back in the woods but now that Eitak had put himself on offer for a wash, he bounded over and knocked, Eitak straight off his feet and then with one front paw planted firmly either side, he bent down and licked Eitak all over his face.

Suddenly, there was a familiar sound which reverberated around the wood, it was the sound of a hunting horn and within a second, the Hagraals were gone. Eitak stood up from Hunter's enthusiastic welcome and wiped the slobber from his face.

"Something's wrong," Klum bellowed. "That was an alarm cry, a warning, and it came from inside Kidder Doon."

Eitak quickly climbed onto his Rhinamoth and the group rushed to the pass, leading through the volcano which they found was open. Concerned with what they might find, swiftly they continued on through the mountain tunnel to the other side.

As soon as they stepped from the gloom and into the light of the village, an enormous cheer erupted and there in front of them, the entire village of Giants had turned out to welcome them back from their journey and at the front of the gathering was King Gom and Queen Min.

As the cheering died down the king and queen stepped to either side of the road, the crowds parted and there stood in the middle of the dusty track, leading through the centre of the village was Bones and either side of him were two of the most beautiful female giants who had ever lived.

"Bones!" shouted Eitak and he ran forward past the crowds, he was about to grab his friend with a heartfelt hug when the two beautiful women put their hands down and gently stopped him.

"You must be careful, Eitak. He is still weak and the wound has not yet healed," said one of the girls concerned for Bones' welfare.

"Sorry, oh, yes, of course," Eitak replied, embarrassed by his display of affection and lack of thought. "I didn't mean to…"

"I understand," said one of the girls softly and they removed their huge hands, allowing Eitak to see his friend for the first time since the battle.

"It's fantastic to see you on your feet, my friend, and how nice it must be to have such lovely bodyguards," Eitak said looking at the two beautiful giants. "…Put it this way, they are a lot better than some I could mention."

Bones eyes widened and as discreetly as he could, he shook his head in very small quick movements, desperately trying to stop Eitak from saying anything else.

Eitak looked at him and raised one eyebrow, confused by what Bones was trying to tell him without actually saying anything.

Eitak looked over his shoulder towards the king and queen who were still stood at the front of the crowd talking to Sirod and when he thought that they couldn't hear, he whispered in a low voice, "So what happened to Luj and Noj?"

Bones thrust his head and eyes first the right and then to the left and then said, "You wouldn't believe me if I told you."

Eitak looked at the two exquisite women either side of Bones. They had long silky, dark brown hair and hazel-coloured eyes. They were both slim, although curvaceous and voluptuous and both wore the same bright orange- and yellow-coloured dresses that he had seen Luj and Noj wearing the first time that he met them, only now they were considerably more tailored and fitted. Eitak studied the two beautiful giants and the more he looked, the more he realised that there was something very familiar about them and then like a lightning strike, it came to him and as he turned his head to look at each one, his thoughts left his mouth.

"Luj, Noj?"

The two girls looked at Eitak, and then at each other and giggled.

"It took you long enough," Luj said still, half sniggering at Eitak's awkwardness.

"How…I mean what happened?" Eitak said uncomfortably and then realising how he must have sounded, continued, "…What I'm really trying to say is…" All of the other giants had heard Eitak's exchange and the entire village erupted with laughter and then King Gom came over and stood beside him.

"Allow me to introduce you to my daughters, Luj and Noj. You see, what you probably didn't realise about giants is that beauty comes from within and when our women feel beautiful and loved on the inside, then it shows itself on the outside and the more in love, they feel, the more beautiful they become."

Eitak was stunned and looked from Luj to Noj and then to Bones. "Well, all I can say is that Bones must love you very, very much." Gom gently slapped Eitak on the back and the whole village burst into a round of laughter and cheers.

"Who's hungry?" Enquired the king and once more another cheer erupted and then the entire village followed Gom to the green. Before long, the smell of roasted meats filled the air as the companions sat down to another giant feast.

With a full belly and a warm heart Gom stood to make a toast. "Friends, old and new," he began, "today is the first day we can truly celebrate victory, the Golden Army has been defeated, the last of the rag-tag guards have been driven out of Illya where Thaddeus and his men have decided to make their home, our people have returned from battle unharmed, and our guests have returned victorious from the marshes. Usurpus has been defeated and now we have a souvenir of that victory in Sirod."

The giants looked over to Sirod, raised their glasses and laughed at the king's joke.

Sirod sat next to Noj. "Where is Malarog?" he asked having not seen his old friend since they had arrived back in Kidder Doon.

"He went back to Illya with Kram, he said he needed to collect something," she replied.

"And now my future son-in-law is back on his feet…" the king continued, "…and my daughters are happy for the first time in living memory…" the crowd burst into laughter once more. "…I am not only a happy king and a triumphant king but I am also a king in a new world where man and giant, Wirral, Nagraal, Dust Dweller and Whisp can live as one and walk the lands freely and without fear of one another and I say let's drink to that."

As the sound of cheering and the clinking and clanking of glasses filled the air, the king held up his hand and silence fell. "And tomorrow we will make ready for the wedding of the year and what I say is who will drink to that?" A huge cheer erupted again and Sirod leant over to Bones.

"So just how is this going to work?" he asked curiously.

Bones was already quite drunk, having not quite mastered the art of how full to fill the giant-sized wine glasses.

"I'll work it out...somehow," Bones replied slurring his words, not really interested in the details and just living for the moment.

As the flames of the bonfire danced into the nights sky, Eitak approached Arwie and stood next to her. "All this talk of marriage..." he began.

Arwie turned and looked at Eitak and their eyes met as they sparkled in the firelight. For the first time Eitak looked in through the windows of her soul and at that moment he realised that he wanted to spend the rest of his life with her, but as much as he wanted to, he just couldn't bring himself to tell her, there was something holding him back and as he watched everyone having a wonderful time; he knew what it was, it was rejection. He had lost his mother and father at a tender age and he didn't want to commit to anyone, only to lose them further down the line.

"Yes?" Arwie replied.

"I was just wondering..." he continued now having lost his nerve and being desperate to think of something else to say. "How did you get your scar?"

Arwie took a step back, lifted her shoulder and covered her cheek. "I got it in Rampor," she replied in a deflated tone. Arwie loved Eitak too, she desperately wanted for there to be something more between the two of them and just when she thought that he was going to ask her something important, he asked her about her scar. Was it her scar that put him off? Was he going to ask her a special question and then changed his mind because he couldn't live with her face? These were all questions that swirled around in her head as Eitak continued.

"I thought you got it in Bagdoon along with the ones on your back?"

"No, I got it from an Umberjax when I was with Mia." Arwie thought of her best friend who, by a strange turn of fate was now Ember, and she walked away from Eitak, with tears rolling down her face. She heard Eitak follow after her and she showed him the back of her hand as she held her arm in the air and then continued to walk into the shadows.

As Eitak watched Arwie walk away, he thought for a moment what was he thinking of...he loved Arwie, he was certain of that. But even so there was still another matter clinging to the back of his mind, there was that slight doubt that niggling concern over the rumours surrounding the Wirral. After all, no one had ever seen a Wirral man, legend had it, that once a Wirral woman had taken a mate, he was taken off never to be seen or heard of again. What did that mean and was he really ready to find out?

Of course, he was, he didn't want to lose her and he decided it was now or never, this was the moment he needed to be a man and tell her how he really felt.

"Arwie!" he shouted as he ran after her. "That wasn't the question I wanted to ask, what I really wanted to say was, that all this talk about weddings has made me realise that I love you more than anything in the world and I never want to lose you. I have been a fool and a coward and realise that I just need to ask you and there is no other way to say this, will you be mine? Forever?"

Arwie dried her eyes and as she looked into Eitak's, she saw her own reflection mirrored in the dancing light. "If you are asking what I think you are asking then the answer is yes, I accept, but are you absolutely sure? What about my scar?"

The scar didn't bother him at all, he had only mentioned it because he wanted an excuse and something to say but what did concern him was the legend of the Wirral.

On the other hand, if this was going to be a double wedding then Sirod, Bones and the rest of his friends would be there including Klum and the rest of the giants. How much safer could he be.

Eitak shook the thoughts from his head and looked directly at Arwie, he bent down on one knee, held her hand in his and said,

"Arwie Willowbreeze, you are the most beautiful woman I have ever met and will you do me the honour of becoming my wife?"

Arwie smiled, she had never been so happy, she truly loved Eitak and wanted to share her life with him.

"Yes, yes, I will."

Eitak rose to his feet. "Where shall we get married? Rampor or Kidder doon?" he asked.

"It will have to be Rampor, there's no question about it," Arwie replied forcefully.

"My, you seem quite certain about that, why must it be Rampor?" Eitak asked, slightly uncomfortable at Arwie's quick response.

"All will become clear in the fullness of time. We must speak with King Gom but not tonight, tonight is for the king and his daughters but if all goes according to plan then I will leave for Rampor in the morning but you must tell everyone to come to the forest in four days from now…for I will need time to inform everyone and make arrangements."

That night, Eitak lay awake in Klum's spare bed and looked up at the ceiling high above. Arwie lay dreaming next to him, smiling peacefully in her sleep. 'Make arrangements' he thought…what did that mean? He desperately wanted to trust Arwie he loved her more than anything in the world but was he really making the right decision to go to Rampor? Or was he being lured into a trap by his emotions and was he about to take everyone else down with him.

The following morning, Eitak and Arwie went to the king's hut. Gom was stood outside with his head in a large barrel of water, wearing nothing but a pair of white long johns and matching vest. As he lifted his head, Eitak and Arwie were drenched by a sudden wave of water.

"Eh? Oh, sorry," said the king, both sorry for soaking his guests and also for being seen out in his under garments. "How can I help you?" Gom spread a huge towel around his middle and wiped the water from his face.

"Your majesty, we were just wondering…" Eitak began.

"What Eitak is trying to say is…" Arwie continued.

"You two are like an old married couple," the king said. "…In fact, I don't know why you don't get married, why we could make it a double wedding." Gom nodded to himself in approval of his own suggestion.

Eitak and Arwie looked at each other in amazement at how easy this had been. "Erm, what a splendid idea your majesty," Eitak acknowledged.

"I suppose you will want to get married in Rampor too," added the king. "I know quite a bit about the Wirral, after all we are almost neighbours and I know something of your traditions. I haven't been to Rampor for years, mind you young lady, you may wish to discuss this with your huntress friends first; as to be honest, I think we all have had enough of arrows for a while."

Again, Eitak and Arwie looked at each other, wondering if the king had been able to read their minds.

As Eitak and Arwie walked back to Klum's hut, the king went indoors.

"You are terrible," said the queen. "Why didn't you just tell them?"

"Tell them what, my love," replied Gom innocently.

"Tell them that with large ears comes good hearing and that we had discussed all of this last night after you 'overheard' their private conversation," Min continued accusingly.

"I know, I know, but it's never a bad thing for anyone to think that a king has special powers." And Gom chuckled to himself as he continued to get ready for the day ahead.

Later that morning, Arwie set off on the short journey to Rampor. She would have to travel to the Plains of Ishtar and then continue north following the eastern face of the Thunder Mountains until she reached the vast sprawling forests and the home of the Wirral.

"I'll see you in four days," Eitak shouted as Arwie disappeared into the darkness of the volcano pass.

Once the passage closed once more, Sirod spoke to Eitak.

"Gom came to me last night and told me his idea for a double wedding. Ember and I talked about it and we think it's a fantastic plan." Sirod then thought about his own relationship with Ember. Sure, they had known each other for the best part of 200 years and surely that would qualify anybody to consider marriage. But something didn't quite feel right and Sirod could not quite put his finger on it. Something deep inside didn't feel as it should and that worried him. It wasn't that he didn't love Ember, because he did with all of his heart. So, what was it? he asked himself. Was it that he had now taken on the looks of Usurpus? Sure, that was part of it and he wanted to see how or if Ember had really adjusted to that, but no, there was something more, something deeper and only time would tell what that was and because of this he thought that now was not the time to consider a triple wedding…two was quite enough. "Besides," Sirod added, "I really fancy the idea of meeting the Wirral again."

There it was again, 'The Wirral', just the very thought of the word gave Eitak butterflies.

Everyone had two days to prepare, the journey to Rampor was two days walk and they needed to be there four days after Arwie left. Queen Min organised the women of the village in creating two magnificent wedding dresses for Luj and Noj and meanwhile the men organised the tailoring of the finest suit of silk for Bones. Just two days later, everything was packed and ready. A huge wagon with the finest meats, cheeses and wines draped with a tarpaulin stood at the entrance to the volcano and together with all the giants, it stood ready for the king and queen to give the signal to leave.

The volcano pass opened and in walked Tum and Malarog back from Illya.

"Malarog!" Eitak exclaimed, pleased to see his old friend.

"There's no time for all that nonsense…" said Malarog as he purposefully marched out of the tunnel. "Am I too late? Don't tell me I'm too late."

"Too late for what?" Eitak asked.

"The wedding, the wedding, of course…" Malarog announced as he looked around for Bones.

"No, you haven't missed a thing; in fact, we are just getting ready to leave for Rampor now."

"Rampor, why would you ever want to go there? It's filled with some very nasty things, you know?" replied Malarog as he rummaged through the pockets of his long coat. "Ah, here it is," he said more to himself than anyone else and he pulled a small bottle of black treacle like liquid from his pocket.

"What in Kennet's name is that?" Eitak asked looking at the black sludge which erupted like over ripe boils in the small glass container.

"This is a wedding present which I really wanted to give to Bones before the wedding, now where is he?"

"A wedding present!" Eitak exclaimed. "…Well, you might want to get two more, that's why we are off to Rampor to meet up with Arwie so that we can get married along with Bones, Luj and Noj."

"Eh, oh, I see very good," Malarog replied, not really paying much attention to anything else other than finding Bones.

"Mind you…" continued Eitak as he looked at the erupting liquid, "…if that's your idea of a wedding present then perhaps I might forgive you for not getting us anything."

"Ah, there you are," said Malarog as he saw Bones in the crowd. "…Here young man, take this." And he handed Bones the foul looking potion which now had steam, rising from the erupting boils of black tar.

"Malarog, glad you made it," Bones said, genuinely pleased to see his Magistanian friend and as his smile subsided, he realised that he was now holding the small bottle. Bones held it up to the sunlight and inspected the contents. "And just what is this?" he enquired.

"That my boy is your wedding present from me, a rare gift which I acquired from a travelling merchant many moons ago. I think that's the right one. Anyway, if it is, then you probably already know what it does." Malarog scratched his head, trying to think if he had brought the right potion.

"What do you mean…you think it's the right potion?" Bones replied. "I have no idea what you are talking about and just what do you expect me to do with it?"

"It looks like plant food to me," said Eitak as he looked into the bottle.

"All I'll say is that you should only drink it if you are absolutely sure that it's what you want," Malarog added cryptically and he nodded his head and he walked off to find Luj and Noj.

"Well," said Eitak, "that was about as clear as the liquid you are holding, so have you any idea what it does?"

"None," replied Bones. "Perhaps I'll feed it to the plants and see what happens."

While Eitak and Bones were debating what they should do with the liquid, Luj and Noj came running through the crowd closely followed by Malarog, Sirod and Ember.

"Have you drunk it yet?" asked Luj clapping her huge hands together excitedly.

"Do you feel any different?" enquired Noj with equal enthusiasm.

Bones held up the bottle of bubbling black sludge. "I was just thinking about it," he replied.

"Well, we all think you should drink it," Luj added.

Bones took another look at the bottle and removed the stopper. He lifted it to his nose and took a small sniff of the contents. To his amazement, it smelt quite nice a cross between chocolate, red wine and liquorice, it just looked like it could kill you.

"Oh, well," he said, "here goes." And he threw the liquid to the back of his throat and swallowed.

The other giants began to take an interest in what was going on and stood in a circle around Bones.

"Stand back," shouted Malarog forcefully and the group took a step back.

"Further," said Malarog, "you really, really do need to give the boy some room."

Bones stood in the middle of the large circle of giants. Luj and Noj stared wide eyed in anticipation of what might happen next and then the ground began to shake.

Cracks appeared in the ground which became wider as the earth beneath Bones' feet dried out, he began to feel very hot and a bead of sweat appeared on his left temple. As the earthquake continued, it spread out and soon the entire circle where the onlookers had stood rippled and contorted as if a catastrophic event was taking place below ground.

"What have you done?" Eitak asked Malarog.

"Well, it would seem that I did bring the right potion after all, unless of course I got it mixed up with the tunnelling liquid," Malarog answered considering the possibility.

The shaking gradually intensified and then the very fabric of the soil changed as the energy was sucked out of the ground and beneath Bones' feet, the once rich brown soil turned into a halo of white dust.

Bones stood still, wide eyed and startled, he looked up at Luj and Noj until the energy transfer from the ground reached saturation point and he began to grow.

The ground soon looked further away than he remembered and instead of staring at his fiancée's knees he was now eye level with their hips, and then their belly's, their breasts followed by their necks, their eyes, their foreheads until he could see over the top of their heads and in a very short space of time he finally stood as tall as Klum.

Bones looked down and realised that he was now totally naked. Eitak, Malarog, Sirod and Ember stood below him, the tops of their heads reached just beneath his knees, Ember looked up and very soon wished that she hadn't and turned away from Bones naked body, shielding her eyes from the view.

Luj and Noj looked on their eyes wide open and then they giggled.

At first Bones wobbled uneasy at the sudden increase in altitude but when he realised what had happened, he held out his huge hands and turned them over looking at each one. He then patted himself all over, first touching his head then his face and body, just to make sure that everything was in its rightful place and not out of proportion with anything else. As he got to his belly, he found to his surprise and satisfaction that the stretching process had made him a lot slimmer than he was and just as he was about to smile about that it dawned on him that he was still totally naked and was standing in his birthday suit in front of the entire village.

Quickly Bones covered his modesty with his hands.

"Wow," he boomed, his voice now as loud as a foghorn. "Is this permanent?"

"As permanent as you want it to be," Malarog shouted as he rummaged through his pockets once more.

"This was the other option," he announced holding up another small bottle, this time with a glowing pink clear liquid. "I could have given this to Luj and Noj but I've only got the one bottle and I didn't think the king would approve. But I suppose you should look after it, just in case you change your mind."

King Gom stepped forward and handed Bones a towel which he quickly wrapped around his waist, he then looked at his future wives who were still giggling and threw his arms wide open. Luj and Noj rushed forward and melted into his arms and began to kiss him all over his face and neck.

"I think I'll stay just as I am…for now," Bones announced contentedly.

The entire village of giants began to cheer and closed in on Bones and slapped him on the shoulders and back as they welcomed him into their lives.

Bonsai and Jangles who had been watching the proceedings from the safety of a nearby hut swung down and climbed up Bones' legs as if they were tree trunks until they reached his shoulders where they happily sat either side of his huge head.

Bones looked at his two furry friends and said softly, "And you two will always be my special friends no matter how big or small I become."

"You really are full of surprises, aren't you?" Eitak said to Malarog, amazed by Bones' sudden transformation.

"Well, to be honest, I had my doubts that it would work," said the Magistan as he pulled out a third bottle from his cape. Malarog looked at the clear liquid removed the stopper and took a sip.

"What does that one do?" Eitak asked his eyes widening at the thought of another earthquake.

"This? Oh, this one is just a little something to calm the nerves," Malarog replied and he replaced the small bottle back into his cape.

"Right…" said the king, "…who wants to get married?" A huge cheer echoed through the volcano pass and the giants slowly moved into the darkness. "Don't forget…" added the king, "…be on your guard, Rampor is a very dangerous place, there are creatures that even giants are afraid of…after all it's not the hunting ground of the Wirral for nothing."

Eitak remembered Arwie's words when they first met in Illya, she had told him that the great forests were home to the creatures of nightmares but he hadn't really thought about that until now. He turned to Sirod. "So, not only may my wedding day be my last but now we might die before we even get that far." And he held his head in his hands as he wondered again if he was doing the right thing.

King Gom and Queen Min led the way through the pass, followed by Kram and Klum and most of the other giants. Luj and Noj walked either side of Bones who had his great arms around them and then Eitak, Malarog, Sirod and Ember brought up the rear. As they entered the tunnel, a voice shouted out, "Wait for me." And Tum came running up from the other side of the village. As his massive feet thundered through the main street, the entire Hagraal pack materialised next to him.

Hunter walked alongside Eitak and turned to look at him. "You're not bringing them, are you?" Eitak asked wondering how the Hagraals would be received in Rampor.

"Of course, they are part of the family," replied Tum rather hurt at the idea of leaving his hunting dogs behind.

Eitak looked at Hunter and the rest of the Hagraals and suddenly felt a lot safer. As he entered the gloom of the mountain pass, he turned to take one last look at the village and as he did the strangest thing happened, the white halo of drained earth began to sink.

The two-day journey to Rampor turned out to be just one as Eitak hadn't allowed for the fact that giants walk faster than humans plus he, Sirod and Ember had accepted a ride on the huge wagon full of food.

15. The Forests of Rampor

The road to Rampor took the wedding party back to the Plains of Ishtar and then northwards following the Thunder Mountains until they came to the vast dense sprawling forests that the Wirral called home.

"Be careful…" said the king, "…there are things in these woods that even I dare not disturb." And with that, 81 giants, five Hasty Hagraals and four humans entered Rampor.

The forest spread from the Cylesian cliffs on the northern shores of the continent all the way south, where they almost met the Plains of Ishtar. Rampor was an ancient forest of massive trees which towered above the giants and made them appear as tiny insects as they meandered their way north. After a while, Klum began to sing and before long the entire village joined in and the forest murmured as the huge trees caught the deep sound of the Giants song.

Eitak listened to the drone and was just about to join in with the chorus when he heard another sound coming from the east. It was a rhythmic thumping sound, mixed with a faint cracking noise. Eitak looked along the line of giants to see if anyone had brought with them a drum and when he was satisfied that they hadn't he thought it best to mention what he had heard.

"Can anyone hear that?" Eitak asked. 'No' reply, the giants were far too busy singing to pay any attention to his tiny voice. The noise grew louder and now Eitak was sure that he could see movement far off into the darkness amongst the trees to his left. "Can anyone hear that?" Eitak shouted at the top of his voice.

Hunter looked at Eitak and then followed his gaze into the woods. The huge Hagraal stopped, threw back his head and howled, Eitak had never heard a Hagraal howl before and now that he had, he decided that he never wanted to hear it again. He put his hands to his ears to muffle the shrill noise, an invasive, piercing and deafening sound that entered the body, shivered the spine and made every hair stand on end. The other Hagraals saw what Hunter had seen and within moments, all five Hagraals joined in and howled into the woods.

King Gom threw up his hand. "Stop," he shouted and all the giants came to a halt.

The Giants strained to look between the trees as the noise grew closer. Soon the thumping noise turned to a thunderous boom and each cracking noise was followed by a dreadful creaking sound and a massive thud. Eitak peered into the gloom and then he saw the cause of the noise.

"Umberjax!" shouted Gom. "Hide." And the entire village of giants ran to hide behind any tree large enough to disguise their huge bodies and as far from the crashing sound as they could find. Eitak, Sirod, Ember and Malarog stayed together and hid behind a particularly enormous tree. Bones, Luj and Noj selected a large tree each, quite close to each other. As Bones brushed against the thick bark, he snagged his shirt ripping a gaping hole in the back. Eitak had no idea what an Umberjax was and decided to sneak a look around the massive trunk.

The Umberjax blundered its way, obliviously through the forest ignoring everything and anything that happened to be in its path. Twice as tall as a giant, the Umberjax was the largest creature Eitak had ever seen.

"I thought that giants were supposed to be the biggest living things," Eitak stated as he turned to Sirod.

"Why how big is an Umberjax then?" Sirod asked having never seen one.

"You'll see in a moment because it's coming this way," Eitak replied with the panicked voice of concern.

The Umberjax continued through the forest, pushing aside any tree small enough for it to break and avoiding the larger ones. Eitak had seen a Snowjax before when the avalanche engulfed it on the Mountains of Light but this…this was a different thing all together. The Umberjax was totally hairless with yellow leathery warty skin. It had large warty feet with huge yellow claws, thick, muscular wart covered legs which had boils and erupting pustules all over. It had a large hunched fat body with a huge sagging belly and pendulous wobbling breasts. Its arms were warty and muscular and its hands had claws which matched its feet. To complete its look, the Umberjax had a massive wart covered domed head with a single horn growing from its forehead. Its mouth was a huge gaping maw with broken and jagged yellow teeth.

As the repulsive creature ponderously made its way closer, uprooted trees snapped and fell all around the faint path which the companions had been following through the forest. Quietly, everyone sidled their way around their respective trees and kept out of the Umberjax's sight. As the great beast reached the path, it suddenly stopped, sniffed the air and headed straight for the food wagon. With one powerful swipe, it bowled over the cart and noisily scoffed down all the food it could eat. Once full, the Umberjax continued on through the forest, leaving behind it a trail of destruction in its wake.

Once the coast was clear, the wedding party emerged from the trees.

"What was that?" Bones asked as he looked at the upturned cart.

"That my boy was an Umberjax," Gom replied. "Peaceful unless provoked, or angry or tired and if any of those apply then you run fast in any direction… In fact, it's best to avoid it I'd say."

"Sounds like good advice to me," Bones replied as he looked through the swill of mixed food on the floor. Some of the giants came over and righted the wagon but the axle was now broken and everything would have to be carried for the rest of the way.

"At least the dresses are OK," Noj said as she picked through the rest of the belongings that were strewn about the forest floor.

"Well, if that's a taste of things to come, I wish I'd stayed in Kidder Doon," Eitak said as he picked up his haversack of belongings.

The party continued on through the forest until evening came. "I don't fancy the idea of camping here in the middle of the night." Eitak announced. "This forest seems to go on forever."

They carried on walking for another couple of hours until Hunter stood still and sniffed the air. Eitak looked around with a heightened sense of awareness and listened in case another Umberjax was about to appear. The huge Hagraal looked up and cocked its head to one side and then the other as it looked high into the trees.

"Today is the day that the Hagraals are being watched," Klum said as he too scanned the forest canopy.

Bones was just about to bite into a nice juicy alder fruit when an arrow whistled through the air and embedded itself right through the centre of the core. Bones startled by the sudden appearance of the sharp object, lost his balance, dropped his apple and fell to the ground, tearing his trousers on a large tree root as he went.

"Woah!" he bellowed loudly as he looked up. "We are on our way to a wedding." And he picked himself off the ground and stood in his ripped and tattered clothes.

Moments later, six young women swung down from the tall trees on twisted vines and stood before the group with bows and arrows poised at the ready.

16. The Weddings

Gom stepped forward. "I am Gom, King of the giants and am here for the wedding of Arwie Willowbreeze to this young man." And he bent down and patted Eitak on the back.

"We have been following you since you entered the forest," announced one of the girls. "The Umberjax made quite of a mess of things back there didn't it?"

Eitak looked at the four girls. They were all aged between 20 and 30 years of age and were scantily dressed in green and brown clothing. Covering their skin, they wore body paint which meant that they blended in with the forest almost completely. One of the girls had fiery red hair like Ember, one had blonde hair like Arwie and the other two had brown hair like Luj and Noj. As Ember stepped forward, the girls immediately recognised her.

"Mia!" One of them exclaimed and was just about to embrace her old friend when she suddenly held back and with a slightly deflated tone added, "Princess Arwie is waiting for you all, you had best come with us before it gets dark."

"Princess Arwie?" Sirod repeated slowly as he turned to Eitak. "I'd say my friend, that you have just made it in life."

"I promise you, I never knew, Arwie never told me anything about being a princess, honestly," Eitak replied reeling and stunned at this new revelation.

The wedding group struggled to follow after the lithe huntresses, who made their way through the trees like water flowing downstream. It was the ponderous giants who had the most difficulty as they collided with trees and tripped over stumps in their attempt to keep up but eventually they came to a clearing and in the middle was the largest tree that anyone had ever seen.

The huntresses walked across the clearing and made their way to the other side of the huge tree which had a girth the size of the green in Kidder Doon.

As the wedding party followed the girls, to their amazement on the other side of the tree they found themselves staring at the eastern face of the Thunder Mountains.

"I didn't realise we were that close to the mountains," Gom announced in surprise.

"There are many things here that may surprise you." Came a familiar voice from behind. Eitak spun around and there walking from a doorway within the huge tree was Arwie.

Arwie was dressed in brown leather sandals, attached to her feet by a series of intricate straps which were tied up her legs to a point just below her knees. She wore a short skirt made from a series of leather straps fastened to her waist by a gem studded belt, her belly button was highlighted by a single red glowing gemstone and on her top, she wore a short tight fitted, green coloured top which was emblazoned by hundreds of tiny red gemstones.

Arwie had tied her hair back in a plait and as she moved, it swayed from side to side and glistened in the fading light. On the top of her head was a simple golden crown, encrusted with three large red gemstones.

"You look beautiful…your highness," Eitak said mesmerised by her beauty. "Why didn't you tell me?"

"Because I thought it might frighten you away," Arwie replied quietly.

Sirod turned to Ember. "I think we could be the poor relations at this wedding."

"I don't know, you almost took over the world that must count for something," Ember replied and then laughed at Sirod's expense.

Arwie approached her guests. "Welcome, everyone," she announced. "…You are safe here. Tonight, we will feast and tomorrow we will marry, rejoice and celebrate from dusk until dawn but before that, I have a little surprise for you all." And with that she waved her hand and from within the tree stepped Thaddeus, Lucius and Felix.

"Thaddeus!" exclaimed Eitak, pleased to see his old friend, "…I'm so glad you could make it."

Behind Arwie the door opened once more and a group of young women walked into the clearing, carrying huge sides of meat and various fruits and vegetables. Before long, several fires were lit, the food was served and fine wines flowed in great quantities to quench the almost insatiable appetites of even the Giant guests.

The huntresses of Rampor made wonderful hostesses, they were lithe, athletic and extremely beautiful but not only that, they were also talented and intelligent as well, the male giants found it very easy to make friends with the pretty girls whilst the female giants swapped hunting stories and discussed matters of the mind and by the end of the evening and with the addition of the wine, everyone was the best of friends.

Wirral tradition dictated that Eitak and Arwie would have to spend the night before the wedding apart and as midnight fell, Arwie entered the huge tree and retired for the night.

Bones although not completely drunk was feeling quite merry. As he laughed and joked with the other giants, a thought suddenly entered his head and panic immediately set in. "What am I going to get married in?" he said. "My wedding suit is no longer going to fit me as the one made for me back in Kidder Doon was when I was smaller!"

Gom was the first to answer and said with a broad smile, "That's OK, my son, you can borrow my second-best outfit." And everyone roared with laughter.

The morning brought with it glorious sunshine. Everyone awoke early, some feeling slightly the worse for wear of the night before but by midmorning, Arwie was ready to address her guests. "Gom, King of the giants," she began, "…when I was in Kidder Doon, you spoke of the peoples of Kennet joining as one, I agree with you…for too long have we all stood, separated by our prejudices, now is the time to put aside any differences that once existed as we enter a new age of unity and to celebrate that unison, I invite you to share with me a secret we have kept for generations now…who will follow me to meet the real Wirral of Rampor?"

Arwie threw her arm towards the Thunder Mountains and the huntresses ushered the wedding party around a granite outcrop which jutted out obscuring the view of what lay beyond.

Eitak's heart raced, was this it? Was this the moment that his life was about to end? He walked towards the outcrop and turned the corner but to his surprise, there was nothing but a hidden narrow pass through the mountain.

Arwie walked to the front of the group and led the way through the narrow passage. After a short walk, the path came to an end and opened up onto what Eitak could only describe as paradise. The view beyond the mountain was amazing. Beautiful colourful birds flew above a silver shimmering lake, fruit trees grew in full blossom. Green grass lay underfoot and all around in the distance, the entire landscape was surrounded by tall mountains.

As Eitak scanned the area, he became aware of several plumes of white smoke which rose into the air from various small but immaculate buildings. They had been difficult to see at first as they blended in so well with the surrounding countryside and beyond the buildings, reaching high into the sky was a multi towered castle, the like of which Eitak had only ever seen in books.

"Welcome to Rampor," Arwie announced as she strolled along a brick path which led towards the plumes of smoke.

The wedding party including all the Giants, Hagraals and Humans followed after the princess and soon they arrived in a small but beautiful town which had been completely hidden from view by the contours of the land. At the far end of the town, above all of the other buildings was the multi towered castle that Eitak had seen from the mountain pass.

"Don't you think it's a bit strange that we haven't seen anyone else yet?" Malarog asked Sirod as they walked through the centre of the town.

"I didn't want to say anything in case it upset Eitak," Sirod replied thinking the very same thing.

Once they reached the steps leading to the castle, the main doors burst open and out marched two women dressed in very long and multi coloured striped coats. In their hands, they held long trumpets and once they had positioned themselves at either side of the doors, they blew a fanfare which resounded around the town. Almost immediately and all around, doors opened and closed as people, women and children of all ages began to rush forward, dressed in their finest clothes. Several of the children, all of whom were girls, pointed to the giants and whispered comments amongst themselves but before long all the towns folk congregated at the foot of the stairs with the wedding party. Sirod was just about to speak to Malarog about being wrong when the King of Rampor stepped out of the castle and stood at the top of the stairs, looking down upon the crowd.

"I am Theon Willowbreeze, the King of Rampor and on behalf of my daughter, Arwie, I welcome you all. You may have heard the tales and legends of our kind and that is what has helped to keep Rampor hidden from the outside world for hundreds of years. The truth is far simpler. You see as soon as our daughters reach adulthood, they are sent to the forests where they learn to hunt and once they find a husband, they come back to Rampor where they live out their lives in paradise."

"So where are the men? And what do you suppose happens to the boys?" Malarog whispered to Sirod curiously.

Sirod thought for a moment and then replied, "Don't spoil it, you, old fool, there's probably a very good explanation for that."

"I understand there are to be two weddings at midday," Theon continued, "...so I suggest that we all get ready and feel free to use whatever you need."

As everyone prepared for the weddings, half a world away and on the other side of Kennet, a solitary figure fought against the icy winds of Sivestol. The rag-tag guard dressed in heavy furs leaned forward against the harsh ice storm as he battled his way to the home of 'The Queen of all that is white'.

Syagonus Sly stared into her jet-black eyes as she stood in front of a long mirror and admired her own reflection. Mother had always told her that she was beautiful and how right she was. She considered as she brushed her long ice white hair. Tall and slim with plenty of curves, it was true that she was a wonderful specimen but unfortunately, her personality did not match her outer beauty, for inside that alluring, exterior was a soul that was as cold as the icy world which she now called home.

As the ice palace of Sivestol drew closer, every breath was an effort. For two days, the rag-tag guard had marched south and now he was on the very verge of collapse, the icy polar winds blew with great strength against him, hindering his progress and now every ponderous step sapped what little of his strength remained. "The reward," he said to himself, "just think of the reward."

The ice palace stood alone in the bleak white wilderness. Constructed from huge slabs of carved ice, it was the only bastion of salvation against the severe polar winds. Built centuries ago, the palace had many turrets of differing sizes and this design had stood the test of time as the harsh southern winters had done nothing to detract from its beauty and had only added to its strength by reinforcing the walls with further layers of ice and snow.

The guard had now reached the palace gates and called out one name, 'Usurpus', before he collapsed, unconscious in the snow.

Midday arrived and everyone was prepared for the weddings. Eitak and Bones stood at the foot of the steps leading to the castle. Eitak was dressed in black trousers, a flamboyant shirt of fine white silk and a black leather hat with a single large feather that the giants had fashioned for him back in Kidder Doon. It wasn't until the night before that anyone had considered that Bones would no longer fit into his and so he now stood as if dressed from a jumble sale with mismatched clothes of different colours, styles and sizes that he had managed to borrow from some of the other giants. The outfit promised to him by the king was way too big and there was no time to make that many adjustments before the main event. He had, however, managed to have a haircut and shave and that made him look several years younger.

"I feel like an idiot," Bones announced as he looked down at his multi coloured clothing.

Eitak looked at Sirod and tried to stifle a laugh. "You look just fine," he said as he sucked in his cheeks and re adjusted the shape of his mouth.

A noise from behind caught Eitak's attention and as he turned, he saw two female trumpeters with long brightly coloured coats, stood at either side of the castle door and once again they raised their trumpets to their lips and sounded a harmonious fanfare.

Eitak looked at the trumpeters and then looked at Klum. "See, it's not so bad, bright colours seem to be in this year."

Bones stared back at Eitak and said nothing.

Once the fanfare had finished, the townsfolk left their houses and joined the giants and their new friends from Monrith. They took up a position in a large semi-circle in front of the two grooms.

Eitak looked at Bones who stared back and said nothing.

"What?" Eitak said, "It was only a joke."

Bones couldn't contain himself any longer and burst into infectious laughter which soon spread to Eitak and Sirod and before long, all three friends were stood at the foot of the steps, laughing uncontrollably.

The trumpets sounded once more and from the distance, a crowd of people advanced on the town; as they gathered with the other townsfolk, Sirod couldn't help but notice that although there were plenty of women and girls, there was not a single man or a small boy amongst them.

The trumpets sounded harmoniously for a third time and the castle doors opened.

The first to emerge from the castle and walk down the steps was Arwie. She was dressed in a traditional wedding dress, befitting a princess of the Wirral. The whole sleeveless dress was mint green in colour and had a fitted bodice which was sequinned with tiny emeralds, the narrow waist was tied with a large mint green bow which was tied vertically down her back and the gathered and ruffled train cascaded to the floor like the waves of the ocean. As she walked down the steps, she was joined by the king who held her right arm in support and they slowly made their way down the steps towards Eitak. As they walked, Bonzai and Jangles wearing matching waistcoats, skipped along behind hanging onto the material of the train as it cascaded after her.

Last were princesses Luj and Noj, both of whom wore matching purple-coloured dresses with white diamond encrusted boned bodices. Their ample bosoms were accentuated by a pleated bustier which was also emblazoned by white diamonds. The waist and train were a series of gathered ruffles which hung from the dress like small hammocks attached at either end by a diamond cluster stud. As they walked down the stairs, King Gom came and stood between them.

The crowd remained silent as the three beautiful brides came to stand beside their future husbands.

There was not a dry eye in the town. As Eitak looked upon Arwie and Bones upon Luj and Noj, each privately thought they were the luckiest men that ever lived and with tears rolling down their faces, they each held the hands of their soon to be wives.

Each of the grooms now faced their brides as a very tall, thin man with a long thin nose and who was dressed in a white robe and pointed white hat walked down the steps.

The man stood on the sixth step from the bottom so that he both looked up to Bones, Luj and Noj and looked down upon Eitak and Arwie.

"Let me introduce myself," the man began with a deep voice that didn't seem to match his thin frame. "I am the Cylesian minister of matrimony and we are all gathered here today to celebrate the marriage of these fine men to these even finer women."

Half a world away the rag-tag guard awoke, he found himself slumped in a chair within a huge frozen hall in the ice palace. In the centre of the room was a large square pit and in the bottom of that pit chained to a metal ring was a very angry looking Snowjax. As the guard came around and familiarised himself with his surroundings, the sound of footsteps filled the room. Two soldiers dressed in white fur trousers and jackets entered ahead of Syagonus Sly. She was dressed in a long soft black fur coat which brushed the icy floor and stood in stark contrast against her snow-white hair.

"What news do you bring?" she enquired in a short-clipped voice as her jet-black eyes met those of the guard and pierced deep into his soul.

The man spoke in the common tongue of the peasant guard, "Not good, I'm 'fraid, Its Usurpus, see…"

"Usurpus?" The queen snapped. "What of my brother?"

"Well, 'es dead, killed by them, what's with the Giants?" the man replied.

"Dead…" Syagonus screeched and immediately realising the guard had brought her quite possibly the worst news she had ever received, she waved her hand in the air and hissed, "…Throw him to the Jax."

"No, what 'bout me reward?" The man protested and screamed loudly as the two fur clad soldiers grabbed a hold of either of his arms and dragged him to the pit, where they unceremoniously shoved him firmly down into the Snowjax's lair.

The queen of all that is white was livid. "My brother…" she screamed, "I must avenge my brother." And she rushed from the hall, leaving behind the sound of crunching bones.

"Do you, Eitak Ladoog, accept this woman, Arwie Willowbreeze, into your life, to love her and protect her from this day until the end of days…" the minister of matrimonies asked.

Eitak looked into Arwie's blue eyes and to him, she looked as beautiful as the day he met her. "Of course, I do," he replied.

"And do you…Bones take these women, Lujinda and Nojanda of Kidder Doon, into your life, to love and protect them from this day until the end of days…"

"Lujinda and Nojanda?" Bones repeated as his eyes widened and his voice raised an octave. He looked at his beautiful soon to be wives, the disapproving way in which he had asked after their names had stuck a nerve.

"Nobody liked our names when we were young and everyone made fun of us," Luj said, beginning to snivel as a wart suddenly appeared on her nose.

"Luj is right, we were always made fun of and now even you…" Noj added as a hairy wart appeared on her chin.

Bones realised what he had said and felt dreadful at having upset his two fiancés. "I didn't mean…that I don't like your names, it's just that you had never mentioned them before. The truth is I love them, I love them both as I love you both." Luj and Noj looked at bones and saw that he really meant what he said and as quickly as they had appeared, the warts disappeared, leaving behind beautiful skin which was even smoother than before.

"Who has the rings?" the minister continued.

Thaddeus stepped forward and handed Eitak a simple white gold ring which he turned in his fingers. It looked like the halo of white soil back in Kidder Doon Eitak thought.

Across the Thunder Mountains in the volcanic village of the giants, the halo continued to sink. The cracks that had appeared across the surface of the soil had widened to such a degree that steam began to rise from deep underground and between the cracks, molten lava and magma flowed. Kidder Doon had awakened once more, the river of fire under the village flowed with great speed, building in pressure and then like a great plug being pulled from the wrong side of a bath, the halo of soil disappeared into the magma and was carried away by the liquid stone. The lava now had a means of escape and great bubbles of fire erupted from the unplugged hole and then like the tide of the sea, it withdrew. Deep underground, an underworld of fire was exposed, plateaus of rocks jutted out at different levels and a huge burning chasm was revealed as the river of fire retreated.

As Syagonus Sly made her way through the frozen palace corridors, her long black coat brushed the floor behind her like a fur wedding train. Eventually, she came to a spiral staircase leading down deep underground. She hesitated a moment but then rushed down the steps which led to a long wide corridor. At the far end through an ice arch, the ground opened up to reveal a huge cavern which was lit by several blue Orillion crystals. Syagonus took a deep breath and then walked across the cavern floor until she came to an altar carved out of the ice. Above the altar and suspended from the ceiling by huge chains was an enormous block of ice. And frozen within that ice with its wings outstretched and jaws open, was a crystal dragon.

"Do you, Arwie Willowbreeze, take this man Eitak Ladoog into your life, to love and protect him from this day until the end of days?"

"I do," Arwie replied excitedly.

"And do you," the minister concluded, "Lujinder and Nojander…"

Bones squinted and checked that no more warts had suddenly appeared.

"…Take this man, Bones, into your life, to love and protect him from this day until the end of days?"

The two giants looked at each other. "We do," Luj said smiling.

"Very much so," Noj added also smiling.

"Then you may place the rings," the minister confirmed.

Syagonus stepped onto the altar where underneath the huge ice cube, there was a large metal cauldron containing firewood and coal which had a raised domed roof above it. She thought for a moment but then reached into her pocket and took out a tiny Orillion crystal which she tossed into the large pot. There was a bright flash and then slowly the wood began to crackle and spit as the flames took a hold.

The two grooms slipped their rings onto their fiancé's fingers.

"From this day, you shall no longer walk upon Kennet as two but as one…" the minister concluded, but as he said this, he looked at Bones and corrected himself. "I mean three…and one." He then realised that this was wrong too as Eitak would no longer be walking upon Kennet as one, but then no matter what he said, the holy words of matrimony seemed wrong. "What I really meant to say was…from this day, you will walk upon Kennet as one and I pronounce each of you husband and wife…I mean wives."

A huge cheer erupted as Eitak kissed Arwie and Bones, kissed both Luj and Noj and Bonsai and Jangles hugged each other and grinned.

Syagonus Sly stepped back from the Altar as the ice cube began to melt and water hissed on top of the raised cover as it turned to steam. "Soon, my lovely, soon you will rise and help me take back what is rightfully mine."

After a long kiss on the castle steps, Eitak held Arwie's hand and was just about to mingle with the crowd of well-wishers when he looked up to the castle doors. The trumpeters had left their posts and had retired to the castle. Just as the doors closed, he saw one remove her long coat and much to his surprise he noticed that underneath her coat, the trumpeter was wearing the standard dress of the rag-tag guard. Eitak pondered for a moment but then brushed the thought aside as Arwie took his hand and pulled him towards the cheering crowd.

It was now late afternoon and everyone was feeling rather hungry. King Theon, together with the townsfolk had arranged a huge outdoor banquet within the grounds of the castle and before long, everyone was enjoying a feast of the finest meats, fruits and vegetable that the forest had to offer.

Malarog stood next to King Theon. "I was just wondering," Malarog began, "…I don't see any men or boys amongst the crowds?"

Theon's eyes narrowed and his face turned a little pale, but after an awkward moment when he appeared to stare into Malarog's mind and said nothing, he replied to the question, "that, I'm sorry to say, is the curse of the Wirral, only the girls survive and so it has been for as long as I can remember."

King Theon then apologised and walked back to the castle.

Strange, Malarog thought and he went to find Sirod.

Eitak sat down with Arwie. "This is the happiest day of my life," she whispered and kissed him.

Although happy and enjoying the greatest day of the rest of his life, there was something playing on Eitak's mind and he needed to get it off his chest.

"It's about the trumpeters," he said.

"What about the trumpeters?" Arwie asked wondering if they had done something wrong.

"…Do they live here?"

"Oh, I don't know," Arwie replied, "why do you ask?"

"It's just that underneath their long coats, they seemed to be dressed as rag-tag guards." As he finished his sentence, he realised how silly he must have sounded and almost immediately wished that he had never brought the subject up.

"Now you really are being paranoid," Arwie said. "…We are in Rampor, just try to relax. After all we don't eat people, you know," she continued, trying to make light of the situation.

By evening, the party was in full swing, music played and everyone danced around a huge bonfire that the giants had managed to light in the castle grounds. Eitak held Arwie's hand and watched the dancers mesmerised by their movement and the flickering flames as they danced into the night sky.

Across the Thunder Mountains in Kidder Doon, the unplugged hole grew ever larger as huge chunks of the ground fell into the inferno, which exposed more of the fiery world beneath. Great pressures had built up deep in the planets core caused by the retreating lava flow and then, when it could take no more, the volcano erupted. Like an advancing tidal wave, the molten river of fire raced upwards, forcing great fountains of lava and flame from the pit and within that fountain, a huge fire dragon spread its wings.

As night fell and the party came to an end. Everyone agreed that it was much too late to begin the return journey to Kidder Doon.

"We should camp here for the night around the fire," Gom suggested, "…unless, of course, you would rather have a bit of privacy?"

The newlyweds looked at each other and gave a slightly embarrassed smile.

Arwie composed herself. "That will be fine," she replied and soon everyone was settled down at the end of a very exciting day.

Eitak held Arwie's hand as they looked up at the stars and before long, they were both fast asleep.

Bones lay with Luj and Noj, in each of his huge arms and with a smile on their faces, they too slipped into the land of dreams.

Once Bones was asleep, Bonsai and Jangles seized their opportunity and snuggled up on his massive chest, where they joined their giant friend in his rhythmic breathing of rest.

Sirod and Ember were the last but it was not long before they too succumbed to the excitement of the day.

Rampor was quiet only the deep sound of snoring filled the air.

But suddenly, Sirod awoke with a jolt and sat bolt upright.

"Ember..." he said, "...Ember."

"What is it, my love?" she replied.

"Its Usurpus...he's here with me."

End.

Ingram Content Group UK Ltd.
Milton Keynes UK
UKHW022011100423
419954UK00011B/175